Praise for *Upper West Side Story*

"Susan Pashman's book does what Sue Miller's *The Good Mother* did for an earlier era. It exposes the tensions beneath polite, contented liberal society and how they can explode when something goes wrong. Well observed and heartbreaking."

—Hanna Rosin, Contributing Editor, *The Atlantic*, DoubleX Founding Editor at *Slate*

"What if The Bonfire of the Vanities was set in the present time and told from a woman's perspective? *Upper West Side Story* gives you an irresistible answer."

—Lara Vapnyar, author of *Memoirs of a Muse*

"It's hard to find a novel so candid in its portrayals; so hard-hitting in its examples, and so realistic.... *Upper West Side Story* is the kind of novel that reaches out and grabs you with familiarity—and once you begin its journey, you can't quit. It's that compelling."

—Diane Donovan, *Midwest Book Review*

"Susan Pashman handles a tough and vital subject with unusual daring and sensitivity. *Upper West Side Story* is a gripping novel."

—Hilma Wolitzer, best-selling author of *An Available Man*

"In this powerful novel, Susan Pashman picks up the most delicate–but most pressing–subject in our national discourse and sets it down in the surround of a heart-rending tale of parental love and tender friendship. Everything is here: domestic disruption, generational divides, urban and academic politics, and, most courageously of all, racial resentment and distrust. Pashman knows her way through it all and handles it with intelligence and lovely writing."

—Joann Miller, former Editorial Director, Basic Books

"New York neighborhoods, New York parenthood, race . . . Susan Pashman's powerful story of a fracturing family in a fractured city is fraught with understanding."

—Peter Behrens, award-winning author of *The Law of Dreams*

Praise for *Upper West Side Story*

"Susan Pashman's book does what Sue Miller's *The Good Mother* did for an earlier era. It exposes the tensions beneath polite, contented liberal society and how they can explode when something goes wrong. Well observed and heartbreaking."

—Hanna Rosin, Contributing Editor, *The Atlantic*,
DoubleX Founding Editor at *Slate*

"What if The Bonfire of the Vanities was set in the present time and told from a woman's perspective? *Upper West Side Story* gives you an irresistible answer."

—Lara Vapnyar, author of *Memoirs of a Muse*

"It's hard to find a novel so candid in its portrayals; so hard-hitting in its examples, and so realistic.... *Upper West Side Story* is the kind of novel that reaches out and grabs you with familiarity—and once you begin its journey, you can't quit. It's that compelling."

—Diane Donovan, *Midwest Book Review*

"Susan Pashman handles a tough and vital subject with unusual daring and sensitivity. *Upper West Side Story* is a gripping novel."

—Hilma Wolitzer, best-selling author of
An Available Man

"In this powerful novel, Susan Pashman picks up the most delicate–but most pressing–subject in our national discourse and sets it down in the surround of a heart-rending tale of parental love and tender friendship. Everything is here: domestic disruption, generational divides, urban and academic politics, and, most courageously of all, racial resentment and distrust. Pashman knows her way through it all and handles it with intelligence and lovely writing."

—Joann Miller, former Editorial Director,
Basic Books

"New York neighborhoods, New York parenthood, race . . . Susan Pashman's powerful story of a fracturing family in a fractured city is fraught with understanding."

—Peter Behrens, award-winning author of
The Law of Dreams

UPPER WEST SIDE STORY

A novel

by

Susan Pashman

Harvard Square Editions
New York
2015

Published in the United States by
Harvard Square Editions

ISBN: 978-1-941861-03-5

Harvard Square Editions
www.HarvardSquareEditions.org

Printed in the United States of America

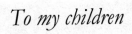

To my children

You have a child. You love him more than you ever dreamed it was possible to love. Never do you take this gift for granted. Not in the city, not on the farm, not anywhere in the world. For nowhere on Earth does a mother feel safe from the monsters who lie in wait. A fever, an intoxicated driver, a knife-wielding kidnapper, a molester. A poorly maintained Ferris wheel, a peanut. Mother love opens us to an overwhelming fear that is ours alone. Once that sticky wet head slips out, trailed by twisted cords that are, yes, connected to us, we are doomed. For it is true that whatever we love with our entire hearts places us in unimaginable peril.

I thought I had vanquished all thoughts of my son's thirteenth year, shredded them and tossed them into my mental trash bin. But then, in a too-thorough spate of housekeeping, I found the journal he'd kept of that year. I lowered myself into a chair, rested the dusty, green-covered book in my lap, and opened it. I hurried past the entries from the year's early months, searching for the pages he'd written in the autumn.

"Thursday, October 7, 8:45 pm. Tomorrow we leave early for our great patriotic adventure," I read, hearing the words in my son's high, tender voice. His young man account continued, and so did I, until every tiny detail came floating back.

MY MOTHER READS MORNINGS. At dawn, she is up, sniffing the air, cocking her head as if to catch the strains of some ghostly tune. Usually she finds the day benign. But at the slightest whisper of disturbance, she dashes about covering things. In the years she spent alone in a New York City apartment, she would throw a second quilt across the bed, a sheet of plastic over the linen tablecloth; she would wrap a silk kerchief around her head and knot it doubly beneath her chin. If the turbulence seemed extreme, she'd drag a wooden stool into her china closet and secure the door from within. As a young girl in Hamburg, she spent weeks, even months, in suffocating spaces waiting for the danger to pass.

On the second Friday of that terrible October, my mother woke to a clear, perfect day and, without stopping to cover the furniture, made directly for the china closet. I knew nothing of this at the time, but, had I known, I doubt it would have changed anything.

That was the day our son Zack and his eighth grade class set off for a weekend tour of our nation's capital. The night before, I had sat on Zack's bed, watching as he stuffed fresh underwear and a sweatshirt into his knapsack. In deference to the trip, his teachers in the Special Enrichment Program had declared a homework *moratorium*.

"From the Latin *moratorius* which means 'delay,' " Zack said, flashing a huge smile. His head still had a lot of growing to do to catch up with his teeth; they seemed enormous and gave him an outlandish grin. He punched his fist around in his knapsack, assessing the space left by removing his textbooks: enough for his chess set, *The Guinness Book of World Records*, and his journal.

I loved that my son kept a journal. At his age, I'd had girlfriends who confided their silly crushes to little leather bound books with brass locks that ensured their secrecy. But Zack kept his journal in a handsome handcrafted book, a treasured gift from his grandmother. Despite a powerful bond with his laptop, he made his journal entries as a serious classical gentleman would, writing out his thoughts in a careful hand.

Once the journal was securely tucked into his knapsack, Zack stretched the canvas to its limits to squeeze in one more slender volume. He had just begun Latin in school and had fallen madly in love with it; for his trip to Washington, he decided he must also have the battered, soft-cover copy of *Latin For Life* he'd purchased online.

"I think I could get used to moratoriums," he said.

I grinned back at him. "Moratori-*a*."

This was our lovemaking: Zack being smart, me loving it, him knowing how much I loved it and loving me loving it, loving being able to please me so by fanning himself out in all his child prodigy glory.

"Auditori-*um*," Zack said, strutting, "auditori-*a*. Moratori-*um*, moratori-*a*."

He draped a thin, sallow arm about my shoulders, dropped his chin to his chest, and fixed his huge blue eyes on me.

"Now, you be careful while I'm away," he said gravely, "and don't think you can stay up late just because I'm not here to wear you out. And make sure Dad's careful when he drives."

He would have gone on but we both burst out laughing. My thirteen year-old son was not only saying he was worried by our impending separation, but also reminding me that he could read my thoughts, say before I could myself, how much *I* would worry about *him*. For the rest of my days, I thought, his mind would track mine as faithfully as a baby duck waddles after his mother.

I first understood that when I curled Zack against me and rocked us in the painted wood rocker my mother had bought at the Salvation Army. She had them hold it until Zack actually arrived, warning it was bad luck to set up the nursery before the baby was safely born. In the hours near dawn, I'd rock Zack and smell his milky breath and know that it was he, not my husband, Stephen, who was my life's completion.

Simply put, Zack was *my* child more than he was Stephen's. Stephen and I had always known this. We never spoke of it; parents rarely do. But it is true in every family that each child belongs to one parent more than to the other, and although parents do not confess to this asymmetry, children understand it early and ponder it as they drift off to sleep.

The next morning, as Zack and our daughter, Hallie, made their way to school—as my mother remained shut in her closet, a blue scarf double-knotted beneath her chin—I stood at our bedroom window waiting for Stephen to finish in the shower. It was easy to lose myself at that window. Stephen and I both treasured our eighth-story view of Manhattan. We congratulated ourselves regularly for having persevered through more than a decade, moving three times to increasingly more desirable apartments within our building, tipping the superintendent excessively for even the tiniest service, and being, in general, disgustingly obsequious so that we might finally clinch this plum.

I checked our bedroom window each morning, if only glancingly, to reassure myself that our neighborhood was still the bright and quirky place we'd said good-night to. And there it was, New York's Upper West Side spreading itself out before me: a patchwork quilt of rooftops studded with air shafts, water towers, storage bins, all laced about with clotheslines; the wide, north-south avenues, traffic islands banked by worn wooden benches where long-time residents liked to sun themselves. This is the place Midwesterners have in mind when they talk about the "East Coast." If I press my face to the window pane and turn slightly, I can glimpse the hulking Cathedral of St. John the Divine anchoring the neighborhood as those medieval cathedrals did in their fortified hill towns.

Amid the morning bustle, I saw that Nelson, our resident blanket man, had survived yet another night and stood beside our corner lamppost, his accustomed spot. A purloined supermarket cart he had long ago made his own was stacked with frayed blankets and neatly folded corrugated cartons; one hand clutched a cardboard coffee cup, the other was raised prophetically to give emphasis to his declamations.

"What makes a neighborhood?" I was once astonished to hear him ask as I hurried past. I felt compelled to stop and hear his answer; but Nelson's oration—dozens of hundred-dollar words soaring on intricate rhythms and sprinkled with references to Nietzsche and Marx—veered off as usual, leaving me dazed.

Stephen was taking his time in the shower that morning, most likely letting the hot water pound his left trapezium; that muscle was always so tight I could hear it crunch when he rolled over in bed. And, down on West 103rd Street, Nelson had ceased his morning sermon and was hunched beside his shopping cart, poring studiously over a rumpled magazine. Coming from another sort of place, from a rural village or a suburban town, one might wonder how a real community could possibly take root in our miles of dirty, cracked pavement, in our teeming apartment buildings, their long corridors of identical doors recalling a nightmare. How do we find one another in such a place, a stranger might want to know? Where is the glue that could bind all this? Yet, over the years we do, in fact, forge friendships so close and nourishing that this crazy mix of people and odors and sounds eventually fades into the background, and this place becomes our own small town.

My husband grew up in the outer borough of Queens and spent his college years at M.I.T. training to be a chemical engineer, so he is not so much a creature of this place as I. I spent even my earliest years here. I understood the answer to Nelson's question in my bones, although I could not explain it in so many words. For never, I knew, in any small town in this country, could I have found the extraordinary friendship I had found in this Manhattan neighborhood.

The closest friend I ever had in my life was Viola Nightingale, the black woman who was the mother of my son's best friend, Cyrus. Our friendship had developed imperceptibly: maybe she'd said something at a P.T.A. meeting that rang true, or we may have nodded hello at the market. I know I saw her carrying a placard during a rent strike, and that I stopped to wish her luck. I remember her relentlessly interrogating the candidates before a school board election. And then, we were suddenly partners in developing a plan for the school's new Special Enrichment Program and it was as if we'd already exchanged life stories, worked out secret signals for use at public meetings, sorted the other parents into camps of the good, the bad, and the convertible. In our first actual conversation we spoke as old friends. Women do this all the time, secure mighty alliances in the moments between things.

The real closeness, of course, took longer to develop. After all, there were differences between us that would, with two other people, have made a friendship impossible. Viola was from the Deep South, from Georgia, and product of intense racial struggle. I, the daughter of Holocaust survivors, was the sort Viola might have disdained as yet another white do-gooder. And I have to believe that there were, at first, deep chasms separating our two boys. But as Viola and I grew closer, so did our sons. They played chess together, led their class in every subject, shared secrets Vi and I could only guess at. When Viola's husband, Phil, fell dead in the subway, his heart suddenly strangled, Stephen and I swooped in to embrace her and Cyrus. By the time of that fateful October day, we'd morphed into one beautiful rainbow-colored family.

I heard the water sloshing over the sink, Stephen clearing away the thick nubs his razor had dropped. His mother had made him a far better housekeeper than I was, or maybe it was Stephen himself, more attentive to detail, more disciplined than I could ever be. Soon I heard the bathroom door groan on its hinges.

In the street below, Nelson had decided to take his cart for a stroll. Two young Puerto Rican women who held animated conversations on the steps of their tenement each morning were at it once again, and the white-haired Italian woman in the ground floor apartment had her solitary window open and was planting red, white and green plastic flowers in her window box, poking little American flags down among them. Columbus Day. There would be a parade on Sunday. Stephen's boss, the mayor himself, would march in it.

"Bettina, I'm done." Stephen called out to let me know the bathroom was free.

"Yes, I'm coming," I murmured. It was my turn to move into the day.

Freshly showered and zipped into our business clothes, Stephen and I slid silently around the kitchen avoiding each other's eyes. Our marriage had been spiraling downward for months. We'd barely spoken since August. I was going to be late to my Feminist History seminar but an intense pressure was mounting inside me that wanted the silence to end.

I let my fingers graze his arm as he wriggled past me to the coffee.

"Stephen," I said, "we should get away. It's a three-day weekend. Zack will be gone till Monday night . . ."

". . . but Hallie won't." Vacant. Sullen. He'd been that way for weeks.

"It's leaf-time, Stephen. We could go to Vermont . . ."

"Vermont" meant the home of our friends, Clive and Selma Haselton who, until two years earlier, had occupied the apartment just below ours. The Haseltons now had a cheese farm with a sprawling white house, a flock of brindled goats and, of particular interest that morning, a nine-year-old daughter named Maddy. Just before the Haseltons moved, Maddy and our daughter Hallie had become sisters in a ritual involving embroidery needles, a jar of Vaseline, and several drops of blood. If Maddy could take Hallie off our hands, Stephen and I might mend things between us.

"Vermont." Stephen's voice was non-committal as he slouched behind the Times.

We needed to get a jump on the Friday exodus north or we'd exhaust ourselves in traffic. "Can you get home by two?" I pulled hard on his arm, forcing him to look up at me. "Stephen, say 'yes!'"

Stephen looked thoughtful. I know what you're trying to do here, that look said. "Okay, two."

As soon as Stephen was out the door, I phoned Selma Haselton and told her to expect us for supper. "I've got to get Stephen to come back to me," I remember telling her.

All through the summer, Stephen's job had hung on City Hall negotiations too complex and far too mired in corruption for me to follow. Every night, depressed and disgusted, he'd trudge in after the children were asleep. His eyes turned bloodshot; his chestnut hair became greasy with sweat, and it smelled of other people's tobacco although smoking was prohibited in government buildings. I'd hold my breath as I tousled his hair, wordlessly suggesting a shampoo before bed.

He'd comply, knowing how much I hate the smell of cigarettes, but knowing, too, that his hastily blow-dried hair would flatten as he slept, making his head one of those sideways-leaning pumpkins in the morning.

During those months, we had said less and less to each other. Stephen was shielding me from the squalor of city politics; I couldn't trouble him with the trivialities of university life. (Academe, Stephen once told me, is an inconsequential little world where viciousness intensifies inversely as the square of what's at stake.)

I began to read the newspapers selectively, avoiding the *Metro* section. By the middle of August, Stephen thought the mayor was about to strike a deal and shift money from the school cafeteria budget to the experimental sewage treatment plants Stephen had headed up for almost a decade. But the week school opened in September, three black youths walked into a school cafeteria in Brooklyn and opened fire on the cafeteria workers, leaving one in a coma, inflicting serious wounds on two others. Marcus Hake, the city's most powerful black leader, rushed to proclaim it "an unfortunate and yet predictable response to the oppressive reality of hunger in our city." The mayor couldn't touch the cafeteria program while the police commissioner was crying for more troops to keep peace in the schools. Environmentalists, the deputy mayor pointed out, were *white* people. Sewage treatment, Stephen was informed, was a *white* issue. Not the sort of thing you shift money to in the midst of racial uproar.

Stephen responded that the city had already spent thirty million dollars of *everybody's* money to research and develop the plants, and that the health problems that would ensue if outmoded treatment systems were kept in place would most adversely impact Hake's poorly nourished, poorly inoculated community. But long-range consequences, Stephen told me wearily, were not a priority while the headlines were screaming hate.

"But you *do* see their point," I said quietly one fateful night. "Drugs, crime, child abuse, police brutality . . . In the vocabulary of poverty," I said, "'environmentally-sound-sewage-disposal-system' is just a fancy, unpronounceable word. And when you're as poor as those people are, an unpronounceable word is a dirty word."

"Whose side are you on?" Stephen bellowed, and stamped out of the room.

"You might try to see it from their side," I called to him.

"Good," Stephen shouted back, "you see it from their side, Bettina, from the theoretical viewpoint of an academic! I'll take my own side, thanks, and keep trying to feed our family—if you can still bear to live with such a contemptible realist, that is!"

That's when the corrosion that had been accumulating for years came sailing headlong through the pipes and made the machinery of our marriage cough so hard it damn near stopped.

In the feverish years of our falling in love, the path of goodness and justice had seemed plainly marked to us both. But that autumn, when I looked into my husband's angry face, I missed the man I'd married. Stephen thought academic life had kept me from growing up; I believed politics had made him a player. We were growing apart, coming apart and, in that heated little exchange, we could hear the first bolts and screws shake loose from their moorings and roll across the floor.

Things had resolved for Stephen in the end. On the final day of September, he had called to say his program was safe for another 27 months. He'd have the job for which he is brilliantly suited by both temperament and education—the job that put most of the bread on our table—until the city got a new mayor and a whole new game at City Hall that would drive us crazy once again.

But the ugliness that had surfaced between Stephen and me did not recede so easily, and by the time the budget settlement came, I knew I had to act quickly to breathe life back into whatever was left of us. I believe I would have rushed us up to Vermont that Friday even if I *had* known my mother was locked in her closet, wishing the danger away.

Hallie had been dying to see Maddy, and chattered cheerily in the back seat all the way up to Route 7.

"I'm not wearing my retainer," my daughter announced as we turned onto the unpaved road that curved up to the Haseltons' big white house. "I'm having plain normal teeth for the whole visit and you're not telling Clive and Selma anything about it. And you're *especially* not telling Maddy. Ma, do you understand? I'll tell her myself when I'm ready, so you're not telling *anyone*. You hear me, Ma?" She leaned forward from the back seat, speaking directly into my ear as she loves to do. "You hear me, Ma? MA?"

It turned out that Maddy had been fitted with a retainer of her own which greatly deepened Hallie's affection for her. The girls spent their time inventing a new sisterhood ˙ ritual involving hooded plastic rain ponchos and an exchange of orthodontic hardware, a pseudo-religious activity that required the full three days to complete. It turned Maddy into the perfect sitter.

And the Haseltons, unsurprisingly, were perfect hosts—knowing when to pour more wine with the cheese, when to let us wander alone across the goats' meadow, when to leave us for a few hours in the ruddled heap of a barn on that part of their property that lay across the road. As we made our way toward the barn, Stephen reached for me, scooping his hand around one of my buttocks, his favorite part. "Dark eyes, a turned up nose, and a turned up ass," he'd told me shortly after we met, describing his feminine ideal. My nose does not quite turn up, but it does not hook downward either, and so I pretty much filled the bill, I'd concluded with glee. I'd been thankful, too, that he did not care much for breasts, my most worrisome deficiency. My behind, the part I'd tried as a teenager to hide in softly-shaped dresses, was indeed his favorite place to start.

In the barn, the tickle and scratch of straw on our bodies launched an awkward tumble: Stephen and me, striving for that easy, riding-a-bicycle lovemaking we knew we were good at, and not finding it. What we found instead was uncertainty, and the modesty that protects wounds before they're fully healed. Still, it was a start, a softening of the frozen ground, and when we were finished, we lay, staring up at the rough wooden beams, two old acquaintances feeling their way back from a long separation.

Vermont had indeed been a good idea, I decided as the city rose up to greet us. On the back seat beside our sleeping daughter were paper bags stuffed with cheese and apples, and jars of syrup that we didn't believe you could buy in the delicacy shops along Broadway. The apples pumped their perfume into the car and it hovered there. Certainly, we'd gotten lucky with the girls.

We turned off the Henry Hudson Parkway at 125th Street. Harlem. Our road home wended past teeming front stoops and neon-lit *bodegas*. We inhaled the fresh apple scent one last time and let Vermont slip back to the Haseltons, let ourselves come home.

Before the Haseltons' move, the four of us used to debate obsessively about the best possible place to raise a family. Did suburban tranquility make for happy children? Or would children be healthier in the country, the *real* country? The Pacific Northwest? A commune? Almost daily, it seemed, we'd be forced to reconsider the question. We loved New York for ourselves, of course, but would the gargantuan effort we had to make to keep a family going there yield sufficient benefits for our children? It was critical that the children not merely survive city life, but benefit from it. There must be something of inestimable worth to offset the loss of fresh air. Over sushi, over coffee, over the phone, we enumerated the advantages of having tough, street-smart kids with tolerant souls, eager minds and—it was a phrase we could never utter often enough—*the right values.*

Our discussions ceased abruptly when both Clive's parents died within a single month, his father of a stroke after being robbed at knifepoint in the Bronx, his mother, Clive said at her funeral, of a broken heart. With the insurance money, Selma and Clive purchased a powerful guarantee: pristine meadows and mountains, safe from the sort of random urban deviance that had ravaged their lives.

But although we no longer argued the point with the Haseltons, every time Stephen and I visited Vermont, we'd embarrass ourselves in spates of anxious self-validation. So it was to reassure ourselves, not to impress Clive and Selma, that Stephen, for example, mentioned Hallie's ballet class at Carnegie Hall, and I let it drop that Zack's chess team had made it to the city playoffs at Madison Square Garden, that Zack's co-captain on the team, a brilliant black child named Cyrus, was also Zack's best buddy. Even Hallie caught on to our game and mentioned on the way to Ben & Jerry's Ice Cream Factory the Ethiopian delicacies she'd recently downed at a funny little place on Broadway and Ninety-first. We were firmly in favor of raising urban children, but the piney air of Vermont could still stir doubts.

At last, we stood in our lobby waiting for the elevator. Like many of our neighbors, we cherished our pre-war building for its thick plaster walls, but they were no protection at all from the cooking smells and the musty odor of ancient lead plumbing from the basement catacombs. Together, they made up the smell of home.

Stephen looked haggard, distinctly yellow under the harsh fluorescent light, his shoulders sinking beneath the weight of two overstuffed duffels. I felt a sudden rush of love for him, for the disheartening life of the high-minded public servant that was his chosen path. I watched the lines that had vanished from his face over the weekend work their way back into his jaw and brow. He shifted his weight and gave the elevator button a second poke.

As I studied Stephen's face, I struggled to keep the kindness in my own, even as my mind began its furious homecoming business of making lists: Get the kids showered, separate out the dirty clothes, pack tomorrow's lunches, check Hallie's homework . . . Had she done any homework? Zack would arrive from Washington brimming with stories. It would be futile to mention homework then.

I'd also have to review my notes for Tuesday's seminar in Feminist History. They'd make no sense; a previous year's class notes never did. I'd pull out a few phrases to mull over as I sank to sleep, babble to myself on my way to class in the morning, and pray my students had worked harder over the weekend than I had. My brain was tugging itself into position, feeling like a foot at summer's end that had to squeeze into a new leather pump.

Stephen, growing restive, banged on the elevator door. It was my fault. I had engineered the trip that would leave us all disorganized at the start of the new week.

"I'm going to walk," Stephen said. Eight flights of unyielding marble. It was a threat.

"No, Daddy, don't!" Hallie hurled herself against his legs. "It *has* to come soon. I have to pee." I remember thinking that long after she reached maturity, my daughter would continue to view herself as the moral and causal center of the universe.

Stephen reached down to stroke her hair, his eyes rolled toward the ceiling. I tried to resist the urge, but my hand moved automatically to the chipped black elevator button and I rapped it impatiently. It was Stephen I was summoning, of course, not the elevator car. For Stephen was, with each passing moment, slipping away from me and back to where things had stood before.

We both smiled down at our daughter, grateful for her having played so happily with Maddy all weekend, relieved that she'd more or less disappeared.

"Almost there," Stephen said softly, smoothing her hair once more.

"I kno-o-o-w," Hallie said. "That's what makes it so ba-a-ad!"

By the time we reached our floor, she was bouncing up and down on the balls of her feet. I glanced at my watch. Eight-thirteen. We'd arrived home much later than planned.

"Good thing I left Zack some supper in the fridge," I said. "He must have gotten home an hour ago."

"Not necessarily," Stephen said.

"The bus was due in at six-thirty . . ."

"It's a holiday weekend," Stephen said. "You saw what the traffic was like. And they have to get the kids off the bus and sort the baggage." He shouldered up the duffels again, leaving the shopping bags for me. "Please, Bettina, let's not fry our nerves about Zack. He'll be home soon enough."

"Ma loves to fry her nerves," Hallie said, bouncing more vigorously. "She always fries her nerves about Zack."

"That's enough, Hallie," Stephen said.

"She hardly ever worries about me, but she *always* worries about Zack." My daughter was being her usual unflinching self, the sort who derives more comfort from knowing—and uttering—a painful truth than from burying it in the little lies most of us rely on. "I'm going to wet my pants, Ma," she sang out. "Hurry up!"

I had the wrong key in the lock. Hallie's voice rose to a shriek.

"Okay," I said, "okay, here we are." We seemed to have a knack for getting places just in time. Out to the country. Home again. Always in the nick of time.

The note I'd left for Zack was still on the refrigerator door and the sesame noodles still in the covered glass bowl exactly as I'd left them. I had imagined him beaming with pleasure when he found them, knowing I'd anticipated exactly what he'd want for supper, understanding he could always count on me to know him.

I got busy unpacking, stashing cheese and apples in the fridge, laundry in the hamper, worrying all the while that I was forgetting something: Some item, I felt certain, would slip off my mental list and be forever lost.

I unwrapped the package Selma had fixed for my mother. More cheese.

"Cheese," my mother would say when I finally coaxed her out of her closet. "The air last Friday was thick as cheese."

The phone rang. "That's Zack," I called out as I dashed for it. I was imagining his yellow hair, his big smile full of teeth. As I picked up the receiver, I could see the answering machine's signal blinking madly. We'd somehow disabled it before we left!

I was suddenly confused and embarrassed. What if something had happened to my mother while we were gone? What if a neighbor had wanted to leave us a message?

But we'd never even tried to pick up our messages! And our cell phones had remained switched off the entire time! We'd been too busy repairing our lives, giving them oxygen.

"Hello?" I was scolding myself for being so neglectful, me with a deranged mother . . . and with a son off traveling in another state . . .

"Mrs. Grosjean? Mrs. Stephen Grosjean?"

"Zack!"

"Your son isn't hurt, Mrs. Grosjean. This is Lieutenant Vicarelli down at the 23rd Precinct. I have to speak with you about . . ."

"Where's Zack? Put Zack on the phone! What are you doing with him?"

"We need for you to come down here, Mrs. Grosjean . . ."

What he said next toppled everything.

-2-

IN MY MEMORY OF IT, the 23rd Precinct has the look and feel of an hallucination. Some parts of that memory—Lieutenant Vicarelli, Zack, the papers on the Lieutenant's desk that Stephen and I had to read and sign—are huge, like the grotesque, helium-filled balloons in a parade. And other parts, things I know must have been there, have vanished completely. Adrenalin is nature's response to danger, and mine was pumping fiercely, calling forward what I needed for survival and blotting out the rest. Within moments, I could see only Zack, and I rushed toward him and pulled him into my arms.

"Thank God you're safe," I said in a half-whisper, half-growl. In the fifteen minutes it had taken to race down the stairs, out onto Broadway and over to the station house, my hormones had turned me to mostly animal.

Zack was weeping and his skinny body pulsed against mine like a raw beating heart.

Stephen handled the business end of things. There had been an accident. A child had been hurt.

But not Zack. Why were they holding Zack?

I released my mother-bear hug and looked down into Zack's face, put both my hands on his moist cheeks. "What happened?" I asked. "What is this all about?"

Zack's sobs gave way to wailing. "It was an accident, Mom, I swear. We were playing around. He was running after me at the Port Authority terminal and he chased me up the stairs. I stopped at the top and he smashed right into me. I bumped back at him. Like a sort of fist bump. Like I was just saying 'Hey, guy, watch where you're going.' I was running so hard, I was so out of breath. I fell over and bumped the front of my leg on the top stair. And then I got up and looked behind me and Cyrus was—oh, MA!"

My heart plummeted. Zack was the first fruit of my womb. But Cyrus Nightingale was a son to me as well. His mother, Viola, was practically my sister. And now Zack had injured Viola's child. Two young boys horsing around. But Zack was safe in my arms, while Cyrus was . . .

"In a coma," Lieutenant Vicarelli was saying.

Dear God! Cyrus! Viola!

I shuttled Zack into a corner of the police station. "Zack, you have to tell me every little thing that happened today. What were you doing on a staircase in the bus terminal anyway? Why were you even there?"

A shadow flitted across my son's face and he hung his head. Silence.

"You have to tell me, Zackey," I said. "That's the only way I can help you."

Zack sucked in a long breath. "Cyrus was talking to some kids who don't like me, and I walked over to them and they started yelling out a lot of stupid stuff, calling me some bad names. They do that sometimes but I just ignore them. But then Cyrus did it too. He called me a mean name, too."

"Cyrus wouldn't do that, Zack. I know him. I know him as well as I know you."

"Well, he did, but only because those kids were leaning on him. I could see his face. He was, like, trying to tell me that he was only kidding. But after he said it, they wanted him to come after me, too."

"How did he fall down the stairs, Zack?"

"I just told you!" Zack's tear-stained face was flushed and hot. "I told you the whole thing! We started chasing around and I found the staircase and ran up and Cyrus came up behind me. He ran right into me. So I did a little bump back at him and I guess he lost his balance or something because when I turned around he was ... at the bottom of the stairs! I couldn't believe it, Mom, I swear. I didn't mean to hurt him or anything! We were just goofing around and it happened!"

I knelt down on the floor beside Zack and took him into my arms. His damp hair and neck smelled of thirteen year-old boy and harrowing pain and dread. "It's okay, sweetheart," I said. "I'm sure you didn't mean any harm. It was an accident, a terrible accident. As soon as Daddy reads and signs those papers, we'll all get out of here. It'll be fine, sweetheart. Just try to calm down."

"But Cyrus! He's in the hospital, Ma. He couldn't wake up!"

"I'll go to the hospital as soon as we're done here. I'll find Viola and see what's happening."

"I have to go with you," Zack cried, grasping my wrist.

"You can't come, Zackey. They won't let you in. I'll talk with Viola and when I get home, I'll tell you everything, I promise. It'll be fine, you'll see. It will all be okay."

You say these things to your children, constructing about them a protective shield of stories you know are lies. A human mother and a lioness are the same at certain moments: We both do whatever is necessary to protect our young— outlandish, unrealistic things that we ourselves don't understand. It's a reflex. Hormonal. A maternal mechanism. "It will all be okay," I told Zack without ever consulting reality.

Stephen set some papers before me. An accident report. I signed just under where he'd signed, and he showed Zack where to put his own signature. He handed the sheaf back to the Lieutenant and then, as my memory recorded it, we were out on the dark street and Hallie was asking if Zack would have to go to jail, and we were all relieved and grateful for a reason to laugh.

"But there was another report," Zack was saying. "The one from the Port Authority. There were these two guys down there who kept trying to get me to say I pushed Cyrus, but . . ."

"We only had to sign the accident report," Stephen said. "Any other report was just a couple of guys in uniforms pretending to be big shots."

"But they tried to make me say I pushed Cyrus," Zack said again.

Immediately, I my old instincts kicked in. "How dare they?" I shouted. "How dare they harass Zack, put words in his mouth? Those bastards! He's only a kid! They had no right!"

"Let's all calm down, now," Stephen said wearily. "They were just jerking you around."

Stephen put a heavy arm around my shoulder. "It's nothing, Bettina. Just some hyperactive bureaucrats. We can all go home now. It's over."

But it wasn't at all over. It was only just beginning.

-3-

Monday October 11, 10:20pm

I'M SO FREAKED OUT I could die. I'm waiting for my mom to call and if I don't keep writing I could blow up. My dad saw me on my bed with my journal and he said, "Go to sleep and don't worry." But I can't do that. My heart keeps pounding. What about Cyrus? I can't get him out of my head.

Cyrus Nightingale is the coolest kid. He might be small, but his head is ginormous. His forehead sticks out over his eyebrows like a boulder. He's got a brain as fast as lightning. He totally mentally destroys me every time we play chess.

You look at Cyrus and you just know he's awesomely smart.

The thing about Cyrus, though, is he's beyond smart. He's *wise.*

The Nightingales like "ethical values." They hit on the name Cyrus because of Cyrus the Great of Persia. He was the wisest king ever. He brought peace to the ancient world and got famous for his tolerance and high ethical values., Cyrus is not a Persian. He's an Afro-American Baptist. Mrs. Nightingale, the information technology lady at our public library, is an uber strict widow. When Viola Nightingale thinks high ethical values, she thinks Cyrus better give twenty-five percent of his allowance to charity, and baby-sit the neighbor's kid for free. She thinks Cyrus better head to the Amsterdam Avenue Library straight from school so she can make sure he copies over his class notes neatly before he even starts his homework. If I want to do my homework with Cyrus or maybe hook him into a little chess, I have to hang out for an hour first so Mrs. Nightingale won't hook *me* into the note-copying thing. Cyrus's mother is mega tough, but she loves him more than anything. She says he's her whole world. I'm wigged that maybe something terrible is happening with him. What if what I did ruined Mrs. Nightingale's whole world?

If I believed in magic, I'd say Cyrus has magic powers, but probably it's just his mega smartness that makes him do some super-incredible things. Like, last week we had to watch this lame DVD in our Health class about gums. The junk they show in that class is always so boring that even the teacher ends up zoning out. I was feeling around in my book bag for a pen so I could doodle and I found an old spit-out piece of gum instead.

Cyrus has a front seat in every class because he's short. In Health, I sit in the next row and two seats behind, a perfect diagonal from my mouth to the back of his neck. The healthy gums infomersh is so boring, I have to do something just to stay awake so I shoot the wad of gum and pop! get him right where I aimed it.

Cyrus doesn't even look back to locate the source of the projectile. He dips a hand into his book bag, pulls out a rubber band, tears off a wad of paper and chews it to soften it up. Then—and here's the totally outrageous part—without even turning around, he makes a slingshot with his fingers, loads up the chewed-up spitball and fires backward over his shoulder. I don't bother to duck because I can't believe this is going anywhere. But, whoa! if that thing didn't hit me smack on the forehead!

So, of course, I have to chew up some paper and dig around for my own rubber band so I could send one back. I line up my slingshot, load up the spitball and let go. And, *mirabile dictu*, just at the second it's going to pop him on the neck, Cyrus-boy ducks down. The big wet ball goes splat onto the monitor screen and the class goes ape.

I got this ridiculous extra homework to write an essay about gums. The whole time I was writing it, I kept wondering how Cyrus did that. Like I say, he's sort of a magical kid and I am amazingly lucky that he's my kemosabe. This is why I'm out of my skull now, waiting to find out if he's okay.

A few hours ago, we were just arriving at the Port Authority from a trip to D.C. with the best teacher in the entire universe, Mr. Anthony Michael di Perna, and everything was fine. Now, I'm freaking because I think I majorly hurt my best friend of all time.

When I saw Cyrus lying at the bottom of the Port Authority stairs with his head and shoulders on the floor and his feet sticking up at me, I ran down to him. I think I was still laughing. I yelled, "Hey, Cyrus!"

Cyrus just laid there which I thought must be him putting me on. I said, "C'mon Cyrus, cut it out." I shook his arm. Then I pulled on it real hard. I could tell he wasn't kidding because he didn't pull back. I thought he'd passed out or something.

I started slapping his cheeks with both hands the way they do in the movies. Then I stood up and yelled at him, "C'mon Cyrus, man! Stop goofing around!" Then I felt sick in my stomach and ran to get Mr. di P.

Mr. di P told Mrs. Mejias, the trip mother, to round up the kids in the big station lobby while he went to check on Cyrus. I ran back to the stairwell with him. I was totally freaking by then. But when we got there, Cyrus was sitting up, rubbing the back of his head and saying he didn't know what happened. Some guy brought Cyrus a bottle of water and some ice wrapped in a rag. Cyrus held the ice on his head and drank the water. Then he got up and he said everything was cool.

Mr. di P said, "Okay, you two. Go sit on a bench out there and calm down. I'm going to see if there's a medic on duty."

A guy in a blue uniform came over and took Cyrus's pulse and shined a flashlight in his eyes and told Cyrus to move his head left and right. Cyrus told the guy everything was fine. Hundreds of people were going by with their suitcases. Then, while Mr. di P was filling out some forms, Cyrus leaned his head on the back of the bench and closed his eyes.

When I saw Mr. di P waving us over to get on line, I said, "C'mon Cyrus. Gotta roll." Then I shook him. Then I felt sick in my stomach all over again and started calling for Mr. di P because Cyrus wasn't waking up.

The bus terminal guys came with a stretcher. Outside the terminal I could hear the ambulance sirens. They sounded mega scary. I was starting to get dizzy like I was going to throw up. I was thinking: I did this. I did that little bump that made him lose his balance and fall, and that's why he can't wake up. I'm the reason Cyrus is going to the hospital on a stretcher.

Mr. di P gave Mrs. Mejias some money and told her to send the kids home in taxis. He gave me his cell and said I should call my parents to tell them I'd be late because we were going to have to answer some questions. I really had to talk to my parents just then. I called them at home but the machine didn't pick up. Then I called my mom on her cell and got the message that the cellular customer was unavailable and it went right to voice mail. I sure wasn't going to leave a message. I kept on trying, though, because I needed to say hello really badly. I had a lump in my throat that wouldn't melt down. I was still trying when the two Port Authority guys told us to come into their office.

That office had lights so bright I wanted to close my eyes, but I was afraid if I did, I could start to cry. So instead, I thumped my hand on my thigh real hard. Mr. di P told the officers what happened. I figured since he was the teacher that would be it.

But after they finished with him, they started all over on me. I said it was pretty much what Mr. di P said. The first guy, Officer Lunney, wasn't buying that. He said I must know more about what happened because I was in the stairwell when Cyrus fell.

My shin was hurting where I bumped it, but my neck started to hurt much worse. It hurt like it did in the Citywide Spelling Bee when they asked me to spell "scimitar." My Dad says my neck muscles scrunch when there's only one right

answer and I can't count on my prodigious vocabulary to talk
my way around it. Lunney and the other guy, Officer Thomas,
started blasting me with questions. My neck began to scream.

"Did you push Cyrus down the stairs?"

"I stopped near the top and he smashed into me. I would
say we sort of *collided*."

"He didn't ask what you would say. He asked what you
did."

"We collided."

"How did Cyrus fall down a whole flight of stairs if you
didn't push him?"

"I don't know."

"Why was Cyrus chasing you?"

"Some kids told him to."

"Why?"

"I don't know."

"Which kids told him to chase you?"

"I don't know."

Well, really, I *did* know. My neck muscles were screwed so
tight, my head was ready to pop off. I did know, but it just
wasn't the kind of knowing I could come right out and say.
Not with Officer Lunney and Officer Thomas eyeballing me
like that. Not with their secretary shaking her head every time I
said something. Not with Mr. di P and me being the only white
people in the room.

What I knew was that the kids who got Cyrus to come
after me were some black kids who are totally not down with
Cyrus being friends with a white kid. They're not down with
him being a kid with high ethical values either. And what freaks
them the most is Cyrus going to the Amsterdam Avenue
Library to do his homework right from school instead of
hanging out in the school yard with them. Plus, they got totally
disgusted last month when he refused to run for a second term
as class president. They yelled, "Go for it, Cyrus," but Cyrus

said it was time to give someone else a chance. That was Cyrus being mature, but those other kids thought it was wimpy.

Ronnie Holmes is the leader of that group. He once told Cyrus in private he thought Cyrus was a pussy dweeb. None of them would say that around me, though. Around me, they act like Cyrus is their homey, like they're all in totally tight with him.

While we were hanging in the lobby of the terminal, Ronnie came up to me and said, "You're a really stupid kid, you know? A total tool is what you are."

I said, "Yeah, Ronnie, you're correct. I'm irrefutably a slack-brained, hebetudinous, impercipient, blathering lout."

Then LeVar Morrison got into my face and said, "You're a dumb-ass, snowflake. A loser, boy."

I said, "I'm sorry, LeVar. I know that's how it must appear to a puerile, jejune, congenital cretin, but what else can one expect?"

So then Louis Byrne started mouthing off and said, "You can expect that Cyrus is gonna whip yo' sorry ass in the chess tournament at the Garden next week."

Then Ronnie said, "You don't seriously think Cyrus is any friend of yours, do you, faggot? He's just getting tight with you so he can figure out all your moves. That's so he can burn you in the championship."

Then Louis said, "Cyrus not gonna let no snowflake beat him, no way. He not no friend with no wimpy-ass neither. No way!"

Louis and those other guys speak perfectly good English but when they hang out in the schoolyard, they start talking black. Black kids in the Special Enrichment Program are always checking themselves out to make sure other black kids don't think they're turning white just from being in our class. And that's pretty bizarro because only four kids in our class actually *are* white.

Ronnie really cut me when he said Cyrus wasn't my friend. None of those guys can stand me playing chess with Cyrus. They hate Cyrus shooting baskets in Riverside Park on Saturdays with my father and me. They got mega steamed when they found out Cyrus's mother invited me to a Broadway play for Cyrus's thirteenth birthday. I wouldn't ever put that around, but Cyrus wrote about that play in a homework assignment he read in English class and he said I was there with him so then everyone heard about it.

Anyway, Ronnie dumping on me and Cyrus being friends really hit me hard. I walked away and yelled back at him, "Why don't you ask Cyrus if he's my friend? Just ask him!"

A little while later, those three guys were standing together, talking to Cyrus, probably bad-mouthing me some more to make him feel bad about being my friend. So I decided to walk over to them and try to get Cyrus out of that mess they were putting him in, making him choose between me and them.

When I got up to where they were standing, Louis yelled out, "Here comes White Boy, better get the roach spray, call the exterminator!"

Then the other two called out some bad names and I could see they were shoving Cyrus, pushing him up against one of those fat columns in the lobby. That's when Cyrus looked up and saw me and looked down on the floor and said, "Yeah, here comes Pinky," and they all just started laughing like that was the funniest thing they ever heard.

"Pinky" is the name of the rat in our science room who runs around all day on a wheel in his cage. A *white* rat.

Next thing you know, Louis and Ronnie and LeVar were yelling "Go get him, Cyrus! Make him run! Go get Pinky!" and some other stuff that was off the wall.

I'm taller than Cyrus and even though I'm not so buff, I can always outrun him. But they kept yelling, "Get him,

Nightingale," and "Show him who's the champ," so Cyrus started after me.

Once, I turned around and saw Cyrus. He was grinning and pumping his eyebrows up and down, meaning I should help him put on a show for the homies because what else could he do? It's tough for Cyrus having me for his best kemosabe with those other kids hating on me all the time.

I paced myself so we could give the guys a thrill. Then I ran through the exit door and up the stairs, and Cyrus came running up behind me.

In the Port Authority office, Officer Lunney kept it up about me pushing Cyrus. He and Officer Thomas wanted Mr. di P to say I had some grudge against him. But Mr. di P said I was Cyrus's best friend and I'd never hurt him. He said it was an accident. It was.

When Lunney and Thomas finally quit grilling us, I was totally ready to go home. But then Lieutenant "You-can-call-me-Al" Vicarelli showed up in a police car to take us to the 23rd Precinct.

Mr. di P called his wife. He looked really stressed when he hung up. He said he had to get home right away.

I said, "I better go home, too, you know. It's really late," but Al said he'd call my parents from the station.

So there I was at the 23rd Precinct with Mr. di P wanting to get back to his wife, and Al saying we both had to write some statements about how Cyrus got hurt. I wrote everything I told Thomas and Lunney and the stuff about Cyrus falling asleep, but I said nada about the guys who got Cyrus to chase me around, and I didn't write about the name Cyrus called me either.

I have nothing to say about that, not even to my mom. She and Viola had the idea for the whole Special Enrichment Program and they put every hour they could into making it happen. They would never want to know what goes on between those guys and Cyrus and me, and how things are not really working out the way they were hoping they would. I never complain about those guys at home, and I don't think Cyrus does either, because the program our moms dreamed up is a very good thing anyway.

While I was writing my statement for the Officer Al, he kept trying the phone at my house that never picked up, and also my mom's cell with the message still coming on that the customer was unavailable.

When Mr. di Perna and I finished our reports, Al gave us Cokes and told us to wait while they got typed up. Mr. di P's report was done first. He signed it and started pacing and looking at his watch so Al let him go. That's when I started feeling all cold and the room started looking too big. I felt like throwing up.

Every five minutes, Al called my house and my grandmother's house because my grandmother's number was the emergency number on my school record. It's truly awesome that the cops can get that information even when your school is closed. It's this kind of thing that makes my mom freak. She once got arrested at a student rally or something and says the F.B.I. still keeps a file on her and even now, they probably know what we eat for dinner every night. It doesn't creep me out, though. I actually think it's pretty cool.

When I told Al my grandmother never answers her phone, he wanted my Dad's office number. I said my father works at City Hall as Director of Environmental Affairs.

Al said, "That's nice. Do you know the number?"

I said, "City Hall is closed for Columbus Day. My mother's cell is the best idea."

When my accident report was ready, Al told me to read it over and sign at the bottom. I checked it out carefully. I must have my mom's view of cops.

I said, "I don't think I should sign anything until my parents get here."

Al said, "It's only an accident report, kid, not a confession."

I said, "Still, I'd rather not sign."

I was feeling totally zonked. I said, "Maybe my folks took my grandmother for Chinese food. They do that sometimes. I have a key. I can get home from here myself."

Al said, "Don't worry, kid. Your folks will show up soon enough."

At five after nine, my whole family *did* show up. Even my bratty little sister who kept asking if I was going to get locked up. I just wanted her to un-exist.

Now, my mom's at the hospital with Mrs. Nightingale and Cyrus. I just wish she'd call and tell me Cyrus can come home tomorrow. I was mad at him before, but not just because he called me the name of a rat, or because it was a *white* rat. I was mostly pissed because he let LeVar and Louis and Ronnie think they were onto something when they said he wasn't really my friend. He was hanging out with them even while they were bad-mouthing me with their whitey-boy stuff. When he smashed into me on those stairs, I wasn't in any mood for fun because all that stuff down in the terminal wasn't very funny. At least, not to me.

So maybe I wasn't feeling like a great friend of Cyrus just then, and maybe that's why I bumped back at him. It was like I wanted to tell him to get off my back because it was enough already. But I never thought he'd fall down. I wouldn't ever try to hurt him. I just wanted him to know I wasn't down with the way he'd been treating me.

Jesus, I am so, so, so sorry. And scared. We were just goofing around.

I wish my dad would come back in here so he could see I'm still awake. I need him to sit down on my bed and tell me Cyrus is okay and everything's okay.

I never felt so horrible in my whole life.

-4-

I ASKED STEPHEN to take the children home so I could hail a cab to Harlem-Manhattan Hospital and find Viola. Somewhere in that spiritless place our other child lay in a coma and his mother, who I loved as a sister, was—

I could not imagine what I would say to Viola.

The triage nurse did not look up when I blurted Cyrus' name. Her eyes remained fixed on her charts; her nostrils, however, flared slightly. I was speaking out of turn; she had not yet asked what I wanted. I would be punished by being forced to suffer an unbearable wait. The nostrils conveyed this. In New York City, you learn to decipher the faint twitches of people in small but critical positions, those bridge-trolls who can keep your life forever on hold.

But I was in no mood to take instruction. "I'm here to see Cyrus Nightingale," I said. "I'm his aunt. My sister, Mrs. Nightingale, is expecting me."

"Yeah," the troll drawled, "and I'm the boy's uncle." My punishment now, I understood, would be merciless. But I had to see Viola, I had to see Cyrus.

"I'm Bettina Grosjean," I began again. "My son Zack is…"

"… the kid who broke that poor little boy's head!"

Who had told her that? Could they have given her *names*? *Zack's* name?

"Have a seat," she said, motioning with her head. "He's on critical care. I don't know if they're gonna let you in."

Harlem-Manhattan is a hideous micropolis of sooty yellow brick high rises encircled below by a sprawl of tenements that have been turned into clinics and offices. The whole affair is enclosed by a twelve-foot high cyclone fence and illuminated by powerful kliegs. On the ground floor of

Butenweiser Pavilion, an overlit, shapeless space serves as the waiting area. Traumatized patients loll on gurneys parked along the walls; interns, stethoscopes dangling from their necks, hurry past, bumping into nurses' aides who are in no hurry at all. I lowered myself into a black leatherette armchair and tried to breathe deeply. Close by, a janitor sloshed a mop in broad arcs sending up a stink of disinfectant. I sat, numb and frightened until I heard my name blasted through a loudspeaker.

The moment I entered Cyrus's cubicle, I knew I was too small and stupid to be of any help. I stared in awe at the machines, obscene gray-shrouded beasts, their brightly-lit screens displaying graphs—bars and lines—that chugged up and down. I glanced at the skinny steel pole with its hooks and plastic bags, liquids coursing in and out, and at the jungle of electric wires coiled all around.

Cyrus lay absolutely still, his eyes closed as if in sleep, his dark, feathery lashes soft on his cheeks. That big, gorgeous head, enlarged by a white gauze turban, was all you could see of him, his head and some rumpled blue pajamas. One of the plastic tubes led to a spot near the back of his head, and one had been inserted into his throat just under his chin, held in place with a neat square bandage.

Viola sailed to where I stood and took my arm. She is a short, round woman and, as she came to greet me, the thickness of her body and the smooth, deliberate way it moved conveyed her solidity. Viola had always caused me to wonder how I would carry *my*self without a husband to balance my checkbook and to keep me from frying my nerves. I had always marveled at the deftness with which she ordered her household, her desk at the library and, I felt certain, all those inner files and cabinets where our lives are stored.

I took her in my arms and, for a while, we stood together, simply holding on.

"How is he?" I whispered.

"You don't need to whisper," she said.

"Oh, God, Viola . . ."

"They say he can't hear us. You can speak normally."

I placed my hand over hers where it rested on my arm. "What else did they say?"

"His eyes move a little. They don't open, but the eye movement underneath is a good thing." Her voice was colorless, flat as a board.

I patted her hand to thank her for saying something I wanted to hear.

"They'll know better in thirty-six hours," she said. "They drilled a hole to relieve the cranial pressure and gave him something to dissolve blood clots. They keep doing scans. They need thirty-six hours to see what develops. Meanwhile, they're helping him breathe until his brain can take over again."

As Viola spoke, I tried to picture the hole in Cyrus's skull, the fluid draining out. Thirty-six hours would put us at Wednesday morning. With the minutes dragging past like huge dirigibles, Wednesday was unimaginably far off.

A ruddy, bald man in a white coat appeared in the doorway. "Excuse me, Mrs. Nightingale. I wonder if I could ask you and your friend to wait outside while I check the bore?" His voice was delicate, deferential. And behind him, planted stolidly in the doorway, the triage nurse.

"Thank you, Doctor," Viola said. "I'm so grateful for all you're doing." She gestured toward me. "I'd like you to meet Bettina Grosjean, my best friend. Her son and Cyrus are practically brothers."

I shook the doctor's hand, and added my thanks. I turned toward the door to rivet the nurse's face with my stare. "Did you hear what his mother said?" I wanted to yell.

She stared back.

By the time I'd found my way to the street, I felt an irrelevant failure. I plopped onto the cold leather seat of the taxicab. "Oh, God," I sighed before I could give the driver my mother's address. What had I expected anyway? Had I figured I could give Viola a hug that would heal everything? Certainly, I'd hoped to do *something*. I felt thoroughly beside the point.

When I heard the news at the precinct, I responded like a mother whose own child was in danger. But seeing Cyrus with those tubes in him made it perfectly clear: It was Viola's son who was lying unconscious in a hospital; mine was at home in his downy bed. Viola's was the child we might never see again; Zack was the one who was in some way responsible. I could return home to two children and a husband; Viola might come out of this with no one left to her at all. Fate might upset the delicate balance on which our friendship relied; in a single stroke it could all come out horribly unfair.

My cab might have been hurtling through a remote galaxy, the streets seemed so surreal. I felt suddenly estranged from the woman who was practically my sister.

In our work for the Program, Viola and I often spoke several times a day. We took to eating Saturday night suppers together while Zack and Cyrus played chess down the hall. We'd stay at her kitchen table or mine, buried in pages of grant proposals and reams of forms from the city budget office until the numbers melted and the words stopped connecting. Then, we'd get down to the personal stuff: our brainy children, our hopes for them riding on our hopes for the Program. Zack, Hallie, Cyrus . . . and the Program to which we were, together, giving birth. Our three glorious children!

At the beginning, I wondered if I could ever do, or be, enough to deserve Viola's friendship. She'd grown up in Georgia in the fifties, and I was in awe of the courage it had taken to walk to school in the company of state police. In those early days, we told each other our deepest secrets, unzipped our souls until we stood, almost literally, heart to heart. I had believed, as I raced to the hospital that night, that Viola and I had forged something so indestructible that we could overcome the events of that day. But, sitting powerless in the back of that yellow cab, I knew that friendship had its limits. I sensed it in the coolness of Viola's hand as she said good-night, and in the absent way it slipped from mine. Two people are always two no matter how close they feel. Would this terrible turn of events tear asunder all we'd so lovingly put together?

As I handed the driver a few crumpled bills, my thoughts darted from Viola and her injured son, to my own son whose injuries were yet to make themselves known. Although I couldn't articulate it precisely in the cab that night, I knew: No matter where things stood with Cyrus at the end of thirty-six hours, my own son would be the worse for this. Something that ran straight up and down inside him would be forever twisted.

Finally, I slammed the car door behind me and turned my mind to my mother. Her injuries were of another sort entirely.

I let myself into her apartment. I had phoned several times from the station house and again from the hospital, hoping she'd give me the assurance that would let me head directly home. But, by the time I left the hospital, I'd reached the conclusion that my mother must be in her china closet, shut away from her phone and from the world to which it might connect her.

I did not bother to flick on the light; I knew the place by heart. Entry hall, coat closet on the right, living room straight ahead, dining room down the hall to the left, my old bedroom on the right. I reached out my right hand and closed my bedroom door. I did not want to see—even dimly in the light from the apartment across the air shaft—my old bed with its red and yellow pillows, my books—some that had been my father's—or the immense doll house with its polished, real mahogany furniture from England and its tiny blue glass dishes from Japan. I didn't ever need to be reminded of the years of hopeful training my mother had invested in encouraging me to care for housekeeping.

I dragged myself into the dining room, turned the little key switch on the floor lamp, and rapped on the china closet door.

"Come out, Ma. It's almost ten o'clock. I'm sorry I didn't come earlier. We were away."

The door creaked open a few inches.

"Come out, Ma. We've been up in Vermont, visiting Selma and Clive. We hit a lot of traffic on the way home. It's late, now, time for bed."

My mother was crouched on her stool, surrounded by shelves of platters and linens. Her moist eyes showed an inevitable fatigue, but her supple white hair remained neatly tucked under her kerchief. Her lumpy nose caught the dim light; it had never detracted from her sweetly pretty face, only lent it character. As she aged, my mother's expression had become increasingly girlish. She hung her head and glanced up at me, all foreboding and dread. "So tell me, what happened to you?"

"There's nothing to tell, Ma. I'm sorry to be so late. We got stuck in traffic, that's all."

"It's Zack, isn't it? Zack is in trouble. I knew it this morning."

"No, Ma, that's not true." My words seemed barely audible, squeezed as they were through a painfully tight throat.

I tugged gently at my mother's arm to coax her out of her hiding place. "But here you are in the closet on the night before I have to teach a nine o'clock seminar. Maybe *you* are a little bit of trouble; do you think that might be it?"

My mother sighed and stood up. She clamped her hands to my cheeks and held my head so that I was forced to look at her. "You look terrible. Why is that? Something bad has happened, I can tell."

"I told you, Ma. We had a long trip home. I am very tired, and I still have two kids to put to bed. So come on, now, let's get you taken care of."

"If it isn't Zack, then it must be Stephen. Usually I don't get premonitions about Stephen, but I've known since last Friday that something was turning bad."

"Ma!"

My mother waved an arthritic forefinger at me. "It's something with a male person. I can tell it's a male. I thought it was Zack."

I placed a gentle hand beneath my mother's elbow and ushered her into her bedroom. I pulled her nightgown from under her pillow and laid it across her bed. Could she possibly have remained in that closet all day?

"Let's wash up and get to bed, Ma," I said. Her apartment felt stifling; the walls were closing in.

Carefully, she unbuttoned her tan cardigan and slipped it off. She was eerily thin and bony, but perfectly straight. She stepped out of her heavy brown shoes, her skirt, her slip. Seeing her there, so slender and small, it was impossible to remember how it felt to look up to her and fear her judgments of me.

"Selma packed you a little gift, but I forgot it," I said once she had her nightgown on. "I'll bring it over tomorrow. Some of their artisanal cheese."

"Cheese," my mother echoed, as she wandered off toward the bathroom. "I can tell, you know . . ."

I walked the two and a half blocks home with my hands crammed into my pockets, gulping down the chilly air. While the elevator climbed to our floor, I tore at an old hangnail on my thumb until it bled and a clear, cleansing pain washed through me.

Zack was sitting up in his bed wearing the oversized gray and blue Knicks tee shirt Stephen had brought home from an evening out with the mayor. In the soft light from his bed lamp, I could see his green-covered journal open on the bed. I sat down beside him and he closed its covers and put the book aside. Then he buried a sorrowful head in my lap and let me stroke his hair.

I told him about the bore in Cyrus' skull, and the gauze turban, and the thirty-six hours. I said that I was hopeful, that Viola was hopeful, that Cyrus' eyes were moving beneath their lids. Then I told him to turn onto his stomach so I could rub his back. I rubbed in big, soothing circles, an activity that was as calming to me as to him.

When I thought he had drifted off, I kissed his hair and rose to leave.

"Do I have to go to school tomorrow?" Zack's voice was thick and drowsy.

I couldn't process anything more. "I'll discuss that with your Dad," I said, and headed for the door.

"If Cyrus dies," my son's voice curled out from deep in his pillow, "will I be a murderer?"

"Of course not, sweetheart!" I dashed back to his bed, stooped to cradle his head in my arms, and pressed my cheek to his forehead. "You didn't do anything wrong! Nothing at all! It was an accident, that's all. A strange spin of fate for which no one's to blame. Certainly not you, I guarantee it." I kissed his forehead. "It's going to be fine," I told him. "Now get to sleep, Zackey. Tomorrow will be a big day."

After I'd closed his door behind me, I stood outside his room for fully a minute or two, stood sentry, I suppose, wanting an amulet, a frightening mask, something that would keep evil from slithering under the door and finding my son.

Across the hall, the ferocious girl-child who could not decide whether to become a prosecutor or a public defender, had thrown her head back across her pillow so that her jaw dropped open; loud snores rumbled past her tonsils and echoed in her lavender room. A pale leg dangled off the side of her bed. I tugged at her pillow, letting her re-arrange herself so the mouth-breathing—which my mother always said could lead to heart disease—would cease. Then I reached down and carefully placed her leg back under her purple flowered quilt. On her shin was a small collage of band-aids—three or four of them—that Selma had fashioned to protect some minor wound incurred at the farm. I kissed the bandage, knowing that Hallie must have impressed Selma with her stoicism when the mercurochrome was dabbed on.

My daughter, who is at core as practical as her father, feels called upon at times to remind us of her femininity in noisy outbursts of hyperbole and demand, but never does she flinch from physical pain. In Vermont, once, we rushed her to the emergency room after she'd slipped on a rock in the Haseltons' stream. A baby tooth had been knocked out, but not before it had chiseled a wedge into her lower lip. I fretted over all the blood on her shirt and on the stainless steel table where she sat, a brave little soldier, showing me up for the sissy I so clearly was.

"God takes care of drunks and children," the staunch New England nurse reassured me.

Hallie, I mused as I tucked her in, would become the rock to which we others would someday cling.

In our bedroom, Stephen was reading. I sat down beside him and let him rub my shoulders while I gave him the news about Cyrus. He held me when I fell in a soft heap against his chest, and asked if I'd like a cup of tea or a dish of ice cream.

He told me Hallie had discovered homework she hadn't done, and it had taken until ten o'clock for her to complete it.

"You should have written her teacher a note," I said. "Zack wants to stay home tomorrow. Maybe Hallie should, too."

"Nonsense," Stephen said. "Tomorrow we'll all have a perfectly normal day."

"Normal!"

"Just put one foot in front of the other," said my husband.

My therapist, Dr. Franks, says I married Stephen to balance my own neurotic tilt.

On a hot July evening in my sixth or seventh year, my mother, my Aunt Charlotte, and I drove to City Island. From the car, I could see the water spread out below the setting sun like a porcelain platter, reflecting a pink and yellow striped sky. Aunt Charlotte turned off the ignition and we sat, the three of us, watching gulls swoop down for shells, then soar up and drop them onto the pavement where we were parked. Aunt Charlotte waved her arms and held forth about the marvels of sea air while my mother, paisley kerchief knotted beneath her chin, distributed egg sandwiches on rye bread. When the sun had almost disappeared, we took off our shoes and stepped out onto the sand.

Instantly, I was surrounded by a million tiny black flies. They crash-landed on my arms and legs, they buzzed into my hair, my ears, my eyes. I cried out, but my mother and Aunt Charlotte claimed to have no idea what I was going on about. They waded through the surf, stopping to point out the Big Dipper and the Bear. I waved my arms furiously and stamped my feet to drive the flies away. Finally, I refused to continue.

My mother said how foolish I was, how spoiled and ungrateful. This entire trip, she reminded me, was for my benefit, so I might see the world beyond the city and experience the Glories Of Nature. My Aunt Charlotte pointed out that discomfort was good for a young girl, taught her a little of what life had in store. Aunt Charlotte, like my mother, neither saw, nor felt, the flies.

Perhaps the swarm of flies parted as the two older women approached; perhaps some hormone in their skin rendered them less appealing to insects. Or perhaps my little girl skin was more sensitive than theirs. My mother, who can pick up the tremors of terrible things to come, barely notices the discomforts of the world she actually inhabits. It's a surprising toughness in her that has eluded me but has passed down, inexplicably, to my daughter.

"Pull yourself together and behave like a normal girl," she told me on that beach, this mother who hides in closets.

I have no inkling of how to account for the rumblings that disturb my mother. And I have no idea how she made her way through those flies, any more than I can grasp how she survived the horrors that befell her family during the War. But I could not continue the walk on the beach that night, and have wondered ever since just what "normality" consists of.

Stephen thought our next day should be a normal one. I could not understand how he could sink into a deep, untroubled sleep while Cyrus Nightingale lay at Harlem-Manhattan, wrapped in gauze and blue cotton, an abominable fluid draining from his brain. And didn't Stephen ache, as well, for our own son whose rough breathing and sudden flaps and tosses echoed down the hall and into our room? I couldn't begin to consider what terror lay beneath those sounds of Zack's, and I doubted any of us would see a normal day for a very long time.

Finally, I hoisted myself out of bed and stalked about the apartment, a mother hen who has heard a fox rustling the grass in the darkness outside her coop. Those horned and hairy monsters we read about with our children really do exist, and when they appear in our lives, they do so by springing suddenly up from their pitch-black hell and tearing the entire world apart in an eyeblink. There is nothing normal about them.

-5-

Tuesday October 12,   8:15 p.m.

THE GREAT AND WISE Mr. di P didn't show today. We had Ms. Seibel, the Home Ec teacher, for Social Studies instead. She told us to write a story about our trip to Washington.

She said, "This is going to count in your mid-term grade so you'd better do a good job." But nobody believes anything a substitute says.

Jenny Yee yelled out, "What happened to Mr. di Perna?"

Ms. Seibel said, "He probably needs a rest after three whole days with you kids. I heard you gave him a lot of trouble on that trip, running wild and causing an accident where somebody got hurt."

That got LeVar Morrison to yell, "Whoa! That was Zack done that. Only Zack and Cyrus was makin' trouble. The rest of us was model kids."

The whole class cracked up then. Except me.

Then Lateesha says with that pouty-lip thing she always does, "Yeah, and now everyone gettin' burned on account of just those two. It ain't fair!" Lateesha ends everything with "It ain't fair!" so now the whole class goes ape.

I couldn't think of what to say about Washington. I figured maybe I'd write about the mint, or the Supreme Court, but all my ideas just slipped away like sand through your fingers. I started to write about the Lincoln Memorial where we saw this awesome statue of Abe sitting on a throne. The place was uber inspiring and Cyrus and I just stared up at him, and Cyrus said, "The air in this place is gold-colored." He was right.

I never got to write down my ideas because my mind kept bouncing back to the bus terminal. I could see Cyrus's eyebrows pumping up and down and feel the hardness of the

stairs under my feet when I ran up to the top and the little
bump when Cyrus got right up behind me. My mind kept
playing this over and over, like a DVD that you stop and
rewind and then play again. I played it so many times the
machine would have broken if it was a real DVD that was
spinning instead of my mind. I made up a bunch of different
DVDs and each one had a different ending. Like maybe if I
just talked to Cyrus about how mad I was about what went on
downstairs, instead of backing up against him like that. Or
maybe if I just dissed him while he was hanging out with those
guys. But I was afraid to mess with the three of them. There
were so many ways that it could have worked out different. Do
over, do over.

Ms. Seibel said, "Zack, why aren't you working on your
essay? You're going to lose points if it's too short."

LeVar yelled out, "He's not worryin' about no points
today, no way! He's buggin' out about Cyrus 'cause he whacked
him and now Cyrus in the hospital. Zack freakin' 'cause he
knows it wasn't no accident!"

Then Louis yelled, "Yeah, he dropped Cyrus 'cause Cyrus
was gonna beat him in the championship at the Garden next
week!"

I turned around real slow and stared LeVar right in his
face. I gave Louis that same look, like I was totally cool, like
those guys were the ones who were wack. Like try to say
anything else. Make my day, Louis.

Everyone says Ms. Seibel teaches Home Ec because she's
afraid of boys. Now, she looked all mashed up. She said,
"Okay you two, that's enough! Get back to work or you'll lose
points!"

Then Lateesha yelled, "How come they gonna lose points
even though they writin' they essay? That ain't fair!"

Everyone cracked up again, and Ms. Seibel started
screaming which is something she is famous for. This is why I

wanted to stay home. I figured this kind of stuff was going to happen. If it had to happen, I wanted it to be in Mr. di P's class because he's an historian like my mom. He knows how people make up facts when they can't be bothered to figure them out. He would have told LeVar and Louis they didn't have a clue of what they were talking about.

After a while, I tuned out all the noise and shut my eyes so I could send mind-waves out to Cyrus and get him to wake up. "C'mon Cyrus, c'mon man," I kept saying with my eyes squeezed tight. Cyrus, man, you gotta wake up so I can say I'm sorry!

Our art teacher, Mrs. Bellisano, said, "Today we're going to make get well cards for Cyrus."

I drew a picture of a chess piece, a king. On the bottom I wrote, "Cyrus, You Are The King." Inside, I wrote, "Get Well Soon." Then I signed my name in ink and folded my arms and put my head down.

That's when I started hearing Le Var and Ronnie whispering stuff about Mr. di P getting fired or transferred to another school. It was knotting me up inside so I told myself to ignore it or they would win this little game of theirs. Inside my head, I was thinking that if Mr. di Perna got transferred, I would transfer to any school he was in. No way, I was going to stay around with these creeps harassing me forever.

Jenny Yee must have heard the whispering too because she raised her hand and said, "Is it true Mr. di Perna is never coming back?"

Mrs. Bellisano said, "Where'd you get that information? Really, Jenny, this is an art class. I can't be bothered with every piece of nonsense that drops off the grapevine."

Jenny turned to the back of the room where Ronnie and LeVar were carrying on and made a so-there! kind of face. But Mrs. Bellisano had not really answered her question.

Mrs. Bellisano collected the cards and said some of the teachers would be visiting the hospital after school and she would deliver our cards personally. I wanted to let her know some things about Cyrus, like about the machines, and about his eyes moving under his lids, but I just handed in my card and stayed under the radar.

"C'mon, Cyrus," I kept saying all day. "Please, please, please!" I could feel my wish fill up my whole body and whoosh out to Cyrus in that hospital uptown. I guess maybe that's what a prayer is.

I didn't get to visit him. *Mater* and *Pater* got Grandma Clara to stay with us and went to the hospital to see how Cyrus was doing. Calling my grandmother to come over is something my mom only does in emergencies. She'd rather not let us stay too much with Grandma because she thinks Grandma will give Hallie and me some wack ideas. She's right to worry about this. My sister already has a lot of my grandmother's ideas.

But Grandma Clara is not totally crazy. She can sleep all night sitting up in a closet, and live for days on bread and water. She also says she can tell what's happening in places she can't see, and predict the future. That's where her story starts getting sketchy.

I wanted to ask Grandma what was going to happen with Cyrus, and whether Mr. di P was coming back, but I know she always predicts bad stuff. My Dad says she relies on the Law of Large Numbers which is if a person always expects the worst, some of what she expects is bound to happen. I don't need any bad predictions right now.

-6-

NUMBED BY FEAR AND GRIEF, I waited in the lobby of the Alma Schomburg Neuroscience Wing. Cyrus had been moved there in the still-dark hours of the morning, no better and no worse than he'd been the night before. Over and over, my mind formed the word "please," but I did not know where to address my importuning. To whom was I speaking? For the first time in my life, I wished I had a religion of some sort, a powerful listener I could believe in.

My parents brought a very small life along with them when they came to America. What was left of each of their families was scattered over England, Lebanon, Israel and even Taiwan. Their wisdom divided the human race between the evil and the impotent; they resolved to keep their heads down and stay to themselves, grateful to have work, and each other, and, eventually, to have me. They had few affiliations beyond my Aunt Charlotte, and Leon Belkin, my father's partner in a small bookselling business downtown. When my father died, there was no ceremony, only Aunt Charlotte, Leon, and my mother, shoveling dirt into his grave. I've been told no prayers were said, my parents having long since parted company with God.

I was left at home that day and was told my father had gone off for a year in a hot air balloon, the religion my mother devised to solace my little girl heart. I never took the balloon story as actual fact, of course; I believed it as I might have believed in God if that were what my mother had served up instead. I accepted the balloon as her gift of comfort and, too, as an admonishment to inquire no further.

Although I did once or twice attend a schoolmate's confirmation, and a midnight mass at Christmas with a

Catholic boy I knew, those brushes with the world's faiths merely advanced my education as might a trip to the Museum of Natural History. When Stephen and I married, we silenced my mother-in-law's pleas for a religious ceremony by threatening not to marry at all and to give our children a pair of unwed parents. Until that afternoon in the Schomburg Wing, I had nothing for my religion but a hot air balloon. And I hadn't, until then, considered myself lacking.

I had been up to see Viola though it was against hospital rules. The receptionist handed me a sign-in sheet and jotted down the extension of the nurses' station, then pointed me toward the house phone. "I hope someone up there can tell you something. Sometimes they do, sometimes they don't." I tried the number several times before my guerilla instincts kicked in.

Double doors in the rear lobby led to a bank of elevators, one for freight, the others "For Staff Use Only." The car arrived carrying a clutch of doctors. Displaying my briefcase, I stepped in.

Along the corridor, in an alcove housing a beverage dispenser, I found Viola. My heart almost raced out of me.

"Viola! How is he? How are *you?*"

"You're not supposed to come up here," Viola said. Her voice was flat and her eyes avoided mine.

"I had to see you," I said, taking a step toward her.

But Viola stepped back. "He's about the same," she said wearily, "and I'm holding my own. How's Zack?"

I was startled to hear her pair our sons that way, as if they'd both come down with a stomach virus at the same time. It was an automatic response, nothing she really wanted to know.

"Zack is hanging in," I said, although that seemed wrong. "Can I see Cyrus?" I searched Viola's face. Cyrus, in his immense bandage and blue pajamas, had entirely occupied my mind all through the night and into the day.

Viola closed her eyes and thrust her chin up as though she were trying hard to swallow. She pressed her thumb and third finger against her closed lids and rubbed them.

"You don't want to go in there," she said. "There's a whole army of doctors checking and measuring. Some people from the church are coming to the hospital chapel this evening. Maybe you could come then."

I flung my arms around her and pulled her close, but her body remained rigid in my arms. "Of course, I'll be there. Of course!"

None of my words would sound like my own that day. I was struggling to be my old self with Viola, but our world had changed and had changed us with it.

"Let me do something, Vi," I said as I released her. "I want to help, even just sit with you if that's what you'd like."

Viola shook her head and urged me toward the elevator.

"I'll be downstairs," I said. "If you need anything . . . anything at all, Vi, even if you just want to talk . . . Stephen's coming after the kids' dinner and I'll be in the lobby. So, don't hesitate . . . please!"

I sneaked off to find Cyrus's room and steal a glimpse of him. His room was easy enough to find: men and women in white coats looking down at him, up at one another, nodding and scribbling on their clipboards, so many of them they spilled into the hall.

Besides the doctors, the room was filled with machines. I understood that what they were measuring were merely the signals of yet another complex machine. What if the body they were all taking such pains with turned out to be like the splendid abandoned armor of the horseshoe crabs Zack and Hallie loved to salvage from the beach at Wellfleet? Certainly, the sturdy arms and legs and all the rest of Cyrus were perfectly recognizable when I scrunched down to catch sight of him between the columns of starched white coats. And certainly it might all keep right on thumping, producing a pulse and fluids with the proper balance of chemicals. But Cyrus, the brilliant chess player with that indomitable wit might all the while have vanished forever. It might be that the one for whom that body had been crafted, to the precise specifications of whose particular nature it had all been fitted out and to whom it had been given at that elusive threshold moment when fetuses turn into children—it could turn out that that wondrous boy was no longer there!

Only a day earlier, I'd felt certain that Cyrus's injuries could not possibly be fatal, that my own son could not so faultlessly fall from grace. But outside that room of white-coated specialists, I felt the truth fluctuate, shallow as my breath. On the intake, Cyrus would surely open his eyes and demand to know where he was; on the exhalation, the church people would arrive in time to learn he'd already "crossed over." When I drew the air in, Zack would emerge more impressed with the world's fragility, and more able to go forward with his shiny young life; then, as my chest sank again, I could see that my son might be ruined beyond repair. Of course, the world had always been like that: It had been possible at every moment for things to go either way. I simply hadn't needed to take notice.

My afternoon in the Schomburg lobby went on forever. I told myself I was grading my students' papers but, although I did, from time to time, glance down and read a paragraph or two, I could not halt the images of Cyrus and Viola reeling through my mind, images of two loved ones slipping away from me.

My class that morning had ended in disaster. I'd assigned *The New York Feminist Manifesto*, a classic. There is an equally classic critique that argues that the New York Feminists failed to consider poorer women and women of color, and it was predictable that one of my students would raise this. But before I knew what was happening, a fight broke out.

Meryl Simmons, a pretty black woman, said, "These so-called Feminists didn't know what was going on. All this stuff about good jobs and equal pay? This stuff about alimony? Unreal!"

"Meryl, I think you have to explain what was unreal, as you put it."

"My grandmother had three different jobs and she thought she was lucky no matter what they paid. And there wasn't anyone she knew ever heard of alimony. All the men just up and walked off and the women did the best they could. Couldn't ever find the man even if you did want to divorce him. So no one was getting any divorces, let alone alimony. Alimony was some rich white bitch kind of thing."

"Cut out that 'bitch' talk," Nancy Hammersmith yelled. "I don't know why all you black women have to call every white woman a bitch. Alimony was compensation for the work women did during marriage because they weren't trained for jobs."

"Well, that's it right there," Meryl shot back. "My grandmother had no more training for a job than any white bitch, but she wasn't getting any alimony either, so she just went out there and hustled. Maybe if your grandmother didn't have alimony, she would have learned to hustle her ass, too."

This conversation was supposed to be about gender, but it had flared into a brawl about race: All the same issues that had been raised back in the seventies were fresh and alive as ever, fueling tempers to the boiling point in my seminar room. And I was a hundred miles away, fearing for Viola and murmuring my silent prayers. As the bell rang, ending the class, I could not even remember the title of the essay I wanted to assign for the following week.

Unable to work in the hospital lobby, I phoned upstairs to Viola. "Why not let me sit with him for a while?" I said. "You really ought to have a break."

Viola sounded very far away. She would not, she told me firmly, leave Cyrus's side.

Over and over, a huge lump rose in my throat that sent me fleeing to the ladies' room to splash water on my face. Back in the lobby, I'd pace. Stay positive, I instructed myself.

Stephen strode through the lobby's revolving door promptly at six-thirty. He carried a paper shopping bag with Chinese food and a Diet Coke for himself, a little tray of sushi and a bottle of spring water for me.

"I called Zack at home," I said. "He was much too quiet."

"He's tired. He got to bed late."

"It's stress, Stephen. The kids were teasing him about Cyrus. And Mr. di Perna was absent. He's terribly upset about that."

"He can handle it, sweetheart. He's stronger than you think."

"Viola's managing, but only barely. These exam papers, by the way,"—I waved the blue exam booklets I had piled on my lap—"are awful. The church people are coming at seven-thirty. There hasn't been a new report so far. . . ."

I could see Stephen pick up on the way my mind was splintering. He was hauling himself back to a place from which he could be the calm commander I would need if Cyrus failed to wake. He handed me some chopsticks.

"I saw him," I said. "I got up to the room—"

"That was foolish. You shouldn't have done that. Let's just have supper, okay?"

"Okay."

I pried open the sushi tray and stared at the raw fish.

"Tell me about your day. The seminar this morning? How'd it go?"

"Disaster," I said. "I started thinking of Viola and how strong she's been since Phil died. She's become an Amazon, you know? She's both mother and father to Cyrus. What'll she do if—?"

"For God's sake!"

I returned to my story of the morning's class, trying to follow the regimen Stephen was prescribing. But the morning had been no better than the rest of the day.

Stephen shook his head and reached out a hand to stroke mine. "Sorry, sweetheart. We knew it wouldn't be easy."

He carried our trash to the bin. When he returned, he stooped to kiss my brow. "We'll get through this," he said.

He's a good man, I thought for the trillionth time, as good a man as there is.

The hospital lobby filled with people wanting visitor's passes. It was useless trying any longer to remain calm. I crammed the bluebooks into my book bag. "C'mon, Stephen," I said. "Let's head up to that chapel."

In the elevator car, I nodded hello to several parents from the Special Enrichment Program: Mimi Yee and LeVar's parents, Wintell and Dorothy Morrison.

The little chapel was crowded when we arrived, people hustling to get the best seats, nodding gently to those they knew and looking solemnly at others they did not recognize. Barbara Schnurr, who had planned the trip to Washington, and Carmen Mejias, the trip escort, were there. So were a few teachers: Marjorie Woods, the music teacher, Terry Avery, the chess coach. I nodded hello and they nodded back.

Viola was seated in the center of the first row. She turned and caught sight of us and then, immediately, shut her eyes. Pastor Ray Oakes, a huge, graying man in expensively tailored clothes, could have been a polished old Cadillac pulled right up in front of her, looking out at the gathering of people from his church and others from the Special Enrichment Program.

Viola caught the pastor's eye and urged him to start. But another knot of visitors suddenly appeared hurrying toward the front of the chapel. Four or five nattily-groomed black men.

Stephen exhaled audibly. "Oh, Christ!"

I leaned my head on his shoulder and glanced up at him. "What?"

"Marcus Hake," Stephen whispered. "He sure does get around."

So that's Hake, I thought with a secret thrill. Stephen's nemesis in the city's political sphere, but a man I'd secretly admired for years. A strong voice for his community and, often enough, a broker for peace. I thought I might want to introduce myself later if time permitted.

Pastor Oakes acknowledged the new arrivals, then nodded to Viola. Stephen folded his arms around me and clasped his hands beneath my chin.

Oakes began: "Lord Almighty, *hear* your children . . ." I stared at Viola. Her shoulders sagged, but her back was perfectly straight, her head tilted slightly to one side.

"We beg you, O Lord, pre*serve* for us your most *pre*cious child. Wake him from his sleep and re*store* him to your servant, his *saint*ly mother, Mrs. *Vi*ola Nightingale. For his mother has *suf*fered, Lord . . ." I closed my eyes and imagined the blue paper legs of Cyrus's pajamas, the flannel blanket neatly folded across the foot of his bed. Oakes' voice, like a locomotive, was gathering steam.

What could I say in my own voice? Bring Cyrus back to us, O Medical Science, O Technology? How I longed for the assurance I saw on the faces around me. Not a single tear!

Oakes' voice and arms rose and fell in unison. Cyrus is "a *beau*tiful child," "a most *pro*mising student," "his blessed mother's pride and joy." Yes, I agreed, he is all of that. "O,

Cyrus," I said in my inside voice, "you must come back, you must! For Viola! For Zack! For us all!" My original prayer. "Amen," I said with the others.

Oakes' words had imperceptibly become a melody, a hymn I didn't know. Stephen and I stood to join the others who were singing along with the pastor. Why couldn't they sing "Amazing Grace," a song to which I knew all six verses? I didn't bother to move my lips. People can always tell when you're faking.

Marjorie Woods' rich mezzo-soprano voice rose above the others. Mr. Avery knew the hymn, and so did the Morrisons. I could see Dorothy Morrison far to my right; her mouth was tight, angry-looking. From time to time, she raised her eyes in Marcus Hake's direction. Hake knew the words, and he sang off key just enough so you could pick out his separate voice.

I felt relieved when the hymn was done. I had passed the singing time with my jaw set hard against the impulse to cry.

Stephen maneuvered me through the crowd to Viola and I squatted down in front of her. "It's going to work," I told her. "He's going to wake up soon, I can feel it."

Viola did not look up. "We'll see what the new day brings," she said. Her voice was husky. I could smell her sweat and her souring hair cream.

"I love you, Vi," I whispered, and kissed her cheek.

On the way out, I shook the pastor's hand. His handshake was vague, and he looked past me into the crowded room. He knows, I decided. I lack faith. Stephen lacks faith. We are being polite, but we're placing our bets with the scientists and their flashy machines. We haven't got the music in us, we didn't even know the words.

In silence, we walked across the lobby and out onto the street.

"The pastor doesn't like us," I told Stephen. "He knows we're non-believers; I could tell from his handshake. Did you sense it?"

"That wasn't the problem," Stephen said flatly.

"What was it then?"

"I don't know. Maybe he's queasy with Hake and me, two political enemies, in the same place at a time that's supposed to be sacred. Maybe he knows something I don't. I'm not sure what it is, but it's not what you're thinking."

"Well, he didn't want us to feel welcome, that much was clear."

"We weren't welcome, I agree," Stephen said. "Just forget it, sweetie, okay? No point making things worse." He walked to the curb and hailed a cab.

I held myself rigid in the taxi, resisting the lurches and screeching turns. We had stood on the bridge between life and death. It was like nowhere we had been before; we could not give it a name. So we rode in perfect silence. When I stepped out of the cab, I threw up. Bits of salmon and eel and flecks of rice. And then, water and mucous. Then, simple dry retching. Then tears.

Hallie opened the door for us. She was wearing her expensive pink flannel pajamas with sheep printed all over them, a present from Stephen's mother.

"Did he wake up yet? Is he okay?" She bounced on the balls of her feet.

Zack ambled in behind her, his hands crammed into the pockets of his corduroys, and struck as careless a pose as he could manage. "So, Mom? Is he?"

"There's still time," I said. "We have to be patient."

I dashed to the bathroom to rinse my mouth. I could not let my children smell sickness on me.

Stephen urged my mother to get herself together so he could walk her home.

"It's not good, what's going on here," she told him. "I knew this, you know—"

"Thanks for coming over, Ma," Stephen said. "It was a big help. Really."

"You should listen to Grandma, you know," Hallie said. "In the War, she learned to see things other people can't. She can see the future sometimes."

"For heaven's sake, Ma!" I said. "What are you doing to their heads?"

"Grandma is a very wise woman," Hallie said. "She knows practically everything. You shouldn't ignore her like that."

My mother held my face close to hers. "That's a smart daughter you have there," she said. "She has a good future, that child. You go to sleep now, precious," she told Hallie. "You're a beautiful girl. Strong. Smart." She turned back to me, still holding my face. I sucked in my breath lest she discover my secret.

"Good night," I said, and kissed her on the ear. Her skin was still firm and smooth.

Stephen led my mother to the door. When they were gone, I turned to my children. Hallie came easily into my arms smelling like fresh laundry. But I had to coax my son.

"I want to see him!" Zack cried. "I want to talk to him!"

"You have to be fourteen," I said. "Anyway, there's nothing you can do, sweetheart. The doctors are the best in the world. We just have to hope..." Each word landed with a thud. As the world gets more immense, our words for it can't keep up. "Come," I said, "let's have a hug."

But Zack pulled away. "They have to let me in," he insisted. "I'm his best friend. I'm the one who.... Mom, what if he DIES?"

"We'll all be the saddest we've ever been."

"But . . . MAH-OM!" Zack turned abruptly and ran to his room.

I released my daughter and sprinted after him.

"Mah-om!"

I sat beside him on his bed and switched myself off. I turned on my mothering machine, the answers I knew I should give no matter what I was feeling. "If Cyrus dies," I said as evenly as possible, "we will all be very, very sad. And you will be one of the saddest. Eventually, things will get easier, but you'll always remember this and feel sad about it." I laid my hand at the nape of his neck, coaxing him to rest his head in my lap. "Anyway, we're getting way ahead of ourselves. Cyrus might wake at any time. No one can say when it could happen."

Zack reared back and stared into my face. "But Ma! What if he doesn't, what if . . .?"

I had no further answers and I told him so. I pulled him close and rocked the two of us. It was all I could think to do.

All that second night, I drifted from Stephen to Zack and back again, a nocturnal ferry, picking up and delivering consolation. I'd stretch myself out beside one, then the other, unwilling to close my eyes and unable to keep my thoughts from traveling back to Viola.

I was alone again in the Schomburg lobby the next morning, trying to learn something about Cyrus's condition. All the man at the front desk would say is that Cyrus had been moved to the I.C.U.

But why? What had happened during the night? I received no answers. Once again, I ducked into the elevator reserved for staff. Scarcely breathing, I rode to the floor where the I.C.U. was located.

In an alcove just around the corner from the elevator bank, I found Pastor Oakes pacing about, drinking iced tea from a can.

"How is he?" I asked, hoping to be recognized and not have to identify myself.

"Not good," said the pastor. He shook his head from side to side. "He's on some kind of breathing machine."

I began to walk away. I had to find Viola. I had to let her know I was there for her, rooting for Cyrus, praying for him.

"You can't go in," Oakes called after me. "They won't let you through the door. Viola's got her sister, June, with her now. Flew in last night from Georgia. That's two of them and that's all that can go in there."

I returned to the alcove and sat down on one of the worn plastic chairs. Stephen would soon arrive from City Hall and I supposed he'd find me there. I checked my watch, then stood up and walked down the corridor and back again. The Pastor crumpled the tea can and set it down on the plastic table that stood between our two plastic chairs. It seemed an hour had passed since I'd arrived.

At last, I began another walk through the corridors. I had to find Viola. Outside the I.C.U., I rinsed my hands at the soap dispenser and, as a visitor exited through the electronically-controlled doors, I slipped in.

In the center of the wide, brightly-lit space, a vast nurses' station was banked with computers and scattered with files, in-boxes, out-boxes, clipboards. Phones rang insistently. Surrounding the station, in a horseshoe formation, open-ended cubicles were hung with blue privacy curtains, most of them pushed back to expose the intensive care patients to constant observation. As soon as I entered the area, my eyes lit on Viola, perched on the edge of Cyrus's bed and, cautiously, I made my way toward her.

Cyrus's gauze turban was gone. Only a lonesome brown head, tucked up almost to its chin in a mound of soft white sheets, rested on the pillow. The tracheotomy tube was still stuck into his throat, connected, now, to a ventilator, a small one I supposed had been designed especially for children. The machine kept up an infernal hum, a sound interrupted by regular pings and pongs.

Viola bent over her son and pressed her cheek to his. June hovered close behind, clasping Viola around the waist as if to shield her from the hurtful room. On the other side of Cyrus's bed, a nurse checked her clipboard chart and then the dials and levers on a wall-mounted machine.

June stood up and saw me inching closer. Her face turned angry and she motioned to me to leave. When she saw that I would not, she came over and introduced herself. "It's not so good, today,' she said. "He won't breathe right without the ventilator."

I told her I was Viola's best friend.

"I know who you are," she answered, ruefully.

"He needs more   time," I said. The words came automatically and I knew my voice lacked conviction.

June blinked hard and shook her head impatiently. "You need to leave here," she said. "You can't stay in this place." She looked up beyond me toward the nurses' station and I knew she was about to call for someone to show me out.

"Please kiss your sister for me," I said.

June turned abruptly to return to Cyrus's bedside, and I slouched back to the electronic doors and left.

When Stephen finally arrived at the little alcove, I felt he must have brought something benevolent: a potion, a charm—something that would alter the balance of good and evil in that terrible place. I introduced him to Pastor Oakes and told him about June. Stephen had already succeeded in getting an update on Cyrus's condition; he knew all about the ventilator.

"Does this mean . . . ?"

Stephen put his finger to his lips. There were no questions to be asked because there were none that could be answered. Nothing meant anything. Everything was an unknown.

Time moved both very quickly and very slowly, as if someone were messing with the clock of the world.

Suddenly, a surreal bleeping split the area where the three of us stood, urgent and demanding, a single note that seemed to grow in intensity. The nurse I had seen in the I.C.U. with her clipboard dashed past us, followed by another I had not seen before. I heard the P.A. system announce a "Core Zero" and then the name Nightingale. Within moments, medical personnel—what seemed a dozen of them—emerged from every direction, streaming through the corridor toward the I.C.U. Pastor Oakes started as if to join them and then, remembering where he was, hung back. Stephen and I, immobile, held each other. But then we, along with the Pastor, drifted toward the I.C.U. as if carried on the powerful currents of a river in floodtime.

We knew that inside the unit the well-drilled, perfectly-coordinated team was going swiftly, efficiently about its work. In my mind's eye I could see the doctors yank down Cyrus's bed sheets and thump on·his small young chest. We had all witnessed this particular scene on television too often not to grasp what was happening.

When a second surge of medics rushed past us, we followed in their wake and sailed with them into the I.C.U. At Cyrus's bedside, they went to work, each at his assigned task, highly-trained experts trying their utmost to restart Cyrus's heart. Chest compressions, blood pressure readings, the bright monitors being checked as every second ticked by.

I held tightly to Stephen's hand, as the heroic team, moving in a perfect choreography, tried, and tried, and tried yet again to revive the failing heart. So small a body, so small a heart.

But even as they leaned in, throwing their collective energy toward the still, dark child on the bed, I knew. And Stephen knew. He turned me toward him so I could no longer watch. But I did not have to see it to understand what was happening. I tried to force a different scene into my mind but the truth came barging through: The brave little heart was giving out.

The doctor at Cyrus's bedside straightened and backed away from the bed; his arms hung limp at his sides and his head sank to his chest. He could not even manage to say "I'm sorry." No one could utter a word. Viola covered her son with her body and wept. June knelt and held her sister.

Stephen wrapped himself so tightly around me that I could barely breathe. I took tiny sips of air from his warm armpit and let go little exhalations that each formed the silent word, "No." No. No. No, no, no, no, no!

"I'm sorry, but you are not allowed in here," I heard a nurse say. Her voice was gentle but firm.

Pastor Oakes, in his clerical garb, was permitted to approach the cubicle. He bent over Viola and gently urged her away from the bed as he began his prayer.

"You need to clear this area," The nurse said, more insistently this time. "Only immediate family, please."

But I could not move, even as I felt Stephen tug at my arm.

The clipboard nurse stepped in front of Pastor Oakes. Painstakingly, she peeled back the little square bandage at Cyrus's' throat and extracted the plastic tube. The ventilator had already been switched off. The windows showing the digital graphs had already gone dark. Freed of this last connection to the world, Cyrus floated out into our somber space, lingered a moment, and was gone.

-7-

Sunday, October 17, 4 p.m.

THE WORST HAPPENED.

I can't believe he's dead. I can't believe any of this. It still feels like he's here.

I wish they had let me see Cyrus when he was in the hospital. He couldn't talk, but at least I could've tried talking to *him*. I could have told him I'm sorry and asked him to forgive me. I didn't even get to say good-bye.

Some of the people who went up to see him in the coffin talked to him there which was seriously weird.

My mom said, "You don't have to go up there if you don't want to."

My dad said, "You can look if you like. It's up to you."

My sister ran up to the front of the church and pushed into the line. She grabbed a look at Cyrus and ran right back to the pew where we were sitting. She said, "He looks just the same to me." That's my sister.

I thought maybe Cyrus would look different, but he didn't. He just looked like he was sleeping. He was wearing a suit, and I wondered when he got it. My first suit is the one I wore today. I only got it yesterday when my mom took me downtown. We also got some black shoes which are hugely stiff and heavy.

Cyrus's mother was standing next to the coffin and she yanked me into a hug. She said, "Oh, Zack! He loved you so much! When I think about you two playing chess . . ." Then she started to cry, and I didn't know what to say so I just stood there letting her hug me. I wished like anything she'd let me go. That hug was hurting my whole body.

I started crying when I got back to the pew. It was Mrs. Nightingale saying that about chess that did it. I don't know what I'll do when I grow up, or even what I would want to study in college, but I guess I always figured Cyrus and me would be playing chess together, even when we got real old.

Looking at Cyrus in his coffin totally creeped me out. I don't get how someone can be running up behind you on the stairs one day, doing his eyebrow thing, and then he's totally gone. Death is something I don't exactly understand yet.

When they started up the singing, I felt like Cyrus might be sitting next to me, like when I came to church with him sometimes. But then the pastor started talking about him and I snapped back. Pastor Oakes does this up-and-down thing with his voice so all his speeches sound the same. He was going up and down telling about Cyrus and I kept looking at Cyrus's mother even though that was the last place I wanted to look. I wanted to make sure she wasn't looking at me, the kid who knocked Cyrus down the stairs. He was her whole entire world. And I am the one who took him away.

The pastor went on and on about Cyrus being in the Special Enrichment Program, and being a chess champion, the president of our class and an all-around uber great kid.

Ronnie Holmes and Louis Byrne were sitting with Ronnie's mother, wearing white shirts and ties; when they caught me looking at them they stuck out their chins and turned away like I was some kind of lowlife. LeVar was there and he wasn't acting too friendly either. Jenny Yee had her mother and father and grandmother, and some patent leather shoes with high heels that I figured must hurt her feet as much as my shoes hurt mine.

I think our whole class was there, and all the teachers, too. Except Mr. di P who was still missing in action. It was like one of those celebrity funerals where everyone was coming to say how much they loved Cyrus. And I knew they were all hating on me because it was me that killed Cyrus. *Mea culpa.*

I thought of the time I was shooting baskets with Cyrus in the basement of that church. When we got tired of it, Cyrus took out his pocket chess set so we could play best of three. We were up to the second game when, bam! the lights went out. The janitor must have shut down the power or something, and then he went home. Trouble was, he locked Cyrus and me inside.

It was already dark out and there was a huge amount of snow. We thought we'd call my mom or Cyrus's, but the pastor's office where they have the phone was locked, too. Upstairs, we found a window we could open. We jumped out onto the roof of a lower part of the building and looked over the ledge to see if maybe someone would come along to help us.

I checked things out on all sides. I said, "It looks like that iron fence with the tall spikes goes all around the building."

Cyrus said, "Yeah, they got to protect everything around here, or homeless people get in and mess the place up."

I said, "We might have to spend the night in this place if nobody shows up down there."

Nobody came and we were getting hugely cold. We figured we could jump from the roof to the sidewalk if we could clear the iron spikes.

I said, "I vote we do it. I'm hungry and I want to go home."

Cyrus said, "Me, too. I vote we do it." Then he made those funny eyebrows and he said, "Well, that's it then. The motion carries."

We picked a place where there was plenty of snow piled up. I jumped first and landed on my book bag. I stood up so I could break Cyrus's fall, and when he jumped he landed on top of me and we both went down in the snow together. Lucky for us, we didn't get impaled on the spikes. We both could have died right there. But it was a truly great escape!

We swore we'd never tell our parents about any of it. When I got home, I wanted to tell them but I knew they'd just get steamed. Cyrus and me talked about it the whole next day. We decided to call it "The Thing." Sometimes, when we were walking somewhere, Cyrus would just say, like out of nowhere, "Remember 'The Thing?'" And when someone told some great story at school, I'd whisper, "That's not as good as 'The Thing.'" But we always kept the secret.

Now, it's a secret I will have inside me forever, just me and "The Thing" and no one to say it to.

"The Thing" was uber dangerous, but no one got hurt cause I landed on a pile of snow and Cyrus landed on me. If only I could've been at the bottom of those stairs in the bus station instead of up at the top when Cyrus fell.

My parents were the first ones to go up to the front of the church when Pastor Oakes got done with the sermon. They hugged Mrs. Nightingale and her sister and everyone cried. I stayed in the pew. I was thinking how it's going to be when I'm back in school, everyone hating on me, no Mr. di P, and Cyrus not being there to hang out with. I wish I had something of his I could carry around with me, like a good luck charm or something so I would feel he was still there.

I feel like getting lost somewhere that no one will find me.

-8-

THE DAY AFTER CYRUS WAS BURIED, Stephen came home early. He seemed startled to find me there. I usually have office hours on Monday afternoons, but I'd cancelled them.

There was no hello kiss, no "How are you?"

"Better sit down," he said.

"What?"

The funeral still hung thick around me: the sight of a child in a satin-lined box, the coldness of Viola's hand. When I called that morning to check on Viola, June told me, coldly, I thought, that Viola was asleep, would be asleep for a long time because she'd been given medication to calm her down. I should not try to call again that day, she'd said.

It was an anxious, miserable woman Stephen found when he arrived home.

He said he'd been called in to see the mayor, an emergency conference. Marcus Hake was there, Stephen said, to discuss the case of the three boys who had shot up the cafeteria. I wondered what that had to do with Stephen.

"He wants an investigation into the accident."

"What accident?"

"The accident."

"*Our* accident?"

"He wants the D.A.'s office to look into it."

"What? Stephen!" I sprang out of the chair and lunged toward him, "Stephen, this is crazy! What is there to investigate? Zack has been through enough. We all have!"

In the days following Cyrus's death, I'd kept Zack at home. Even Stephen had agreed Zack needed time off. The principal was bringing in a grief counselor to help all the kids adjust, but I had taken Zack to a private therapist, a man recommended by Dr. Franks. I'd told him Zack had turned silent and had virtually stopped eating.

"That's normal in this sort of situation," the therapist said, "but he'll come around in time. You're doing the right thing bringing him here. Just try to keep his days as normal as possible, keep things moving."

I didn't believe the therapist could do enough. Could a child of thirteen come to terms with the ambiguity of accidents, with feeling himself to be the cause of his own unfathomable loss? Zack needed time to make peace with all that had happened. He was writing twice a day in his journal, hopefully working out the difficult concept of "unintended consequences."

"There are some kids in the class who claim they saw it," Stephen was telling me. "They say it wasn't an accident." He looked down at a crumpled paper in his hand. "Louis Byrne, LeVar Morrison and Ronnie Holmes. Hake says they witnessed it, and he brought them into the D.A.'s office to make their statements."

"This is *insane*," I said. "There was no one in that stairwell but Cyrus and Zack. Zack knows there was no one else there with them."

"Nevertheless, Hake wants an investigation. This is his new cause."

"His *what*?"

Stephen began to circle the room; it's his habit, when he sorts through something difficult, to drop his jaw to his chest and clomp around in circles.

"Of course, in his view, it's connected to his other project," Stephen said, his head still sunk low, his brow deeply furrowed. "He wants the three kids who shot up that school cafeteria charged as juveniles, not adults. They were fourteen and fifteen. The D.A. is charging attempted murder and will ask for a blended sentence. That means that eventually, they'll serve time in an adult prison. Hake wants an investigation into Cyrus' death so he can set up some sort of deal . . ."

Stephen rambled on, trying to figure out what Hake was up to. He paced round and round, setting out arguments, weighing the pros and cons. For years, he and Hake had opposed one another in City Hall budget struggles, and for years Hake had been on Stephen's enemies list.

It was just "hypothetical," Stephen kept saying, but I stopped trying to follow him. My mind was flooding and I feared I might soon fly up and wreck his neat stacks of premises as if they were so many houses of cards. But still, what would Marcus Hake want with our son?

"You see?" Stephen finally stopped and looked at me. His hair was greasy with hand-sweat and chunks of it peaked up at odd angles. "Three white victims," he said, gesturing with both his arms to his left, "and three black kids in jail," he said, shifting his arms to the right. "And now, a black kid dies,...and there's this white kid..." He shoved his face forward as if to read some very small print in the air before him. "Believe me, Bettina, that's the way he thinks. To him it's a game: Capture a piece from the other side and then you can work out a trade. That's pure Hake!"

I'd first heard of Marcus Hake when I was in college and he was the miracle boy from Brooklyn. A fatherless kid from a scourge of a neighborhood, he was a basketball star with top grades; there were murmurs of a Rhodes scholarship one day. A guidance adviser steered him to a small upstate college so he would be noticed on the courts but also have time to study. The guy had meant well.

Hake quit halfway into his second semester. He'd been one of three black freshmen; the other two were girls. Depressed and angry, he returned home and enrolled at Brooklyn College where he was kept off the team for a year because his first-semester grades had been too low. He told the sportswriter for The Daily News that he'd been cheated out of stardom by a "white man's scheme to make him into a white guy's idea of success." He soon dropped out of college altogether and disappeared.

But Marcus Hake was endowed with an extraordinary talent for self-transformation, and the next time I had news of him he was running for a seat on the City Council. He soon became a power broker known for calling more press conferences than any other member of the Council. Easily galvanized by racial issues, he could be counted on to muster an impressive crowd at the merest whisper of discrimination and stir them into a frenzy. Getting the charges against the cafeteria shooters dropped to juvenile offenses was merely his latest campaign. I had to wonder how Hake would have come out had he received better guidance in high school.

Stephen couldn't help seeing Hake as obstructionist, an opportunist who seized every imaginable issue, no matter how remote, to put his people and his agenda—but mostly him*self*—into the headlines. As we both well knew, it was Hake who had recently tried to block spending for Stephen's sewage treatment project.

My own view of Hake was more complicated, perhaps because I could view him from outside the fray of politics Yes, he was often rude and belligerent, and it was true he could be a bully. But I enjoyed the way he called the side-steppings of city politics exactly as he saw them, and I admired the deft irony he used to undo the status quo. What Stephen saw as self-promotion, I saw as Hake being smarter than his constituency, understanding their interests better than they did themselves and being a fierce advocate for people who needed one. I regretted that I hadn't introduced myself to him at Cyrus's bedside. But, of course, it had never occurred to me that less than a week later he'd come charging into our lives to threaten our son.

"That's totally ridiculous!" I said when Stephen finished describing what he thought was Hake's strategy. "What happened in that cafeteria and what happened at the Port Authority are two entirely different things. Cyrus died because of an *accident!*"

Stephen nodded sadly. "There doesn't have to be a real connection. This is politics. It's about *perception*."

"But it's a blinkered perception! Zack and Cyrus were playing. Those boys in the cafeteria came armed for assault."

"I'm sure that fact is not wasted on Hake." Stephen's mouth curled in a small smile. "But the way he's going to put it out there, boys were being boys. In both cases. Except if they're black, they get charged with attempted murder, while the white kid gets away with it. He's going to challenge the D.A. to balance that out."

"The D.A. can't charge Zack with a crime just so Hake can get a deal for those delinquents! That's off the wall!"

"The mayor claims those kids saw what happened. I'll bet you anything it was Hake who escorted them downtown to talk to her."

My voice pushed through the tightness in my throat. "Those boys who said they saw it? What, exactly, did they claim to see?"

Stephen shook his head vigorously. "Does that matter?" he hollered.

I wasn't used to him raising his voice, and I winced.

"I've got a meeting with the mayor and someone from the D.A.'s office, day after tomorrow," he said more softly. "The mayor was all sweetness when he called me in, but I'd have to offer him some way around Hake and those so-called witnesses if I want him to turn Hake down. He must owe Hake a lot to have let it get this far. This won't be simple."

I stood up to face Stephen, a lump swelling in my throat. "It *is* simple," I cried. "I can't stand all this conniving and second-guessing when the truth is perfectly obvious. It's always some stupid game with you politicians. But they can't play games with our son, Stephen. That's just not going to happen!"

I tore down the hall to our bedroom and stared out at the city. Down every street, behind every window, lives were being ruined—choked by greed, poisoned by ambition, obliterated by self-interest. The city stared back at me, a professor of political theory, a stalwart campaigner for a more just world.

"Sweetheart," Stephen said gently. He stood in the doorway to our room. "I know this could be a bit hard on Zack, but it'll be worse if we try to head it off. Hake will get the press revved up and *they'll* mix this in with the cafeteria case even if the D.A. does nothing. It's better to let them investigate and find nothing. If we get in his way, Hake will blow things up as he always does.

"The mayor's obviously desperate for a bone to throw to him. The D.A., I'm sure, just wants to keep up the office's image as tough on crimes against kids. She won't be as eager as the mayor is to yield to Hake. It's a game, as you said, but I think we have to let it run its course."

"I won't have our son made a scapegoat! I won't let those games get anywhere near him. We owe Zack some peace!"

I turned back to the window. I felt a tear start down my cheek and brushed it aside. "They have to leave us in peace, Stephen. You and me, but most of all Zack."

There was a time when the neighborhood I lived in was filled with shouting. Stephen insists he picked me out in the crush of demonstrators on the steps of Columbia's Low Library because I was shouting more furiously than the rest, but I'm certain I did not see him until I found myself beside him in the back of a police van. I was so ragged with outrage and fear, I doubt I would have paid much attention to him even then were it not for the way he smelled. I was just fifteen and still attending an all-girls high school a few subway stops downtown. Stephen, six years older, smelled like a man. My father had been dead for several years, but even if he had lived, I doubt he would ever have had the smell that came off Stephen in that van. Stephen smelled like a steel ingot drawn from a furnace, a god rising out of the flames to protest injustice on his campus. In those days, I embodied a willy-nilly sort of anger, more reckless than brave, that rose to any provocation; I was on those library steps for the thrill of the noise and commotion. I'd never encountered anyone as intensely focused as Stephen, and I adored the way his salty body filled that van.

By the time I entered graduate school and married Stephen, he was already a force in city government, the boy wonder of city administration who always had his facts straight and kept to his principles. New York City had been rescued from the brink of bankruptcy, and it was barely supplying the needs of its residents. With Stephen's star on the rise at City Hall and me preparing to teach women's history, we grasped our destiny: Cities around the country had gone up in flames, been wrecked and looted, within recent memory. We would drive our root down in the city we both loved and redeem it. We'd rescue its parks, its schools, its children. We'd have children of our own who would be born in a whole new way; they would herald a more just society. Enough of the hated old order had been dislodged by then that Stephen and I could see the possibility of something pure and good, and could feel at least a little powerful, enough to make a difference.

And I suppose it was also true that we wanted the city to rescue *us*. We were just beginning, and we couldn't allow that the revolution was already over. The city would be the direction our lives would take. We could not imagine, in the midst of this blithe dream, that justice and good deeds might have their own dark sides.

Stephen had given the city much to be grateful for and the mayor much to be proud of. But now the mayor was unloading his Hake problem onto us without a bit of concern for the harm that would result to Zack. Where was the justice in that?

I was horrified that this could happen, and more horrified, just then, to hear my own husband say, "I honestly don't think we have much choice. Hake's getting ready, even as we speak, to go to the papers."

"We can do the same," I hastened to say. "We have our own people in the press, people going way back. We'll fight him *and* the mayor—"

"Let me try to keep this in the back room," Stephen said. "We don't need the papers unearthing old stuff about you or me, stuff from way back."

He was right. We'd have to steer clear of the press.

"Do what you have to do," I said, "but don't let them get near Zack. Those guys at the Port Authority—"

"Let's see what I can negotiate."

"N*egotiate*?" I was sputtering. "Our son . . . is not . . . up . . . for negotiation!"

Negotiation was something Stephen was very good at. He had a temperament well-suited to the games a politician must play, the patience and persistence required for all that horse-trading. And he was willing to settle for the middle ground, something I was never able to do. I, myself, could not imagine bargaining with people who were plainly wrong. Zack was innocent, so there was nothing to negotiate.

Stephen and I were about to be at war—with Marcus Hake, with the District Attorney, with the mayor himself—and at stake would be our own little boy. I had to hope I would not be at war with Stephen, too, someday.

-9-

Tuesday, October 19, 1:20 pm

MR. DI P WAS BACK on Monday. The story is his father's blood formed some kind of clot in his brain and gave him a stroke. It happened while we were in Washington and when Mr. di P's wife called him at the bus station, she gave him the news. That's why he kept leaning on you-can-call-me-Al to let him out of there. When I saw him, I wanted to run up and high-five him. He's the only one in this school who doesn't hate me because of what happened to Cyrus.

So it wasn't because he got fired like Lateesha and some others were saying, and it wasn't because he cut out to get away from the cops asking him about the Port Authority, which is another rumor Ronnie and his homeys put around. Mr. di P didn't show all last week because he's the only one who could take care of his father.

When the bell rang at the end of the period, Mr. di P pulled me out of line and asked how it was going. He said, "I'm sorry I couldn't be at Cyrus's funeral. That must have been a miserable day for you."

I said, "It was my first funeral. It was the worst day of my life."

He said, "Well, I hope you don't have to go to another one for a very long time." Then he gave me a sort of sideways hug to say he knew it must have been tough to have your best friend die. He was sorry he had to stay in New Jersey the day of the funeral. He said, "I wish I could've been in both places at the same time. When it rains, it pours. Take good care of yourself, Zack."

I said, "Thanks. You too."

When I got to Math, they were already doing a new topic. Mr. McNamara asked some questions and everyone knew the answers. I got more confused every minute, so I zoned out and stared across the room to where Cyrus used to sit. Mr. McNamara is keeping that seat empty even though it's at the front. Cyrus's seat is empty in all our classes. It's like the teachers all got together and agreed to do that. It would be creepy being the one who had the seat of a kid who just died. I was thinking that I wouldn't mind having that seat, though. That would be better than looking at it every day.

When I heard McNamara call my name, it sounded like it was coming from another planet and I thought, Oh, dammit!

He made me stand and he repeated the question.

The muscles in my neck started to freeze up. I said, "I don't know what you're talking about. I had to stay at Social Studies with Mr. di Perna so I was late."

McNamara said, "You should raise your hand as soon as you have a question, Zack. Don't I always tell you that? There's no shame in not understanding. The shame is in not trying to understand."

McNamara makes a moral lesson out of anything he can get his hands on.

He made me stand there for about three hours while he explained the whole thing all over again. The Pythagorean Theorem. It's a really great thing. While he was explaining it, the kids started cutting up about hearing the same stuff all over again just because of me.

Louis yelled out, "Hey, Zack! You and Mr. di Perna work out what your story's gonna be?"

I said, "Huh?"

Ronnie started to yell the same thing, but McNamara shut him up, and gave them both three morning detentions. Make my day, guys!

It didn't take me long to figure out what Louis was trying to put across. Pretty soon my neck was sending pains up into my head.

By the time we got to Art, my head was a huge ball of hurt. I asked Mrs. Bellisano if I could get a drink of water. LeVar and Louis and Ronnie started making sounds like animals drinking water. I went out to the hall. The next thing I knew, I was in the nurse's office and she was telling me I passed out.

I said, "Where was I?"

The nurse said, "You were in the hall near the water fountain. The custodian found you. You were only out a few minutes."

I was thinking all I would need now would be Ronnie and his homies putting the word around that I was a cupcake wuss or any other lies about me. I never fainted before. It's not my thing. But those guys would have a real party with the news.

Last night, my parents had a talk with the shrink they're sending me to. They're getting me home-tutored until things quiet down. My mother got a Columbia pre-med who must have signed up to tutor some other Columbia kids but instead he got me. I hope he doesn't think my school work is some boring baby stuff.

Mr. di P called to let me know my assignments. He said, "If there's anything else I can do to help, Zack, just give me a call." Then he gave me his cell number just like he wasn't even a teacher.

I said, "I need to talk to those guys who think I pushed Cyrus down the stairs. They have to say that to my face because it isn't true and they know it. Can you help me with that?"

Mr. di P said, "I think you should stay away from them for now, Zack. There are people looking into this and they will prove those kids aren't telling the truth. *Veritas vos liberabit.* The truth will set you free."

I said, "I wish *you* could talk to them. You're always saying that history depends on who's telling the story. But this story is about me, and I'm the only one who knows what happened. I wish you could help me with this, you know?"

Mr. di P got uber quiet. Then he said, "I'm supposed to stay out of this, Zack, but I understand how you feel. I'll figure out something that'll help you, I promise."

I said, "I'd really thank you for that. They're making a lot of trouble for me."

Mr. di P said, "*Illegitimi non carborundum!*" which he says means "Don't Let The Bad Stuff Get You Down," but I looked it up and really it means *bastards*. Don't Let The Bastards Get You Down.

It's totally boring at home, but it's better than being in school. The whole class must've got the word by now and I'd rather give the wuss story some time to fade.

I hope Mr. di P can get those boys to stop their lies cause it's three against one here and the only one on my side is me.

-10-

THE JAPANESE, I've heard, have a word for "woman" that literally translates as "inside person." A man, they say, is an "outside person." I'm no fan of such crass distinctions, but I think it's true that men, more than women, transform themselves entirely when they stride out into the world to do battle with strangers. Even the tenor of their voices changes. When they return home, the armor falls away. Stephen held firm through those City Hall negotiations that put his job on the line but, as he stepped through the door each night, I could see his "outside person" melt like wax and the inside man, the one I loved, emerge in its place. When he returned home from his appointment with the mayor and the D. A., however, I could not detect that soft look of relief. Stephen greeted me as if he were heading into yet another battle.

"How'd it go?" I managed to ask, although I thoroughly dreaded the answer.

"Well, the mayor didn't show. No surprise there, of course. Why should he dirty his hands with this? It was just me and Marian Lindemann. You remember her?"

Yes, I did remember Marian. Anyone who had ever met her would remember the District Attorney. After chatting with her at a City Hall Christmas party, I'd wanted to describe her as straitlaced, but that wasn't quite right because she was too young for that word. So I'd had to leave it at "straight." Marian Lindemann was, in my memory of her, always perfectly straight up. In part, this was due to her physique: trim and tall with superb posture and the legs of a dedicated runner. But there was a personality there that matched her appearance: elegant, strong-willed, a person you absolutely had to take seriously.

Stephen had once said she reminded him of a nineteen-forties movie star, same finely chiseled features, upswept dark hair and deep red lipstick. He was amazed to find her in the City prosecutor's office because she'd graduated from Bryn Mawr and had a law degree from Penn, the sort of classy training that usually leads to a federal post: a judicial clerkship, maybe a spot in the Justice Department. Lindemann's sterling credentials and her regal bearing were out of place in the gritty District Attorney's office but, as Stephen so wisely noted, that was the source of her power: You didn't expect her.

I was anxious to know how Stephen had fared with her, but I was also secretly pleased to know that she'd be handling this personally. I didn't believe Stephen was right about Marcus Hake being behind those accusations, and I felt certain that no scheme, however subtle, could get past Marian Lindemann. Justice was on Zack's side and Marian was the one who could ensure it would prevail. At least, that's what I believed at the time.

Stephen gestured toward Zack, at work in the next room. "I think we should talk in the bedroom," he said.

More bad news, I thought, and followed him down the hall and shut the door behind us.

He dropped his jacket on our shapeless old armchair and plopped onto the bed.

"Well," he said, "you know how Lindemann is. No nonsense, just the facts. 'There have been some accusations that may require an investigation,'" he said, mimicking Lindemann's stern tone perfectly. "That's all she wanted to say. Didn't matter a bit that she was talking to the father of the target of her investigation."

Target? My face grew hot. In my mind, "target" was a violent word.

I rested my hands on Stephen's shoulders and looked directly into his eyes. "Stephen, is this some serious legal . . ." But even before I could finish the sentence, I knew that that was exactly what it was. Something serious, something legal, something requiring the attention of the straight up D.A. herself. The meeting had not been a mere chat about some story Marcus Hake was promoting. Already the accusations had taken on a formal status. In Marian Lindemann's efficient world, they had been written down on paper. The meeting was a courtesy to the. . . the father of her *target*.

I swallowed hard and tried to continue with Stephen as if I were asking, as I did each evening, about his day at work. Stephen saw right away that I was having trouble.

"She's taken the three accusers' statements and she's sending me the file tomorrow."

Stephen was having as much difficulty telling me this as I was having listening to him. As he paused for air, I imagined a neat stack of manila folders, meticulously cross-indexed and color-coded, all bundled into a newly-labeled Redweld case.

"That file will be full of garbage," I said flatly. "Everyone knows the boys making those accusations have resented Zack's friendship with Cyrus for ages. This is just another one of their pranks, and someone has to put a stop to it. When do we get to call in the people who can say what's really going on here?"

"I told Lindemann all about the situation with the kids in the class," Stephen said quietly. "You know what she said? 'Well you can certainly offer evidence to impeach the accusers' testimonies.' I reminded her this was not a trial, only a *preliminary* investigation. Way too early to talk about 'evidence to impeach.' She said she's always preparing for trial, it's her job to think that way. She's impossible!

"I kept trying to get her to call me Stephen," he said, still fixed upon Lindemann's attitude, "but it was always 'Mr. Grosjean.' That woman never lets down. I reminded her that Zack and Cyrus were the two top performers in the class, best of friends, a pair of champions in the City Chess Tournament . . ."

"And?" I draped Stephen's jacket over the chair back and sat down, facing him.

"And."

"And what did she say to that?"

"She said the chess competition had been mentioned, that it was being considered as a possible motive for what Zack did to Cyrus on the stairs."

"Zack did not try to harm Cyrus!" I yelled and leapt to my feet. "There was an accident! These things happen when boys horse around."

Stephen got up as well and began to pace. He said the whole question Lindemann had to decide was whether Cyrus's death was an accident. That's what would determine whether she'd bring any charges.

"So she's going to decide if that little bump on the stairs was Zack trying to kill Cyrus or just two boys playing around? That's absurd, Stephen. How can you prove that one way or the other?"

I felt my voice wind down because I could not imagine how you *would* prove that one way or . . . the other.

"It's not a trial, sweetheart," Stephen said, reversing direction and continuing to pace, "just an inquiry. They have to talk to people and see if there's any ground for treating it as anything but an accident. Lindemann doesn't believe anyone at this point. She's trying to keep an open mind.

"Anyway, Hake is behind all those accusations, I'm sure of it. That's the layer beneath all this that I have to get Lindemann to focus on. I need her to see she's being manipulated, that Hake is orchestrating this to get the charges against those cafeteria shooters reduced. I started working that line with her today. I'm going to have to keep nudging her along until she sees she's being played. Marian Lindemann is not a person you play."

"Stephen," I said, "I know you can't stand Hake. We both know he's stuck his finger in your eye too many times, and that he tried to put the *kibbosh* on your sewage treatment project.

But he's really not a bad guy. You can't blame him for trying to keep those three kids out of adult prison. It will turn them into hardened criminals . . ."

"They *are* hardened criminals, Bets! Fifteen years old and they shoot up a school cafeteria? Three workers are in the hospital. What do you call that, if not crime?"

I tried to explain—again—that children who are deprived of love and education, of homes, parents, and even food, can't be judged by ordinary standards. Marcus Hake wanted those kids to have the treatment they would receive in a juvenile facility but be denied in an adult prison. He just wanted the system to treat them as the children they still were. I couldn't fault him for that, and I thought Stephen was waging a sort of vendetta in focusing, as he put it, on Marcus Hake. But Stephen knew city politics better than anyone and he let me know it.

"Hake always needs a new way to play the hero to his community," he told me. "He's looking for a high-profile situation, something to get the case for those shooters into the papers and keep it there. And, of course, he wants to keep himself in the public eye, savior to his people and all that. I know him, Bettina. He won't stop."

"Well, it makes no sense to me," I said. "I don't see how Hake can think—or how *you* can keep on thinking—the two situations are related."

Stephen looked at me indulgently. What did I know of the filthy schemes circulating in City Hall? "Those kids accusing Zack live in Hake's district. That's a connection right there!"

"And did you mention this 'connection' to Lindemman?"

"I have to move cautiously with her. I asked her if she thought there might be a connection—"

"And what did she say?"

"I knew what she'd say. She was outraged and indignant at the suggestion that her office could be compromised, that maybe someone was using her for political purposes. She's a good prosecutor, but she's politically naïve."

"And maybe you're politically jaded."

This was me being the out-of-touch academic again, the idealist who didn't understand the real world. But I had spent three years putting together the Special Enrichment Program and I felt sure I knew those kids. I believed I also knew their parents, and how much we all wanted our children to grow up caring about one another.

I was sure the accusations were no more than the mischief of three rambunctious boys who resented Zack and Cyrus as kids always resent the smartest kids in their class. I thought they might also envy Zack and Cyrus the way kids that age are prone to envy friendships that exclude them. It was, as Stephen once said, boys being boys: Zack's horsing around was typical, and so were the stories those kids were making up.

I also believed Marcus Hake had a legitimate ax to grind, and that the D.A. was committed to justice. The way things seemed to me that evening was that a lot of small ordinary things had come together to produce a nightmare for us and our son. I thought if we could simply get those kids to come clean and tell the truth, it would all go away.

"You know," I said, "Marian Lindemann has a reputation for being a protector of children. I'm a fan of hers. She's got children on every side of the issue now. Zack and Cyrus on the one hand, those trouble-makers on the other. And—if you insist on bringing Hake into it—there are the kids Hake wants to see tried as juveniles. I think she'll figure out what's what. She's a pretty smart woman."

"She just needs time," Stephen said, pleased to find something we could agree on. But he was not giving up his precious theory. "If I can just dig up a little evidence for her, she'll stop being so indignant and consider how Hake might be involved. Today, I made just one demand: that her investigation include some intensive questioning of those so-called witnesses to discover their communications, if any, with Hake. For example, how did it happen that Hake was the one who brought them down to her office in the first place?"

Stephen had succeeded in City Hall by being a superb psychologist. He knew how people think and how to steer their thoughts in the direction he wanted them to take. But I kept thinking, as he went on, relishing the way he was "handling" Marian Lindemann, that she was one of those stainless steel personalities, a shiny, flawless surface from which things simply slid away. It worried me to think that in the D.A., Stephen had met someone who would never yield to pressure and could not be seduced into his game of politics.

"But what if you're wrong, Stephen, as I think you are? What if those kids are just being mean without understanding the consequences? What if they're just . . . being kids?"

"That's what we'll find out. For now, I'll continue to assume that Hake is involved."

"And Zack? You know I'm not going to let them start in on him. How do we protect him?"

Stephen had already figured that out. "We'll need a lawyer," he said flatly. "I've put a call through to Dave Rea."

"Stephen . . ."

"I know . . ."

"Zack can never find out about this. He's got enough to contend with, Stephen, do you hear me?"

"I can only try."

-11-

ZACK WAS BARELY THIRTEEN, far too green for what we were about to tell him. I studied my face in the mirror, the face of a mother preparing to tell her son his childhood will abruptly end, a mother who must explain the harshness of justice to a son who has not yet fully comprehended what justice is supposed to be.

"As long as he doesn't feel alone with this, he'll be all right," Stephen had said the night before. He was stroking my back and explaining how the investigation might proceed. "We're all in this together. That's the important thing."

"Yes, of course," I'd said, "but that won't make it easier. I only wanted to keep this away from him. That's all I asked."

I was thoroughly spent by then, but I couldn't let things dangle where Stephen had left them: "Manslaughter, more likely reckless endangerment," he'd said as he slid beneath the covers. "They'd need intent for murder, and they'll never have proof of that."

No proof of intent. Stephen had repeated that last bit of assurance from his old friend, David Rea, the former assistant D.A. he'd asked to protect Zack in the investigation. I'd never much liked Rea, not even back in graduate school, and I'd liked him even less when I learned he'd gone to work in the District Attorney's office. But Rea had since become a terrific defense lawyer, and a partner of Len Jeffries, an equally fine attorney and a black man. I did not disagree with Stephen's choice, but I had difficulty allowing that anyone, even our own attorney, could mention "murder," or even "manslaughter" or "reckless endangerment" in a sentence that included our son.

I would not let Stephen turn out the light. I wanted to be perfectly clear about the accusations against Zack. Were they merely the fabrications of boys in a schoolyard, stories that would fall apart under questioning? Or had one of them actually seen something? Had there been someone else in the stairwell with Cyrus and Zack after all?

"Please, sweetheart, try to get some sleep," Stephen said. "Zack will need us tomorrow. Let's turn out the light."

Dr. Franks was right: I had married Stephen to steady me when I might otherwise fall off the edge. "Unconsciously," she'd once told me, "you rescued yourself when you picked him." Earlier that day, Franks had counseled me to let Stephen do the work for which I'd chosen him. "You need to be more patient and trust him," she'd said. "You married a very competent man."

"I feel so alone, now," I told her. "Viola refuses to see me or even speak to me on the phone. I know she's in a terrible state, but I miss her so much. I always ask June to send her my love but I can tell that even that is not getting through; she slams the phone down as fast as she can. I worry that Viola will *never* forgive me. And what if she won't forgive Zack? Can you imagine what that will do to him?

"And Stephen, well, we really don't see this the same way. Sometimes I feel there's just no one there."

"Stephen is there for you," Dr. Franks said, "but you have to let him be there in the way that he can."

The next day, when Stephen finished telling the children the simple story we'd agreed upon, Hallie was the first to speak. She had looped around her neck perhaps a half dozen ropes of plastic iridescent pearls—pink, lavender, and some she dubbed "bathroom blue."

"Is the District Attorney the lady we met at the mayor's Christmas party last year? The slinky movie-star one?"

"Yes," Stephen said, "you've met her."

"But whose side is she on?" my daughter, the future lawyer, wanted to know.

"There are no sides, Hallie," Stephen said. "It's an investigation. They just need some more facts about what happened in the bus terminal so they can complete their file."

"What kind of file?" Hallie asked. "A computer file or a cabinet file?"

Zack had been sitting with his chin in his hands, staring at the floor. He jumped up and lunged at his sister. "A *nail* file, you dumbhead!"

"Zack!"

Stephen and I exchanged glances, but Zack was already launched.

"Hey, get real!" he shouted at Hallie. "You actually expect me to listen to these Neanderthal questions?"

"I just wanted to know—"

"It doesn't have anything to do with you, anyway. Why should you care what kind of file they have?"

"I would care if they sent you to jail. I would care if you got the electric chair—"

"Hallie!" I cried, my head cranking left and then right, wanting both my children to be very different from what they were just then.

Stephen put a reassuring arm around Zack, but Zack wrestled himself free and came to where I was sitting. He hovered over me, menacing, accusing, my yellow lion cub with a spear caught in his side.

"They're going to investigate *me!*" he wailed. "They're going to try to prove I did something wrong, aren't they, Ma?" He leaned into my face. 'Like the guys at the Port Authority, remember? The guys who had no right to ask me but they asked me anyway? MA?"

Stephen swooped down and caught him in a firm hold while I stood, forming what I hoped would seem a solid circle of parents. But Zack went on struggling, his blazing eyes darting madly from Stephen to me and back to Stephen.

Finally, he settled on me. I was the one who had to answer for this.

"They think I pushed him, don't they?" He tore loose and ran to his room.

I switched on the mother machine once again and slammed it into first gear for a steep uphill climb. I knocked at Zack's door.

"May I come in? Please?"

"Go away!" Zack roared. "You can't help me! It's my life! And it will NEVER BE THE SAME!"

I have no doubt that my own mother wanted the very best for me, and that she provided for me as well as she could.

"You can't overstate the value of a good winter coat," she said, "one that will last several seasons and won't wear thin."

With that in mind, we went early one Sunday morning, up a grimy staircase on West 35th Street to a stockroom on the fourth floor. I followed behind as she tore through rows of coats, pulling out one, then another, for closer inspection. When at last we left, I had a coat with a sumptuous gold satin lining and a sewn-in red label attesting to one hundred percent camel's hair. It was two sizes too large and finally fit me properly when I entered high school, a female institution which required its students to learn both Latin and French. At a school full of pretentious young ladies, I was the only one in a real fur coat.

But my mother failed to provide the one thing I needed most: herself. For not only was she the only mother I knew who often worked late at her job, she was also a woman who presented the world, and me, with the merest shadow of a self. She had obliterated that dimension a person acquires over time; she had become a woman without a history.

My mother and her sister—and my father, while he was alive—simply banished all that had happened before they came to America. Wanting the world to be fresh and rosy for me, they spoke only of the time since their arrival in America—of the sainted Franklin Delano Roosevelt, of Eleanor-the-Benevolent, of Adlai Stevenson, the man of European-style intelligence who should have been President. My Aunt Charlotte made a collage of photographs of the Roosevelts and set it in a frame adorned with red, white and blue crocheting. Beside the portrait of my father that held the place of honor on my mother's dresser, stood photographs of the only other family I knew: the Roosevelts of Hyde Park.

If my mother was determined to shield me from her history, I returned her kindness by never discussing the contents of the ponderous volumes I carried off to college each morning, books so thick Aunt Charlotte pointed out that they would eventually ruin my posture. And although she demonstrated a lively interest in my studies, my mother never pressed me when I omitted details of my reading. Eventually, she took Aunt Charlotte and me to dinner when I graduated with the Ochs Prize in History, and said she was very proud.

My mother's girlhood was shrouded in secrecy and, as an adult, she remained a dark mystery to me. Early in my life, I had vowed I'd fully share myself with any children I might have, that I would give without restraint everything there was inside me.

And I surely believed, when Zack was born, that a new day for parenting had arrived: As a mother, I would be generous, forthcoming, a fount of comfort and compassion.

Yet here was my son, shut away in his room, each of us utterly forlorn.

-12-

WHILE STEPHEN BUSIED HIMSELF trying to prove a connection between Hake and Zack's accusers, I knew I had to get busy myself. My first order of business was to talk to the boys who were accusing Zack, find out just what, if anything, they had seen and what had sent them to the D.A. with their despicable made-up stories. Stephen felt certain it was Hake who had encouraged them to make those reports. I wasn't at all convinced.

Of the three accusers, it was LeVar Morrison I'd speak to first. His parents, Wintell, a manager at a local bank, and Dorothy, a laboratory technician, always seemed bright and engaged; Dorothy was a real cheerleader for the Program. She invited me for coffee and cake after church on Sunday.

She looked positively regal on her suede-fabric sofa in a tailored navy blue suit. Wintell, at her side, was also dressed for Sunday. LeVar tugged on his tie and shifted awkwardly in an immense suede-fabric armchair.

"We're very sorry for all this," Dorothy began. She'd been singing hymns all morning, perhaps the hymn they'd sung at Cyrus's chapel service, and her voice still sounded musical. "You've been such a positive force at the school," she continued. "You don't deserve this trouble."

It should have seemed a welcome bit of comfort but, from the very start, I didn't quite trust it. Dorothy, I thought, was lavishing a bit too much honey on her words, perhaps getting the required courtesies out of the way, clearing a path for something less than courteous. I suddenly remembered that Viola, who knew Dorothy at church, never did like her.

"Thank you, Dorothy," I said, "and thank you for making time for me on Sunday."

Dorothy nodded. It was her sofa, her husband, her son — she owned the hour.

"I need your help," I said. "Yours and LeVar's."

Wintell Morrison edged himself forward on the sofa. "LeVar gave a statement saying everything he knows. I don't see how we can help you, Bettina."

"Would it be okay if I ask LeVar about that afternoon?"

"Sure. Go ahead." Wintell turned to his son. "LeVar knows what he told them downtown. He knows what he wrote down for them, and he's going to say it again to you right here."

I turned to the lanky, uncomfortable-looking boy.

"LeVar, you told the police you saw Zack push Cyrus on those stairs," I said.

"Yeah."

"Where were you standing when you saw that? Were you in the stairwell?"

"We were near there, near enough so we could see what happened."

"It happened at the top of the stairs. Could you see up to the top?"

"Yeah. Yeah, of course."

It was a question I expected would make LeVar uneasy, but he sat perfectly still and looked straight into my face.

"LeVar, did you like Cyrus?"

"Everyone liked Cyrus. I'd say everyone *loved* Cyrus. It's a crying shame what happened, I mean, a boy so smart and talented like that, getting killed so young and all . . ."

"I agree, LeVar. Everyone did love Cyrus. Zack certainly did."

I turned to Wintell and Dorothy. They were nodding agreement, not flinching at the word that had stopped my breath. "Do you think we might speak together alone?"

"LeVar, go get changed out of those clothes," Wintell told his son.

LeVar pushed himself up from the armchair, managing to hold his dark, untrusting eyes on me. He was unbuttoning his shirt as he turned to leave the room.

"Do either of you wonder how he could have seen to the top of those stairs?" I said. I kept my voice as even as I could, as if I were a pollster conducting a survey of New Yorkers' Sunday television habits.

But Wintell lowered his chin to his chest and regarded me with eyes that were darts. "LeVar gave his statement in writing. He's a smart kid, you know, a kid with a future. He's not going to throw it away telling lies about stuff like this. He's not going to lie on an official document."

"Bettina," Dorothy's voice was silky, "we're church-going people. We don't tell lies. If you are saying what I think you are saying—"

"No," I said, "I am simply trying to imagine this and I can't imagine anyone who was not in the stairwell—or even at the bottom of the stairs—being able to see the top. So I was just wondering—"

"You don't have to wonder if LeVar is lying. I know my boy. He fools around a lot, but he'd never lie about this."

Dorothy sat back among the sofa cushions and put her hand over her husband's. She drew her head back and looked at me almost lovingly. Sympathy was plainly what she wanted me to feel, but I felt nothing like that.

Every parent of a teen-ager knows the fertility of the teen-age imagination, and the tendency of an imagined world to eclipse empirical reality. Surely, Wintell and Dorothy had pressed their son each time he claimed to have no homework, each time he complained that all the other kids got higher allowances. I wondered if they had leaned upon him when he told them this story of seeing up to the top of those stairs.

"I'm sure you can trust your son," I said. I heard the sadness and resignation in my own voice. "It's just that I'm having trouble visualizing—"

"I absolutely *do* trust my son," Wintell said. He crossed his legs and eyed me studiously. "It's you who are having trouble trusting him, and you might want to consider why that is."

On this crisp October morning in the Morrisons' plushy living room after church, I suddenly hated Dorothy's husband. A man I'd hoped to know better—I hated him!

I declined Dorothy's cake and coffee, and said good-bye. I pulled on my gloves and jammed my hands into my pockets on the way home, but my hands would not warm up. I was remembering the trip Dorothy and I had made with the class to Safari Park in New Jersey. I'd commented to Zack when we got home that LeVar had a very sweet mom. Zack had said nothing. How strange that had seemed at the time.

Ronnie Holmes' mother, Sheila, said I could stop by around noon on Monday. She was a practical nurse at Mount Sinai Hospital and Monday was her day off. Ronnie would be at school; she did not want me speaking with him directly, she said, but she wouldn't mind taking time from her errands "to get certain things on the record."

Her apartment on the eighteenth floor of the Lincoln Housing Project was cramped but tidy.

"I didn't raise my son to tell lies," she said almost as soon as I arrived. "If he says he saw Zack push Cyrus on those stairs, then that's what he saw."

"But you must know that Ronnie and his friends had some problems with Cyrus . . ."

"No, I wouldn't say I knew that. I would say they might have had some problems with *Zack*, actually."

"What sorts of problems, for example?"

"For example? Zack going off to some fancy places with Cyrus, for example. Some Broadway shows and stuff like that. You know how many hours I put in at that hospital? You know how many hours I have to work to feed these three kids of mine? You think I ever get to take any of them to any shows?

"For example, you think you're doing everybody a big favor down there at the school, putting in all that time for the Program, and you think maybe I don't want to put in that same time. You think maybe I don't care so much about my kids and that's maybe why I don't come down there to all your meetings, for example. But if you had my workload and my three kids to raise by yourself, you wouldn't find time either. So, for example, I'm supposed to be grateful and thank you for what you're doing for Ronnie and the others, helping them get ahead but, for example, you know they're never getting ahead like your son is because when they come home they come here, and there's no one here to take them to any shows. And there's no father here going to take them out for basketball on Saturdays like your husband did with Zack and Cyrus, for example. So what Ronnie and his friends get from that Special Enrichment Program you're running is they get to see how *special* the *rich* kids are, and then they get to see how *un*special they are, and I'm not so sure that makes them feel so special if, for example, you know what I mean."

I drew a deep breath. "I understand your frustration, Mrs. Holmes," I said softly. "You must believe me, I know how difficult it is. But I think you'll agree that your son is better off having the Program than not."

"That could very well be true," she said. "Is that what you want me to say on the record? That Ronnie is getting some benefit from that program you put together? Because I don't think we know how that's going to come out, and I can see how it might be hurting him more than helping, if you know what I mean."

"Yes, I do understand your concerns, Mrs. Holmes, but I'd have to say I disagree."

"Well, yes, we certainly do disagree. I'd say you and I disagree about more than you think."

I let the moment harden off and drop. "You mentioned you thought your son had some problems with Zack. These problems you just mentioned are problems *you* have with *me*, and I can understand them, believe me. But does Ronnie have those same problems with my son?"

"Would you mind repeating that?"

"Do you think your son resents my son, whatever the reasons might be?"

I watched Sheila Holmes' face light with a small, knowing smile as she tilted her head to one shoulder.

"Oh, I see where we're heading with this here. You're trying to get me to say reasons why my son would make stuff up about Zack. Well, I guess I'm smarter than you figured now, aren't I? I'm a nurse, Mrs. Grosjean. I see a lot of people. I've got a lot of smarts, even if I don't have a degree from that university you're working at. I can see what you're up to and I don't like it at all. I don't like it so much that I'm asking you to get out of here, okay? Right now, okay?"

She walked briskly to the door and held it open. "Just who do you think you are, making an accusation like that about my boy?"

Darkness swallowed me as I stood in the hall outside the Holmes apartment, waiting for the elevator down. The walls had been freshly painted over with a thin coat of paint but graffiti bled through—black, maroon and green—making the whitewash hopeless and vain.

Sheila Holmes could be a scary woman, but Sheila, I reminded myself when I reached the street, had always had an attitude. She'd been skeptical about the Program from the start, had hesitated to put her son in it, had had to be convinced by the guidance teacher that Ronnie had the smarts for it and would not be intimidated. There had been a lot of that kind of resistance, parents attributing their own insecurities to their children. Viola had labored overtime selling the program to parents like Sheila, but a few short years had not sufficed to dispel those ancient doubts. Sheila was light years from ever feeling empathy for me, and her son probably felt at least as disconnected from Zack. But did he resent Zack enough to swear out a false accusation?

Stephen scolded me when I told him about my two visits. "We have a terrific lawyer," he said. "Let him examine those boys. Leave the parents alone and just take care of Zack."

"I *am* taking care of Zack. This is how I take care. I get out there and get busy. I can't leave it to other people. I don't know any other way."

There was both frustration and anger in my voice. I heard it and so did Stephen.

"You have different styles of coping," Dr. Franks said at that week's session. "You've always had different styles. This sort of crisis tests a marriage. It's why so many marriages fall apart with the loss of a child. Different styles of grieving. Each partner feels the other doesn't care. But it's just different styles."

"Whatever it is," I told Franks, "I can't stay at home with Zack while the lawyer does his thing."

"Perhaps you're also doing this for yourself," said the woman I was looking to for comfort. "The lawyer will get to all those same people eventually, and he'll know what to ask and how to get answers rather than provoke personal attacks. But perhaps all this activity keeps your anxiety in check."

"Are you saying I should stop?"

"You are doing what you need to do. This is how you cope."

"I am trying to be a good parent!"

"And you are also parenting yourself. That's good."

"You make it sound selfish. I'm not being selfish. I've always taken up causes I deem worthy. Now it's my own son. I can't wait around for the city's wheels to turn."

"You raise some very interesting issues, Bettina. A crisis like this brings up a lot of old issues. Your need for moral vindication—"

"My need for *what?*"

"The moral high ground. It's one of your deeper issues, and we should talk about that again sometime. But now, our time is up."

"Whenever you say we're at something deep, I can count on our not coming back to it."

"We take up whatever you bring up."

"My need for moral vindication? Did I bring that up?"

"I'm sorry, Bettina. Our session is over."

I left our session thinking of my father. In the very few years I shared with him, he managed to leave his mark. On Sunday mornings he'd take me with him to the bookshop. The smell of aging paper, binding paste, and the worn oak floor that held onto dust with its splintery fingers returns unbidden in libraries, and even in the antiseptic megastores that have replaced small shops like his. Then, I hear the crunch of steel wheels like roller skates over the wooden floor, my father letting me ride atop the book cart as he pushed through the aisles, re-shelving the books his patrons had mislaid. I'll never know the method he had for locating those thousands of volumes, out-of-print first editions, each one an old friend.

When my father died, Leon bought out my mother's share, handing her the funds that would someday send me to college.

Besides his love of books, what I took from my father was his passion for a cause. I remember listening at my bedroom door to the conversations in my parents' kitchen. Long into the night, over steaming tea and rolls, fists pounded the table, voices rose, one above the other, as my father, Leon, and Leon's brother considered the fate of Communism after McCarthy. There was no disagreement among them, only ferocious concern: The cause might be lost, the new vision might never be realized, it might be stifled it before it had a chance. Why, look at what they did to the Rosenbergs!

Sometime before I was born, a cousin had arrived from Russia. Over tea and plum wine, he'd told of the *gulag*, of persecutions and firing squads. He begged my parents for help.

But my father read *The Worker*. It was published by good people my father had followed for years. This ragtag cousin from Russia, what did he know? And what did he want anyway? A job? Money? They all want something, these gypsies!

"He's a liar," my father had said when the cousin was gone.

But years later, my parents began to understand that their cousin had told the truth, and their mistake haunted them. My father died in a torment of confusion and guilt, leaving me to take up the fight for justice.

Stephen, on the other hand, grew up in a leafy neighborhood of private homes. His wrath had been aroused by an immoral war; it had fueled his fury at injustices on his campus. But once he'd left campus life behind, Stephen could turn to changing the world in a very different frame of mind; he could accept the notion that you only advance so much in any one day, and in any one lifetime. He had, ever since, contented himself with battles only partly won, with progress that waxes and wanes, with compromise.

It was my father's legacy that I should love a struggle and plant myself squarely in the midst of it. I can't possibly move cautiously and moderately as Stephen does, certainly not when it's my son I'm fighting for.

Dr. Franks knew all this, and still she urged me to trust in Stephen. But it was one thing to trust, and quite another to sit on my hands. There were other parents I could talk to, and teachers I knew I could count on. First, though, I needed one more talk with Zack.

"Zack, darling," I said as I entered his room. It was late in the evening and he had finished his homework and was poring over one of those thick books he loved, *The Book of Lists*.

He looked up and let the paperback flop closed. "Yeah?"

"I'm trying to find out more about those boys who are accusing you, and I—"

"Yeah, I heard you talking to Dad."

"Yes, well, I wonder if you could—just one more time, sweetheart—close your eyes and try to visualize that day on the stairs. I know this is hard, but I want to be sure I understand everything perfectly."

"I already told you. I told everyone. I wrote it down." I could hear his throat stiffen. Still so raw. Still my tender child.

"Yes, darling. I know. I just wonder if there's something you forgot, maybe."

Zack closed his eyes and swallowed hard.

"Just tell me, Zackey, was there anyone else in the stairwell, then? Anyone you could see as you ran down the stairs or maybe when you got there?"

"No, Ma, I told you. Those guys weren't there. No one was there. That's why it was so scary seeing Cyrus like that. There was nobody there but me!"

He began to cry. I hated myself for having made him go through it all again.

"I was there, Ma. I was the only one there and I know what happened. If there'd been anyone else, I would have seen them. They have to believe me!"

I took my son into my arms. "We believe you, sweetheart. And everyone else will, too. I'm sorry I made you tell it all again."

Why, then, were those boys making up such a terrible tale? No matter what Dave Rea and the D.A. planned to do, I had to talk to the mother of that third accuser, Louis Byrne. Mothers can sniff each other out, sometimes, in ways other people can't.

Rumor had it that Louis Byrnes' mother, Deandra Phillips, was benignly loony. I had, at first, been curious to meet her, but after my visits to the Morrisons and Sheila Holmes, I had no heart for more anger. Deandra was known to be highly volatile.

She checked me out through the peephole, and then I heard the clicking of four separate locks.

Ms. Phillips is a tiny, painfully thin, woman and I expected a high, shrill voice. Instead, her voice was deep and gravelly, the sort that utters undecipherable imprecations on All Hallows Night. Her apartment was Spartan, yet sparkling and bright, another surprise.

"Can I get you a soda? Or you take coffee?"

"Oh, just some water, please."

"Water?"

"Okay, maybe some soda. Anything that's convenient, thanks."

"Louis already told the police what he saw down there at the bus station," she said handing me a glass of orange soda.

"Yes, I know."

"So then, what you want from me? I can't say nothing about it. I wasn't there. How you think I can help you?"

"The plain truth is I really don't know how you can help," I said. "It's just that I've given a lot to this community—"

"And so now you come calling to get something back!" The voice was something of a cackle.

"We're a single community, you know. Our kids are all in this together. They're all grieving a terrible loss. My son perhaps more than the others."

"Well, yes, they're all upset, poor things. But what you think I can do for you? What's any of us got to give to you and your boy?"

"A little support, I would think. A little openness. A willingness to consider what we've gained from our experiences together…"

Deandra slammed her glass down on the Formica tabletop and stood up, her hands on her hips. "Hah! Missy, you are breaking my ear with those preachy-speechy words."

"I'm sorry. I didn't mean to sound like that. I don't know how to—"

"I believe you know a lot more than you're saying. And if you won't come out and speak plain, there ain't no reason us going on."

"Funny, I was going to say something like that to you. You know Louis and those others didn't see anything at the top of those stairs. They *couldn't* have. How about you tell me what you know about what's really—"

"What *you* know and ain't saying is how that program you started got going in the first place. You knew it wouldn't do my Louis no good being in with a group of kids much smarter than him. Wouldn't do him no good being showed all that privilege, getting taken down to the opera house and seeing how some other folks spend their money that he's never going to have."

"That's unfair, Deandra. The whole point is that talented, bright children like Louis can use that enrichment to make their way up."

"If my boy don't get thrown in jail by the time he's seventeen, he's going into the Marines. What's the opera and the art museum and the trip to that science place in D.C. gonna do for him, huh? Tell me that, Bettina Grosjean! Tell me what all this is doing for my Louis besides making him feel like the poor, dumb kid he is?"

"Louis is *not* dumb. He wouldn't be in the—"

"Louis didn't make the cut for that class. You know that. He isn't dumb, you're right about that. But he's no chess champion like your boy and Cyrus. He's no book reader like LeVar and Ronnie and them. He's in that class because you and some other parents needed him to be in it so you could have enough kids for the class to happen. You been using my boy for three years now. He's not getting nothing from it but feeling bad about himself!"

"Louis was in the second cut."

"He isn't right for that class. Never was."

"He is a lot brighter than the kids in the rest of the school. If it were a larger school and the program could have two classes—"

"But it don't, and the truth is—the truth you have known all along is—you put my boy and maybe a dozen others in there so there could *be* a Special Enrichment class. And that's so your boy could have the enrichment and Cyrus and them Asian kids could, and all the time you folks at the school are using my boy and them others!"

"Your son is getting some major advantages. You should come down to the school someday and see what's happening there. You'd be thrilled, I know you would. School today is not what it was when we were—"

"I never went to no school that you were at. You gotta stop saying 'we' 'cause you got this idea about a community that is nowhere but in your head. Black children, the black community—"

"Your son is not being used, Deandra. He's getting the same enriched program—"

"Why you interrupt me then? Why you not let me finish?" She was still standing, a tiny woman hovering over me, pouring out her rage in a dark, raspy voice.

It was true that about half the Special Enrichment class was significantly weaker in reading and math than the other half. It was also true that the weaker half, mostly black children, were necessary for the program to receive state funding. But it was also true that the less gifted half were bright enough to benefit from the program, and that they now tested higher than others their age at the school. Deandra should have been grateful, not to me, but to the school for selecting her son, and to the city for making the Program possible.

"I'm sorry," I said. "I didn't mean to interrupt."

She sat down, sipped from her glass, and stared at the table top. When she finally looked up at me, she appeared terribly sad.

"You know," she said, "I don't blame you for what you did. You wanted the best for your kid. That's just like me. So how I'm gonna blame you? But you and that program of yours are exploiting all the little black kids, except Cyrus and LeVar and Ronnie, and maybe one or two others.

"I don't go down to that school, as you know. I don't go out much for anything. It don't agree with me. Come here, let me show you something."

She got up out of her chair and I followed her to the two rooms beyond her small kitchen. One, with a television in it, was her bedroom. The other, her son's room, had shelves along one wall that were neatly stacked with the sorts of toys and games appropriate for a toddler.

"I take in the little ones from the neighborhood," Deandra said. "Keep 'em while their parents go to work. But I don't go out except for some emergency. Louis does the shopping and the laundry, and takes out the trash. The outside just don't work for me. Maybe if Louis got a mother who could teach him to read before he went to school or someone that could've took him to a museum or something, maybe he woulda come up in the first cut but, you know, most black kids don't have that setup."

"Race was not a factor in choosing children for the Program," I said. "They were chosen for their abilities. Louis deserved to get in."

"You just using him, like I said. Yeah, they go to the concerts and the museums and the trips and all, sure. But, you know, the other enrichment your boy is getting is my son."

"What?"

"You know that, but never talk none about it. Him and LeVar and Cyrus and all the black kids is the opportunity for your son to mix with black folk. They in there to give your son a learning experience."

"Deandra!"

"Now, how you suppose I'm gonna feel about that? How would *you* feel if some black folks took your son in with them so their kids could have the experience of what white folks is like?"

"Oh, God! Deandra! This is really twisted!"

"Sure it is, sure enough it is! All that political correctness stuff is twisted up real bad. And my boy is just one little piece of that scheme you got running. I tell these people that give me their little kids to take care of, I tell them, 'Don't you let them people down at that school use your little ones when they get old enough! Don't you let them take your kids just to show the white kids what a little black child is all about!'"

Perhaps it was because I was already in shreds, perhaps Deandra was making some odd sort of sense. I can't say exactly why, but I suddenly collapsed in tears.

"Deandra, please! Isn't there some way we can help each other? I really want us all to work together. I was hoping—"

"Not true at all! You come here thinking I can do something for you, but you don't hear me telling you: I already done for you! I done gave you my boy so you could get that program for yours! So now I'm done giving. Don't you hear nothin' at all?"

I was reeling when I reached the street. Deandra Phillips was strange, but not crazy; she wouldn't say something just to be hurtful or ornery. How many other parents in the Program felt as she did? Why had none of them ever spoken up? We'd held so many meetings, made so many requests for feedback. We'd never heard anyone with Deandra's point of view. *Using* black children? Why were these bizarre notions surfacing now?

The day Martin Luther King died, my canary Luna also breathed her last. But Luna was old as canaries go, and it was her time.

To my mother, Dr. King was someone she felt unsure of. Unlike me, she had not learned about his dream, and an assassination could not quite stop her heart. In her own early years, many had been murdered. Then President Kennedy, then Dr. King. All in the same untrustworthy world. For me, it was a different matter altogether: King's assassination was the first to really hit me; it had come when I was old enough to grasp the loss.

We got the news on the same April evening that we carried Luna in a Tupperware covered dish to Riverside Park. I dug a hole with a large serving spoon which was the closest thing to a shovel we owned. It took a terribly long time, dislodging rocks and severing small roots, shoving the spoon into the cold ground until my wrist and elbow ached. My mother and I said nothing, only looked respectfully down at the grave for a few moments. I realized then that this was how my father's funeral had been held: a hole in the ground, and then silence.

After the burial, we walked silently home. My mother and I were alone together, no little yellow bird to lighten the burden each of us bore in facing the other. Instead of channeling our love through Luna, we would now have to care directly for each other.

The fact that my mother's sorrow that night was so much smaller than my own, and that she could not understand the grief flooding over me, only increased my sense of isolation. In the days that followed, I sought comfort in the hymns and prayers that resounded throughout the city. On WLIB, "The Voice of Liberty," a black disk jockey became my secret friend. By the autumn of that year, I had pinned my life to the struggle for civil rights.

Oh, Deandra, if only you could really know me! Would you still accuse me of wanting to harm black children? Again, I found myself missing Viola. Viola could tell Deandra Phillips what I could not.

Along Broadway, the stores were decked out for Halloween, cardboard skeletons and scary masks. I hauled myself into the Broadway Luncheonette and ordered a corn muffin and a cup of coffee. I was, that week, beginning World War I with my Modern History class, and I could not help thinking of the tinderbox in Central Europe and the tiny spark that had set it ablaze. Historians, in hindsight, say it could have been foreseen. But, as I leafed back through the short history of the Special Enrichment Program at P.S. 240, I could find no clues signaling the great divide that was threatening the Program and all the good it had already done.

I stirred a second spoon of sugar into my coffee. The accusers were just three boys, only three families out of twenty-eight. Every group has its bell curve. It made sense that the boys who would cook up such malicious reports about Zack would come from the families with the deepest resentments roiling at home. These were, I had to suppose, the bad apples in our basket, no matter that Wintell Morrison was the manager at Amsterdam Savings, and Dorothy had a master's degree in bacteriology.

Stephen was right: They should be left to our lawyer. What I really should be doing with my time was helping Viola to heal. It was Viola's testimony about the friendship between Cyrus and Zack that would make all the difference.

But so far, I'd been unable even to speak with her. June, who continued to man the phone, had turned from chilly to downright hostile.

"Can't you hear me?" She'd sounded a lot like Deandra Phillips. "I'm telling you Viola won't talk to you. I would think you could understand that."

"Viola and I are best friends," I explained softly. "Cyrus and my son Zack . . . "

"If it wasn't for your son, Zack—" June began.

"I'm sorry," I said quickly, and clicked off.

Would Viola never want to speak to me again? Zack should have her forgiveness so he could move on with his life, and I ached to be allowed to help her.

I wanted to believe that this was just an early stage of her grief, something she needed to do for now. But I knew that things could easily remain this way for the rest of our lives. I was the mother in a family of four; Viola had been stripped of all she had. My son had delivered that little push on the stairs, and Cyrus had died as a result. How could Viola bear the sight of either me or my son? We were emblems of all she had lost. I thought I could feel exactly what Viola must feel toward me, and I hated myself.

My cell phone buzzed in my purse. The digital screen said it was my mother. She never called my cell.

"Mom? What is it Mom?"

"I fell down. I couldn't get up. I used the thing you got me . . . the necklace."

"The medical alert. Did they come? Are the emergency people there?"

"They're taking me to the hospital. They say it's my hip."

"Don't worry, Ma. I'll meet you at the emergency room."

Later, in the cab home from the hospital, I succumbed to dread that my mother would not come through her surgery, or that she would not do well in the rehab to follow, that her bad attitude or peculiar habits might keep her hip from mending. But these anxieties did nothing to diminish my pain over what was happening at the school, and over what I felt sure was the loss of my closest friend.

My Aunt Charlotte used to advise me to bite down hard on my lip as she poured iodine on my scraped knees and elbows, but the theory that one searing pain can drive out another is spurious.

-13-

AS OCTOBER DREW TO AN END, I wanted all the bad spirits to depart with Halloween. I wanted the D.A.'s "investigation" and the dark birds buzzing over Zack's head to fly off so that my son could again sleep through the night. I worried endlessly that Viola would never free him from his guilt.

But as the most painful month in our lives began to wind down, the days sinking fast, the only palpable change was the terrible loss of light; some days, it seemed there was not enough to live by. Like a primitive, I began to fear losing it for good.

My mother's lights were dwindling with the world's. Prolonged response to the anesthesia, her doctor said. Her hip was mending, but she herself would come and go. Sometimes the mistakes she made were small—places misplaced, yesterday's news today.

"Dinner was terrible," she told me during one of my visits to the hospital. "Swiss steak again. Every night, Swiss steak."

"But Ma," I said, "it is only two o'clock. You haven't had dinner yet."

"Oh, yes," she said, "it was Swiss steak again. The same supper every night."

The doctor said he saw improvement, that soon she would be her old self.

"She was always somewhat…delicate," I told him. How to describe the shadowy difficulties of a woman who hides among her teacups?

I tried to see her in the morning and again after dinner. My visits were too short, but I wouldn't leave Zack alone more than was absolutely necessary. There were classes to meet, department meetings to attend, a household to manage with a wounded child at home.

My mother was in a hospital several subway stops from home. Viola lived only three blocks away. Several times, I had knocked on her apartment door and handed flowers to June who took them with a surly "thank you" as she slammed the door.

But I persisted, once even setting my foot in the doorway. Little by little, from June and from some other parents in the Program, I drew out bits of information about Viola's progress. Like my mother, Viola lived in a fog but, unlike my mother's, Viola's fog was chemically induced; her doctor was keeping her clouded so that her soul could do its work of mending. She lived in a soft, ambiguous world, a gentle place where she would not unravel.

At the funeral, she'd sat stoically, receiving mourners, hugging us all. She had stood like a rock at the cemetery as her only child was lowered into the ground. But she'd crawled into her bed that afternoon, and had never since tried to get up. She was on a cocktail of anti-depressants, stimulants and sleeping pills, the exact recipe of which was being tweaked every few days. She hardly slept at night, June said, and on the rare occasions when she tried to speak, she didn't make much sense.

The doctor stopped by twice a week to measure with his invisible tape her progress along an invisible line, her slightly increased awareness of the world that had tried to drown her. He wanted to put her in a rest home where he could see her along with his other cases, other people making their invisible progresses day by day. But June had refused, saying they really ought to be going back to Georgia. "Georgia is home," June insisted on a day when I stopped by with daisies. "Soon as I can, I'm taking her back where she belongs."

"You know all you need to know," Dr. Franks told me at our session that week. "I think you have to leave this alone for awhile."

"Zack needs her forgiveness," I said, "and I do as well. And our lawyer says we'll need Viola to testify that Zack and Cyrus were like brothers. What if she never wants to see us again?"

"You may have to get on without forgiveness," Dr. Franks told me. "I think maybe you're asking too much of friendship. This woman lost her only child."

"But there's just no reason to blame Zack!" I cried.

"I agree," Dr. Franks said quietly. "But grief as deep as Viola's is not going to be reasonable."

June's talk of taking Viola back home had set my alarms ringing.

"Do you think they'll leave New York before she can tell the D.A. about the boys' friendship?" I asked Stephen. "Dave Rea said that testimony from the victim's own mother would be the most persuasive thing we could show the D.A. And you know it would establish beyond anyone's doubt that Cyrus's death was an accident after all."

"We have no control over this," Stephen warned. "You can understand how Viola might never be willing to talk about that friendship. She might refuse to testify altogether. She doesn't owe us anything, Betts. We have to remember that."

Even after June finally agreed to stay until Viola was well enough to travel, Stephen continued to caution me about placing too much reliance on Viola. "You can't tell how she'll feel when she comes around," he said. "She could very well decide that Zack was really to blame after all. She might be cursing that friendship the rest of her days. She's lost her son and she'll want someone to pin that on. It would be a normal response. Anger is one of the stages of grief, isn't it? Viola could wake up angry at Zack. And at you and me."

"No, I don't think that would happen. I know Viola," I said, although I could not be sure that was true anymore.

"We have to be prepared," Stephen said, "for the possibility that she'll want to put the whole ordeal behind her and retire to her family's place down South."

That was certainly a possibility. It's what I'd have wanted if I had another place to run to. Even then, as the days grew darker along with my mood, I found myself wishing I could vanish somewhere. That, too, I had to think, was a normal enough response.

As I commuted to and from my mother's hospital room, it sometimes seemed that I had already flown off to an unearthly place.

"Hi, Ma," I said, bending to kiss her brow. "You have to do some walking, you know. Exercise that hip. Come, slide yourself off the bed and get your slippers on."

"I left my slippers in the closet," my mother said.

I looked in the closet and found nothing.

"Not that closet, the other one!" She was growing irritated at my stupidity. But there was no other closet in the room.

"The one with my dishes. With the silverware. You know the one…."

As her confusion became obvious to her, my mother's voice trailed off.

The nurses waved "hi." Other patients greeted my mother by name. I noticed she didn't reciprocate. I could not tell if she was hiding from the world, or if she could not recall the names of the other surgery cases who exercised with her each morning. Three others on her floor had broken their hips; it was a badge of sorts.

"That's Mrs. Flannery," I reminded her. "Say hello."

Once, I thought we'd slid back several notches: My mother mistook me for her sister. "Charlotte, what good are you?" she wailed as I came into her room. "You're never here when I need you!"

"Is it dementia?" I asked the doctor. "You can level with me."

"She's old," he said, "and delicate, as you know. She's on an up curve, though." He patted my hand. "We just need to be patient, Mrs. Grosjean."

It might have been echoes I was hearing when I phoned June later that day.

"She needs more time," Viola's doctor had said.

I mentioned, cautiously, that the District Attorney needed Viola's affidavit before she could conclude a very important investigation. "I wouldn't think of hurrying her. I only wondered if the doctor knows how much longer it might take. Approximately."

"I can't help you there," June said in the irritated voice I'd grown accustomed to. "I want her to get well so I can take her home. But the doctor says it's an individual thing."

"Yes," I had to agree. Watching your son take his last breath. It was an individual thing.

On the day before Halloween, Zack accompanied me to visit to my mother. He brought her his notebook so she could check his progress. Remarkably, her mind was lit with a pure, brilliant light.

"The Pythagorean Theorem," she told him, "was used by the Egyptians to build the pyramids, did you know that? I lived in the Middle East. I saw the pyramids."

My mother did, in fact, stay in Beirut for several weeks after she and my father left Europe. The exact story had varied over the years; it was possible she had visited the pyramids, and it was just as likely she had not.

"The Arabs knew geometry like the Greeks, but also algebra. Algebra is an Arabic word. Do you know algebra, Zack?"

My mother reeled off a few phrases in Arabic. She was as much a show-off as Zack, and Zack was enchanted by her. Stephen said Zack mistook my mother's nuttiness for brilliance.

Zack explained his geometry homework and my mother challenged him with an algebraic equation.

"Ma," I said, "He doesn't need to get ahead of his class."

"He's the smartest," my mother said, beaming at her tow-headed grandson.

But after Zack left her room, her mind clouded over again. It was impossible to know what to think of this. How much was the inspiration she drew from Zack, his grin and his shiny hair? How much was manipulation, my mother delaying her move to rehab where more effort would be required of her? As so often happened when I had to engage my mother, a cloud settled about my own head.

Halloween night, with the children finally in bed after a trick-or-treat tour through our building, I found Stephen stretched out on the couch with the paper. Soon, though, he let the paper drop, closed his eyes and furrowed his brow.

He had spent his morning in conference with Dave and the District Attorney, a status conference Dave had requested in hopes of buying more time.

"Your meeting with the D.A. today, how did it go?" I asked.

I already knew that in order to charge Zack with a crime, the D.A. would need evidence of criminal intent, of Zack's state of mind at the top of those stairs. She would be calling in people to talk to her about Zack and Cyrus, people who knew the two boys and could give her their views of their friendship. Mr. di Perna and Mr. Avery, the chess coach, had already said wonderful things about that. But surely, Viola Nightingale, the person least likely to be biased in favor of Zack, was the one the D.A. should hear from. I had begged Stephen to talk to Dave Rea: They simply *had* to find some way to halt the investigation until Viola was well enough to testify.

"Did Lindemann agree to wait for Viola? What happened this morning, Stephen?"

It seemed Stephen's mind was off somewhere. Either that, or he was reluctant to answer.

"She wanted to go over the accuser's statements again," he said. "I told her not to bother. I've seen those statements a dozen times and they always make me sick. They all say the same thing. She believes they back each other up. I told her that's just evidence there's one shadow actor behind them all. I just know Hake's working this—"

"Stephen, please! Let's not talk about Hake tonight. Did Lindemann agree to put things on hold for awhile?"

"Dave told her it would be an *outrage* to proceed without the mother of the deceased. He was really dramatic. 'Can you imagine Mrs. Nightingale waking to discover what was done in her absence?' Dave said.

"Lindemann didn't budge. She said there couldn't be a *trial* without Viola's testimony, but that the *investigation* could certainly go forward without her."

Stephen looked up at me apologetically. "We'll probably have to proceed without Viola," he said at last. "We'd need a miracle to get her to the point where she could testify in time, and that, of course, is assuming she'd be willing to do it. I just know Hake is stirring the pot down there at the D.A.'s office. If I could only figure out what he's doing . . ."

A familiar sense of loneliness fell over me then. I'd tried to get through to the three accusers, and I was trying get June to believe that Viola ought to testify when she was finally able. What else could I do? Stephen simply had to stop obsessing over his old political battles and turn his energies to something that would really help our son. I was still certain, at that point, that Marcus Hake's campaign for those cafeteria shooters had nothing to do with Zack's troubles.

"What about Dave?" I asked, my sinking spirits audible in my voice. "Does *he* think we can stall the D.A. until Viola's ready?"

"Dave is uncomfortable with Lindemann," Stephen said. "She won't bend or play along with him, you know? He says he just can't read her. Dave isn't used to dealing with someone like that. He needs some wiggle room and she's all business. She sees this whole investigation as preparation for a trial. If you can bring Viola in at a trial, that's good enough for her. She's going ahead with her investigation, Betts, and Dave is resigned to that."

It seemed there was nothing more I could do but wait and pray, and I was really terrible at both those things. Wasn't there something more I could try, something I was failing to think of?

Perhaps I was sleepwalking, moving in spite of my own will. I don't recall why or how I happened to dial Viola's number that night. Like a child in search of a lost teddy bear, in search of comfort she could not find, I picked up the phone and let my fingers tap out the number.

"Are you crazy or something?" June roared.

"Please let me speak with Viola. Please."

"How many times do I need to tell you . . . ?"

I heard muffled voices, Viola and June arguing.

And then, for the first time in many weeks, "Bettina?"

"Vi!"

"I want you to stop calling here and stop coming over. I don't want your flowers. I don't want anything from you, do you understand? Now you leave my sister alone. She's got enough people bothering her, is that clear?"

Oh, God.

"I'm sorry, Vi, really . . ."

So it was true. Viola was lost to me. Lost to Zack. Forgiveness was lost to us both. My dearest friend. Stephen had been right to warn me.

-14-

Tuesday, November 9, 10:20pm

IT'S A MEGA DRAG staying home all day. My homework takes like no time and then there's totally nothing to do. My father bought me an electronic chess game but it just gets me down, playing chess without Cyrus.

I kept chewing over what happened on those stairs and thought I needed some info or I would fry my brains. I got online and found some interesting stuff in The New York State Penal Law.

"Deadly physical force" means physical force which, under the circumstances in which it is used, is readily capable of causing death or other serious physical injury.

So I guess I used Deadly Physical Force because the bump I gave Cyrus caused his death.

I found "Juvenile offender." That means (1) a person thirteen years old who is criminally responsible for acts constituting murder in the second degree as defined in subdivisions one and two of section 125.25 of this chapter.

I couldn't find those subdivisions but I know that killing a cop is murder in the first degree. If it's second degree, since I'm thirteen, it means I could be put away for murder.

"Intentionally." A person acts intentionally when his conscious objective is to cause such result or to engage in such conduct.

The thing that makes it murder is "intent." *Mens rea*. A guilty mind. Did I mean to do it? If I did it with intent, I'm a thirteen year-old kid who committed a murder.

I know it wasn't my "conscious objective to cause such result." But how do you prove that? How does someone get inside another person's mind to see if it's a *mens rea*?

"Recklessly." A person acts recklessly when he is aware of and consciously disregards a substantial and unjustifiable risk that such result will occur.

"Criminal negligence." A person acts with criminal negligence when he "fails to perceive a substantial and unjustifiable risk that such result will occur."

I think maybe I was acting recklessly or with criminal negligence. I don't know.

My father says Dave Rea is a great lawyer. But how does a lawyer prove what I was thinking or what I was *not* thinking? I was *not* thinking that I wanted to hurt Cyrus. I wasn't thinking anything really, just running up the stairs. I "failed to perceive a substantial and unjustifiable risk that such result will occur."

Does it count as intent that I was mad at Cyrus for hanging with those guys, or that I got madder when he crashed into me? Is the bumping back thing the same as pushing him down the stairs? Is it criminal negligence or recklessness? Or is it maybe even criminal intent? *Mens rea.*

Criminally negligent homicide. Is that what I'm guilty of?. A degree of murder? Let the punishment fit the crime. How does a good lawyer like Dave prove Cyrus and me were just fooling around?

-15-

ONE BITTER AFTERNOON in mid-November, I bumped into Yvonne Singh on Broadway. Her son was in Zack's class. Yvonne and her husband, Hari, had phoned us the day after Cyrus died. With everyone focused on Cyrus, the Singhs had sweetly thought to call us, too. I told Yvonne the investigation was continuing while we prayed for Viola to get well.

"Poor Zack must be suffering," she said. "It's politics, you know. Everything in this city is political. But when they put a child into the middle of it, a little boy whose best friend has died? That is just too terrible."

Suddenly, it started to pour and we ducked into the Broadway Luncheonette.

"You know," Yvonne said, leaning across the table, "Hari and I don't think those three boys saw anything at all. They are always making trouble, those three. They tease Little Hari about being chubby, they tell him bad things about me, about my *bindi*. They make fun of things they know nothing about. They are ignorant, bad boys. And what they are doing now is very dangerous indeed."

My ears pricked up and pointed eagerly in Yvonne's direction. I'd promised Stephen I'd leave the three accusers alone, but I had to wonder what Yvonne was trying to tell me.

"Did Little Hari happen to notice if those boys actually followed Cyrus into the stairwell in the bus terminal?" I asked.

No. Little Hari had come down with an ear infection the day before the trip and had been at home.

"I'm sorry I can't help you there," Yvonne said, "but I really do think they are making up the whole thing. Hari and I stay out of politics, but when we learned what they are saying about Zack, we thought we really must get involved. So Hari and Little Hari wrote to the District Attorney. They said the story must be false because we knew Zack would never do anything bad to Cyrus. We told the District Attorney those three boys have always made trouble in the class."

"Yvonne!" I cried, "I'm so touched!"

I understood there was more behind the Singhs' letters than mere kindness to Zack, but that was the first time anyone had tried to do something for my son.

When we stood up to leave, I pulled Yvonne into a hug. "Please tell both Haris how grateful I am. And Stephen and Zack will want to thank them, too."

The D.A., I knew, would ignore the letters from the Singhs, but Yvonne had set a new wheel turning. I wondered why I had not had the idea before.

When I returned home, I phoned Mimi Yee, the president of the Program's parents association. She was a Ph.D. neurobiologist, the most accomplished woman in our group. I left a message on her answering machine and another with her graduate assistant at the university hospital. The next day, I left the same messages again.

"That would not be a good idea," she told me when she finally returned my calls. "The only thing that matters now is the welfare of our children. The school has hired an excellent counselor. We must let her do her job."

"But I really think it might be nice for the children to write letters, each in his own voice, about the friendship between Zack and Cyrus. It would help them recover," I said.

"Bettina," Mimi said carefully, "I do not want the Program involved in politics. That would be very divisive. The children are too young to be caught up in these issues."

"Perhaps we could bring the counselor into it," I offered, "make it a project for the English class, a letter-writing—"

"I think not," Mimi said. "We want the children to put this behind them as soon as possible."

I never could recall who hung up first.

Stephen and I felt blessed that Mr. di Perna regularly called to speak with Zack, but one night Zack was in tears at the end of their call. He ran to his room and slammed the door.

I followed him and knocked gently.

"Go away! There's nothing to talk about!"

"Please say I can come in."

Reluctantly, "Okay."

I walked in and sat beside him on the bed.

"It's nothing you would know about. Just something I thought he could help me with, but he can't."

"So," I said as I stroked his head and neck, "maybe I can help instead."

"No," he said, "you can't. He was going to get those guys to stop telling lies about me. But now the school told him to butt out. I think maybe he'll get fired."

"Zackey, sweetheart, you mustn't expect Mr. di Perna to tangle with those boys. Dave will question them and their lies will all come out. That's not Mr. di Perna's job."

"But he promised—"

"Well, he shouldn't have. He wanted to show you he's rooting for you, and that he believes everything you're saying. But he's a teacher to those boys, too, and you can't expect him to take sides."

"I hate that school! What if they fire him?"

"They can't, Zack. He's in a union. But you mustn't ask him to deal with those kids."

"I really hate that school anyway! I'm never going back there!"

So, then, even my own son was turning against what Vi and I had worked so hard to create.

Next to Viola, Carmen Mejias was my closest friend from the Program. Always ready to pitch in and help, Carmen had been chosen by acclamation to be ombudsman, resolver of conflicts. She'd come up to me after Cyrus's funeral to say she'd be there if I needed anything. "Anything at all, baby, you just call me up." I thought Carmen might be the one to get around Mimi, maybe speak to the English teacher directly, maybe take my idea to the grief counselor herself.

I phoned Carmen and asked if she could meet me for coffee. "Just to talk," I said. "I'm worried about Zack. It seems this investigation is going to go on forever."

Carmen agreed to meet at the Luncheonette the next morning.

I arrived fifteen minutes early and ordered a corn muffin and a large decaffeinated coffee; sleep had become difficult by then. I looked around the familiar old restaurant: All the usual people doing their usual things. How wonderful it would be to have my usual life back! I checked my watch and asked for a refill.

I waited forty minutes and was about to leave when my cell phone rang.

"Oh, baby, I am so sorry. You know, I had to talk to my lawyer and unfortunately he told me not to meet you. He says I can't talk to anyone about that trip. I told him it was just about your son, but he said no, I can't even do that. I feel terrible, honey."

So, Carmen, too, had a lawyer. Understandable, since she was the mother who had accompanied the class; the pressure on her must have been terrific.

"It's okay, Carmen," I said. "You have to listen to your lawyer."

Carmen had been my last hope for the letter-writing campaign. Zack and I were being shut out. I thought I might start to hate that school as much as Zack did.

Later that day, I took Zack along with me to the supermarket. I was double-timing: An hour with my usual chores could also be an hour of mothering. Zack was alone too much, I worried. He needed to get out.

At the corner of 110th Street, we ran smack into Martin Szcepanik, a taciturn widower whose daughter, Annette, was in Zack's class. He was one of the parents I'd never quite gotten to know, a nice man who was always at meetings, sitting quietly in the back of the room. Annette grabbed his hand and lowered her head apprehensively. She nodded mutely at Zack, and then ducked behind her father. I supposed that's what Zack would have had to face each day had we kept on sending him to school.

But Martin wanted to override the impression his daughter was making.

"How's it going?" he said cheerily.

"Oh, well, you know . . ."

"Listen, this has to be very rough for you. Whatever I can do—I mean anything—just let me know."

"I appreciate that," I said. And I did. Just this tiny bit of warmth was enough to make me want to hug Martin Sczepanik.

"You take care now, Zack," he said, heading off on his way again. "Both of you take care. And let me know if I can help you out."

I hurried home with Zack, shopping bags trailing from our fingers and Martin Szcepanik's friendly face dancing before me. There had to be many other parents who would help if only they knew what to do. The Singhs had taken the initiative, but they'd had motives of their own. Other people—most people—were like Martin: They'd wait to be asked. If I couldn't ask the children in Zack's class to write letters, I could organize their parents to do something like that. Perhaps they could write to the D.A. saying what good friends Zack and Cyrus were. Or was there a better approach? I rode the elevator to the eighth floor with a busy mind.

The plan I settled on was to float a petition. Addressed to the D.A., it would say great things about Zack's character and about the friendship between the boys. Everyone would be in it together; no one would have to stand up alone. It was something that people like Martin would be happy to sign. Even Stephen agreed: It couldn't hurt.

I wrote something up. It said very simple, nice things, a petition anyone would be willing to sign.

I called Mimi Yee and asked to speak at the next parents' association meeting. "This is not political," I assured her, "and it will not involve the children. It's an opportunity for anyone who wants to say something nice about the two boys to do so. It'll give people a chance to do something good together."

Mimi hesitated. "There's a lot of old business," she said. "We have a full agenda."

"This is a very good thing, Mimi. I'll only need a few minutes. Less than five. It'll remind everyone of the fine things this Program can accomplish. We all need that now, don't we?"

If she says no again, I told myself, she will be an irredeemable rat. The pause seemed endless.

"Okay, five minutes," she finally said. "Next meeting; Tuesday before Thanksgiving."

The following afternoon, Hallie and Zack accompanied me on a visit to my mother. Hallie's art work filled the walls of the hospital room by then and she had strung all her poppit beads together to make a long rope—pink, pearl, lavender and bathroom blue—which she draped over the dresser knobs.

"Oh, my beautiful child!" my mother exclaimed. "Come here, darling. Kiss Grandma."

But when Hallie bounded to my mother's chair, my mother drew her head back and kissed the air. My mother and Charlotte always kissed the air. Hallie, undaunted, reared back for a new attack and landed her kiss squarely on my mother's cheek. It was a scene that had played uncountable times, but this time, my daughter called a halt to business as usual.

"Now you have to really, really kiss me," Hallie told her.

My mother was abashed and waved Hallie away. No one alive had ever felt my mother's lips in a kiss.

But Hallie was determined. With both her hands, she took hold of my mother's head and lowered her own, firmly drawing my mother's face up to hers.

"Now pucker up and kiss me," my daughter said.

There was a faint popping sound; I wasn't absolutely sure what it was.

"Again!" my daughter said, and pressed my mother's face closer.

This time, the definite sound of a moist kiss resounded through the room.

"Good!" Hallie said triumphantly. "That's it! That's how you have to do it from now on. No more kissing the air."

My mother recoiled slightly and waved her hand as if brushing away some bad smell while I stood, astonished, wishing someone else had witnessed it with me.

Hallie re-arranged her artwork on the walls and on the bureau near my mother's bed, making room for the new day's production. This was becoming a fine art in itself as it was a very small room my mother shared with Mrs. Flannery.

"You're going to need a much bigger room when you get to rehab," Hallie told my mother. "You're running out of space here. Ma, tell them she'll need more space."

She turned back to my mother. "You're going to the rehab soon and you're going to have to work hard there so you can walk like your regular self again."

My mother smiled faintly. She seemed resigned to taking orders from Hallie.

Hallie, it had already become clear, would be a lawyer someday, and at that time she was carefully weighing the relative merits of prosecution versus defense. She was a loyal sister, however, and in Zack's case she was an advocate for the defense.

"Zack could get charged with murder, you know," I suddenly heard her tell my mother. Zack heard it, too. "He could go to jail. He could get *electrocuted!*"

"For godsake, Hallie, that's a very bad joke. You have homework, don't you? Kiss Grandma good-bye. You'll see her next week."

"It isn't a joke," Zack said soberly. "I can't get electrocuted because I'm too young, but I could go to jail."

"Such a smart boy!" my mother crowed. She was beaming gleefully, shaking her head in disbelief at what a genius our family had produced.

"Oh, no, Zack! You're not going to jail," I said, tightening my mouth to steady my words. "Dave Rea is a terrific attorney. It's a misunderstanding that'll soon be ironed out."

"I hope you're right," Zack said, "but I could go to juvenile detention. They keep you there until you're 17, and then they put you in with older prisoners and you get beat up and raped . . ."

"He knows everything!" my mother exclaimed. "He's the smartest boy in his class! I know everything, too!"

"Zack! That's enough!" I said. "That's enough from you, too, Ma. It's time to leave. I'll come again tomorrow. You should get some rest."

In the hospital lobby, I shuttled my children to a remote corner. What could I possibly say? I kissed them both, drew in a long breath, and began: "These are difficult times. We often feel scared. But really, we're safe, even if it doesn't always feel that way. Sometimes, when we're scared, we try to strengthen ourselves by preparing for the worst. But that can weaken us when we need to stay strong. So let's make a promise not to scare ourselves or each other. Let's promise to stay strong, okay?"

That was my mothering machine speaking, and I thought it sounded like Lady Mountbatten channeling F.D.R.

How long had Zack been thinking such thoughts? Oh, my son! Too much grief, too much guilt, too much time to ponder possibilities. Viola *had* to forgive him! Whether she ever spoke to me again or not, she had to forgive Zack. She had to testify to his friendship with Cyrus. That investigation had to end!

But Stephen was still cautioning me not to get my hopes up, and Stephen, it was becoming clear, tended to be right.

-16-

DANNY, THE TUTOR, was off today. I figured I had to get out. I had an idea to go down to 14th Street. I had almost thirty-five dollars in my drawer that I was saving for something special. Today I figured out what that was. I wanted it more than anything, an investment I would treasure for my whole entire life.

I caught the #2 train to 14th Street and walked way over east to a shop I once saw. The guy there said, "What do you want, kid? You're not supposed be here."

I said, "I need a tattoo."

He said, "You're underage, kid. You have to be eighteen. Now get going before I get in trouble. The cops harass me enough as it is."

I said, "I have to get it now. I might not be here when I'm eighteen."

He said, "Oh, yeah? Where ya planning to be?"

I said, " I might be in prison. I killed a kid. I need his name on my chest."

He said, "Right. And I ate an elephant for lunch. You gotta get out of here, kid. I could get fined just for letting you stay here."

I promised not to tell anyone or show it to anyone. But he thought my mother would see it sometime or my doctor would see it when I went for a physical. He kept telling me to get out but I just stood there shaking my head. I had to do this for Cyrus.

He said, "Listen, I'll tell you what. When you get to be eighteen, you can call me from prison and I'll come in and give you the tattoo, okay? But if you're not eighteen, I'll be the one getting punished, got it?"

"I could pay you a lot."

"And who's gonna buy me a new business when the cops shut this one down? Now scram or you'll have two charges against you when the cops come, right?"

"Do you know somewhere they would do it if I'm not eighteen? Cyrus was my best kemosabe."

"Right. But you killed him. I get it."

"It's not what you think."

"Oh, yeah. He was your faggot, huh?"

"Not. That's not it at all. Is there somewhere they would do it?"

The guy gave me a shiny red business card with an amazing black dragon on it. There was an address and a lot of Chinese letters. He said, "You know where that is? Good luck to ya, kid."

It took about two hours to find the black dragon place. It was on a dirty old street that was more like an alley. Wan Lop Toy Trading, Import/ Export. There was no sign about tattooing but the address was what was on the card so I went in. I could tell no one was speaking any English there. I took out the paper I had printed out with Cyrus's name in Gothic font and I held it against my chest, over my heart. I said, "Tattoo?"

The lady ran away and came back with an old Chinese man. He shook his head.

I said, "Please. It's very important. I have money." I flashed my bills.

He said, "Okay, you come with me."

We went down to the cellar which reminded me of the lab in Frankenstein. It didn't look like that, it just reminded me of it. Smelly and full of garbage. The old guy said, "Give me money."

I gave him all my bills and all the change I had and he stuffed it all in his pocket.

He said. "You too young. Come back when you bigger man."

"I need it now," I said. "Please!"

He said, "Okay, I do one letter. Only one. Very small. Which one you want?"

It hurt a lot but that's okay. It's the letter "C" in dark black Gothic, exactly where I wanted it. He gave me some Chinese medicine to put on it at home.

It's not the whole name, and it's not as big as I wanted. But Cyrus would know it's for him and he would know what I meant. Cyrus would know my intention, because your best friend knows stuff about you that other people wouldn't ever know. He would know I had no *mens rea* for hurting him.

-17-

I REMEMBER HOW TOUCHED I WAS when I discovered Zack's tattoo, the earnestness and ardor of his love for his lost friend. And I did smile, I must admit. But I was also dismayed. There is a horror of tattoos that runs in my Jewish genes. A tattoo is a desecration of the human body, the sacred vessel of the human soul; a tattoo is an offense against the Creator. Without harboring any specifically religious beliefs, I still felt revulsion at what Zack had done and alarm at learning where he'd been, the filth and danger of the place. So it was a mixed and overwhelming bundle of emotions that flooded me and lingered, a sense of taint: My son's body, like his soul, was now . . . compromised. Not ruined, nor even damaged. But not the clean and innocent thing it had been before.

This, it seemed, was the case with almost everything else. One Saturday morning, before I could finish my breakfast, Anna Rodriguez, a parent from the Program, called to express her sympathy for what we were going through. When she mentioned Zack's accusers, her language became heated, filled with hate. I was glad for her support but frightened by her vehemence. As the investigation dragged on, it was taking a terrible toll, dividing the Program's parents and imperiling all that Vi and I had tried to build.

I left my morning coffee to turn cold on the kitchen counter and went to wake my daughter. Stephen had worried that we were neglecting her. The squeaky wheel gets the most grease, my mother liked to say. In our family, at that time, Hallie seemed to be the only wheel still whirring smoothly, and it was easy to forget that she, too, needed tending. As I shook her out of her purple-covered bed, I had to admit that I was tending to myself as much as to her: I needed some sun to shine on my gray November day.

We were heading off to Harry's for shoes. Every child on the Upper West Side walked in Harry's shoes. Hallie had outgrown her Mary Janes and was ready for something without a strap, on this much we were agreed.

"And with a heel, too," she'd said.

"You're only nine."

"Almost ten. Just a little something to make me taller. All the girls have them."

"We'll see."

"YES!"

"I said, 'We'll *see.*'"

"Purple patent leather—"

"Absolutely not!"

"Okay, then. Just a little heel in whatever color *you* want."

A natural-born lawyer, my daughter.

We were toting three parcels as we headed to lunch: a pair of bright purple hi-top sneakers; a pair of ballerina-style black patent leathers with low, but noticeable, heels; and a pair of purple suede peeky-toe pumps with sexy ankle straps for me, although I had no idea what I'd do with them.

It was a sooty New York Saturday, and the shop windows were filled with brown and orange paper turkeys and cardboard cornucopias spilling unappetizing fake fruit. But the day suddenly seemed fine It was Hallie who cheered me. I wanted to linger with her as one wants to linger on a beach in August.

"How about the luncheonette?" I said. "They have those enormous layer cakes for dessert."

"Pizza."

"Again?"

"Pizza."

My daughter orders her pizza with several toppings in addition to the cheese, and then peels everything off, separating the toppings and placing them on different sections of her paper plate.

"Ma," she said, stripping back the cooled and partly-hardened mozzarella, "is Grandma ever going to walk again?"

I could feel my jaw clench. "Of course," I said.

It was a question designed to make me say just that. Hallie knows instinctively the lawyers' rule that you never ask a question to which you do not know the answer.

"Of course, she'll walk. The new hip will be even better than the old one. She just has to get used to it." I liked the sound of what I was saying and wanted to say it again.

"That'll take a long time, huh?"

"Well, she'll need to practice walking and she won't like that, but she'll get used to it."

"I doubt that," my daughter said. "She doesn't get used to things. She's going to hate it." She dangled a piece of dripping, greasy cheese above her face and lowered it slowly into her mouth, chewed a bit, and then sucked the cheese from her retainer.

"Hallie, keep your mouth closed when you chew, please."

"Sorry. Sorry. She's going to be *difficult*. She's a difficult person, isn't she?" My daughter scrutinized me with one bright eye; with the other, she watched the next string of mozzarella disappear into her mouth.

"But she's strong. She was a single mother way before that was popular. She could have looked for another man to marry. But she was a working single mother and there weren't many mothers like that in those days, you told me that yourself."

I had always thought of my childhood as deprived, and my mother as stumbling through it. In her granddaughter's eyes, my mother had become a heroine, possibly a saint.

"My mother," I tell Hallie "simply did what she needed to do."

"She did what a strong woman would do," Hallie insisted. "You have a husband. It's easier for you. Grandma was a *real* feminist!"

Unsparing, my little girl.

"You ought to eat some of the crust," I said. "It's actually very healthy."

"It's carbohydrate, Ma. It's fattening. If it was up to you, I'd be eating that layer cake in the luncheonette. Forget it!"

I did. My daughter who was not quite ten was already watching her figure.

I changed the subject to the homework we'd tackle when we got home, something I was actually looking forward to. Her class was studying the Canadian provinces, their capitals and products. The Maritimes. Saskatchewan. Canada was such an uncomplicated place, I thought, a place I'd like to visit, maybe stay.

"What's going to happen to Zack?" Hallie suddenly asked when we were halfway home. "Are they going to put him in jail? Is he going up to Sing-Sing or that place where the juvenile delinquents go?"

"Hallie!"

"Well?"

I drew a long breath. This was not a professional torturer, I reminded myself; this was my daughter asking what, to her, seemed a reasonable question.

We stopped to wait for a light to change, and I took the opportunity to stoop down and speak closer to her ear. "They just need to clear up some details, sweetheart. When they get all the facts, this will be over." The mother machine was kicking in again.

"Everyone's talking about it, you know."

"What? Who is talking about it?"

"Everyone. All the kids in school. The elementary school is in the same building as the junior high, you know. It gets around."

"There's nothing to talk about," I said, commanding my voice to march right up and over the tight knot that was forming in my throat.

"Oh, c'mon!" the prosecutor/child cried. "They're talking about whether Zack *did* it. A lot of them think he did, you know."

Our light had turned green, but I held Hallie back, wanting to finish this.

"They're making it up, Hallie. Zack did nothing wrong. You'll have to stay out of these conversations or just tell them they're being silly."

"It's not silly, Ma. The boys are ganging up on me and some of the girls, too. They say stuff like, 'Your brother's getting sent up the river.' 'Your brother killed a boy.' 'You have a brother who's a murderer.'"

"Oh, Hallie!" I dropped my shopping bags and took her into my arms. "Oh, sweetheart! I'm sorry you had to listen to that. I know it feels awful, but it's just not true! You understand that, don't you?"

"Oh," Hallie said, shrugging, "I tell them it's garbage. I tell them my brother and Cyrus were best friends. It's okay, Ma. Don't let my shoes fall out of that bag! MA! They're going to fall into the street!"

"Just tell *me* about it, Hal," I said, gathering up our purchases. "Whatever happens, tell *me*. I'll take care of it, okay?"

"Yeah. It's not so bad, though."

"I'll talk to your teacher on Monday and get her to crack down on this. You have to tell me if it keeps up, okay?"

"Okay. But don't fry your brains. I just wish Maddy still lived here, that's all."

"You can call her when we get home, if you like."

"Yeah. Okay."

"And *I'm* still here. Remember that."

"Yeah. Watch the shoeboxes, Ma. I need those sneakers, okay?"

As we started back toward home, I could see that my daughter was in as deep trouble as the rest of us, and she seemed to accept that I could not do much about it. The poison was leaching mercilessly down to the innocents in the elementary school, and on and on.

How I wished the D.A. would finish up her investigation! But I also wished she'd wait until Viola could be persuaded to testify. How do you speed things up and also slow them down?

-18-

Thursday, November 18, 2:22 p.m.

THE TATTOO IS SETTING UP REALLY WELL. Mega relief because I thought maybe that old guy used some bad stuff on me or something. The place had roaches crawling all over.

A good thing about the tattoo is that no one can see it but me. I've been checking it out in the mirror. It's way too small. I have to save up some more money and get the rest of the letters. Or maybe an "N" next to it. Cyrus's initials right over my heart. Maybe in a year.

My shrink asked if I would want to visit Mrs. Nightingale. I told him her hugging me made my whole body hurt. I said she made me cry. He said I should think about trying to visit with her, maybe having a little talk or something. He said it will make me feel better this time. I told him I will never feel better around Mrs. Nightingale because I know she must hate me. Anyway, this idea isn't going anywhere. Mrs. Nightingale won't even talk to my mother and she never wants to see her again. So I don't see how she would want to talk to me.

I looked up some more stuff in the New York State Penal Law. Juvenile delinquents. There's a Family Court that can put you away in detention. There must be some mega freaking animals in those places.

I'm thinking I should get some piercings, one in my eyebrow and something in my nostril. Uber Goth. Some black polish on my nails. And a black earring. Definitely an earring. Total ugliness.

I looked up piercings and in New York you have to be eighteen for that, too. Maybe a guy in Chinatown would do it, like, between my toes or in my bellybutton, somewhere my parents wouldn't see it. I have to save up.

-19-

THE MONTHLY MEETING of the Parents Association was held two nights before Thanksgiving, so I was pleasantly surprised to see a pretty good turnout. Mimi opened the meeting in the science room with a little speech about the progress the grief counselor was making, reminding us all that healing takes a long time but that children are resilient. The teachers were all designing special projects to help the children through. Mimi wished Viola who, of course, could not be with us, a measure of peace. She finished with an announcement that she was making an exception to the parliamentary rules to allow time for Bettina Grosjean to address the meeting at the start instead of waiting for "new business."

Her announcement was met with confusion and some anxious shifting about, but a sudden hush fell over the room when I rose from my seat. As I looked around, I noticed eyes lower, hands fumble in handbags. None of the parents of the D.A.'s three "witnesses" was present, I noticed, not even Dorothy Morrison who had never before missed a meeting.

I walked stiffly to the front of the room and forced a small smile onto my face. It was not an appropriate expression, but I could think of no other way to calm the nervousness rippling through the room. I began by eulogizing Cyrus, recounting the ordeal this had been for Viola, and for all our children, including my own. Everyone nodded sympathetically; a few dabbed at their eyes.

The audience was surely expecting the meeting to include some talk about Cyrus, but they had not expected to hear it from me. Some of them plainly did not want to hear anything from me; they did not even want to have to look at me. I decided to tell them I could understand this. Perhaps they blamed Zack and me for the pain their children had suffered, for the disruptions in their lives.

Then, I reminded them of Zack's relationship with Cyrus. I explained that Zack was at home on the advice of a therapist, but would soon be back in class. Finally, I mentioned the D.A.'s investigation. Two of the Asian mothers thrust their arms into their coat sleeves and left by the classroom's back door.

I pressed my palms onto the cold top of the science demonstration table, leaned out toward the audience, and cleared my throat. "I've drafted a very short petition, a way you can show your support for Zack," I said. "As you'll hear, it says what good friends Zack and Cyrus were."

I read them what I'd written, and said I'd leave it on the table at the front of the room. I begged them to sign on their way out, then thanked them, once again, for allowing me to speak. A small, friendly talk.

When, at last, I heard the vote called on the motion to adjourn, I returned to the front of the room and stood, petition in hand, like a mother on the reception line at her son's wedding, waiting to shake hands with the people who would queue up to greet me.

I caught Mimi's eye as she slipped out the door; she sent me a nod and an embarrassed smile. The president of the Parents Association ducking out without signing? Flora Chang, Lyn and Mito Takemura, Mark and Bonnie Hsieh followed, on tiptoe as it seemed to me, without so much as a glance in my direction.

On her way out, Carmen Mejias clasped my hand in both of hers and delivered an interminable run-on sentence about not being near the staircase at the bus terminal and so not really being able to say what happened there, and being very sorry but nevertheless unable—she was sure I would understand the position she was in—to sign something for the

D.A. at this time. "You know, honey, because of my lawyer and all?"

Four other Latino parents smiled as they passed. They promised to pray for Zack and my family. Some others stood clustered around Anna Rodriguez who, when it came her turn, wanted me to know, emphatically, that those three boys were always trouble. "Very bad kids," she said, and her friends agreed in unison.

"I tell my son to stay away from them. It's like gangs, you know? We don't want that kind of stuff here. We have good kids. We want them to get ahead. Our children's all good kids."

Her friends nodded vigorously. Anna signed the petition, but her friends left only their good wishes.

Yvonne and Harry Singh, and Viraj Desai expressed outrage at the injustice of Zack's predicament. They were the only three Indian parents who attended the meeting, and all three signed. I promised myself to learn more about Hinduism if there were ever again a moment of peace. Barbara Schnurr, Martin Sczepanik and Roseanne Yablonski signed, too.

Rosa van Blerkom was a beautiful Trinidadian woman married to a Dutch architect. She was the last to come up to the table, and she leaned in to whisper in my ear. "This is going to get worse, I think, but Jil and I are with you completely. Just let us know if you need anything more." She signed on behalf of herself and her husband, then drew her head back in amazement when she noticed that Jil's name was only number eleven. "They're all scared," she said. "Just let us know what you want us to do."

Her tone was conspiratorial: Us against Them. I'd been away from the school for less than two months. Already the Program was cratering. Or had all these cracks in our community been there all along? How long, exactly, had this been going on?

"How many did you get?" Stephen wanted to know.

I told him.

"God!" Stephen pulled me hard against him and held me tight.

"They filed right past me and out the door. The Asian parents never even looked back. Most of the black parents— more than half the class when you add it all up— were clearly distressed. They were angry at me for bringing this up. Couldn't wait to get out of there"

"I'm sure word is out in the neighborhood," Stephen said, "and everyone's trying to stay neutral. It's about keeping the peace."

"The Williamses signed, of course," I said. The Williams family were Jehovah's Witnesses and had always kept apart from the other black parents.

"There are forty-three parents in the Parents Association and thirty-seven showed up tonight. Of that, only eleven signed to support Zack. What can I do with eleven signatures? It's more damning than no petition at all!"

"The D.A. probably wouldn't have responded anyway," Stephen said as he rubbed my neck. "I'm sorry, sweetheart. You must feel horrible, but it was a good try."

I'd had other disappointments in my years with the Program, but then, I'd had Viola to prop me up. We were always in it together.

I curled into a ball and pulled the covers over my head. Eleven! The number sliced through my brain. Eleven, including Jil van Blerkom who had not even been there!

Mimi had known all along what the outcome would be. She'd agreed to let me address the meeting so I could discover it for myself.

To hell with them, I decided the next morning. The teachers saw the kids every day and knew best how extraordinary the bond between Zack and Cyrus was. As professionals, they would be accorded more credibility than the parents, anyway. Mr. di Perna would do anything he could to help Zack. Mr. Avery, the chess coach, would write a letter praising the teamwork between his two champions. Those two had already told the D.A. some wonderful things about Zack, and now they could help me line up the rest in support of Zack. Perhaps I could start a letter-writing campaign. Something.

I knew Mr. di Perna would be phoning us at home that evening. After my Modern History class, I phoned the school and asked to speak with Mr. Avery.

When he came to the phone, Avery apologized for not being in touch more often. "This must be terrible for Zack. Would you like me to come over some time for a game of chess?"

"That would be wonderful," I said. "He's not much interested in the electronic set my husband brought home."

Then I told him why I was calling. There was, I thought, a slight hesitation. "Yes," Avery finally said. "Yes, of course. No problem. I have to get to class now, though. Can I phone you later this evening?"

"Oh, yes; certainly. Yes!" I practically sang.

The teachers would come through for Zack! At last, a break in the bad weather!

After dinner, when the phone rang, I flew to answer it. It was Mr. di Perna. As I handed the receiver to Zack, I whispered that I'd need to have it back before he hung up.

Mr. di Perna greeted me in the same upbeat tone he'd probably used with Zack, but I knew things were difficult for him.

He asked about my mother.

"She's coming along, thanks. Slowly. And your father?"

"The same. Old age is nothing to look forward to."

"No," I said. Then I told him what I had in mind.

The hesitation was longer and far darker than what I'd heard from Mr. Avery.

"Mrs. Grosjean," he said solemnly, "I want to help you in any way I possibly can. But I can't put anything in writing or do anything official just now. My lawyer is watching everything I do. We're sure Mrs. Nightingale will file a lawsuit. She would sue me along with the city. I was advised to get my own lawyer because it would at some point be me *against* the city. Eventually, I'd be out of it and the city would have to pay, but until it gets to that, I'll be a defendant. My lawyer said—"

"It's okay," I said. "I understand."

"I feel terrible—"

"No," I said, "I should never have bothered you. I'm sorry."

An hour later, the phone rang again. It was Mrs. Bellisano, Zack's art teacher.

"I got a call today from Mr. Avery," she said.

"Yes, I phoned him first because he knew Zack and Cyrus best." I told her what I wanted. "I was going to call you, too—"

"Yes, he told me. I'm terribly sorry about this, Mrs. Grosjean . . ."

I heard the words waft through the receiver like a killing gas. ". . . but as the union representative, I have to tell you that our lawyer has advised us—all of us on the faculty—to stay out of this. Mr. di Perna will probably be sued. We have to stick together, present a united front. We're under orders to sign nothing, make no statements about anything that could be used in litigation. I feel terrible having to be the one to tell you this. Mr. Avery wanted to help, but I had to tell him, 'no.' It's union orders. I'm so sorry."

I was raised to stand with unions.

I'd also be the first to tell Viola she ought to sue over her loss.

In the middle of the night, I woke my husband. "Stephen! They've taken everyone away! There's no one left to help us."

The kids in Zack's class, his teachers, the parents in the Program, even Carmen who had been my friend—everyone had disappeared. Viola might have helped us by testifying about the boys' friendship, but she had made her position icily clear: Leave me alone!

Stephen and I were alone with our lawyer, Dave Rea, and Dave could get no traction with the D.A. That investigation was going to drag on, draining life from my family and leaving Zack on an island of guilt and grief. Thanksgiving was coming. I tried to count my blessings.

-20-

THERE WERE, I decided on Thanksgiving morning, some things I could be thankful for. My son was mending slowly with the help of his shrink. My mother, too, was showing progress and had been moved, at last, to a rehabilitation facility. Hallie loved her purple sneakers and crowed about her high-heeled shoes to Maddy on the phone. Things had stalled at the D.A.'s office which was both a good and a bad thing, but I had done all I could think to do. I counted all these as blessings because I wanted whatever was out there, determining the courses of our lives, to know I was not ungrateful.

Surely, I was glad for a holiday from my classes, even the tiny four-day break. In my Modern History class, the First World War had ended and the world was mired in despair. The old systems of order and belief had collapsed, and nothing good had come to take their place. Tyranny had been replaced with democracy, but democracy was faring poorly. Inflation was rampant, people were starving; in England, there was a severe shortage of men. Freud had vanquished free will, and pessimism was replacing the sense of Man's glory. Nietzsche had said it a few years earlier, but the world now resurrected his banner: God is dead. The cry heard everywhere was the very cry I had heard from Zack only weeks before: It will never be the same!

In my Feminist History class, the world was more hopeful. Germaine Greer was taking on Norman Mailer who, everyone agreed, was a first-rate jerk; when she told him the world will never be the same, my class cheered. But that, I had to remind myself, was the 'seventies, a time of empowerment and dreams.

Although my mother's condition was improving, we could not risk taking her out in the icy weather. Thanksgiving dinner would be in the rehab center's burgundy-carpeted dining room. An institutional holiday feast.

My mother had, astonishingly, found a friend, a diabetic lady named Ruth whose foot had been recently amputated. She spoke fluent German, and that had worked a charm with my mother. She joined us for dinner, rounding out our table of seven, including Aunt Charlotte.

"Will they ever be done with that investigation?" Hallie asked as identical servings of holiday food were placed before us. That was my daughter illuminating for the stranger at our table the dark corners of our family.

"Almost there," Stephen said, without looking up at her.

"Will Viola ever testify?" my daughter asked, drawing our new guest in deeper.

"Very soon, sweetheart."

"It doesn't matter," Hallie said gravely. "It would all be hearsay. You can't listen to hearsay when you're on a jury." She was showing off.

"Why don't you just butt out?" Zack said.

"There isn't going to be a trial," I said for the umpteenth time. While the investigation dragged on, our family fortress was crumbling.

I glanced across the table and saw Ruth pretending not to hear us.

"This is a silly conversation," I told Hallie. "Eat your carrots. They're important for your eyes. You too, Zack. The carrots."

Hallie set her fork down deliberately. "Grandma and I think Zack is in very bad trouble," she said. "Don't we, Grandma?"

"The carrots," I said.

We ate in silence, even through the identical plates of pumpkin pie topped with some nasty hydrolyzed fat. Finally, we bid Ruth and my mother good-bye. "Happy Thanksgiving!"

"Yes, right. Happy Thanksgiving to you, too."

Back out on the snowy street, Hallie slipped one mittened hand into Stephen's and trooped along silently beside him.

"Why are they doing this, Dad?" she'd suddenly asked. "Why wouldn't the parents sign Mom's petition? Why are those boys saying all those things about Zack? They know they're telling lies, Daddy. Why are they doing that?"

"Oh, Hallie, Hallie. I wish I could tell you why."

She pulled to a stop. The snow had started forming a crust on her coat and hair, making her look like a bit of Christmas candy.

"Zack never did anything to hurt them. They got Zack into trouble for nothing, Daddy. Why are they doing that?"

"It's true," Stephen said. "It's one of those true things that has no explanation. I don't know what else to tell you, sweetie."

Before they moved to Queens, Stephen's family lived not far from where our apartment is now, but far enough north that some of the kids in his class lived in Harlem.

In the first grade, Stephen had a friend, one single friend, with whom he played in the schoolyard during recess. Mitchell. Stephen could never recall much about that boy, but he did remember the tentative, hopeful thrill of having a first friend.

One Spring afternoon, Mitchell came home with Stephen after school. Stephen's mother gave the boys cookies and milk, and sent them out to play with Stephen's bike. It was a new two-wheeler with assist wheels on the rear. It had a silver bell that made a beautiful, clear r-r-r-r-r-ing. A birthday present from his grandparents, the greatest treasure Stephen possessed.

All afternoon the boys took turns riding to the end of the block and back, pedaling faster each time. At five o'clock, Stephen's mother leaned out the window to say it was time to bring the bike back inside. Mitchell's mother would be worrying. He had to go home.

On his last run of the day, Mitchell did not turn the bike at the corner to circle back. Instead, he walked it across the street, remounted, and raced away down the next block. Stephen ran after him, calling out to him to stop, but he pedaled much faster than Stephen, short-legged even at six, could possibly run.

When he returned to his mother, Stephen was in tears. She hugged him and said his father would soon be home.

Stephen's father, when he arrived home, showed great distaste for what had to be done, but he made the call. The police showed up and wanted to know Mitchell's last name; Stephen could not even tell them what it was. They wanted to know where he lived, and Stephen didn't know that either. When they asked for a description of the bike, however, Stephen was able to tell them precisely: a Schwinn Junior Eagle, Fire Engine Red.

The following day, when Stephen returned home, his mother said his bike had been found, but that he'd never get it back.

"Why not? It's my birthday present!"

"They took the bike apart."

"Well, we can put it back together. That's what Daddy did when we first got it."

His mother stooped down and stroked his hair. "I'm sorry, Stevie," she said. "We can't do that. There's a ring of kids up there where your friend Martin lives. They sell everything they get their hands on. Bikes, cars. They break them down and sell the parts. The police said it's gone, and that's that."

"But it's my bike! My present from Grandma!"

"I know, Stevie. We'll get you a new one for your next birthday."

That was not good enough, but Stephen could see it was paining his mother to have this conversation, so he ran to his room to await his father's return.

At dinner, Stephen asked why the bike was gone.

"Who knows why they do such things, Stephen? A six-year-old, can you imagine? They're poor people, son. They don't understand what they're doing."

Well, Stephen didn't understand either. If Mitchell had left the bike with him, they'd be riding it together every day. Why had the boy deprived them both of this most supreme of all pleasures?

"They don't do it to have a bike," Stephen's father said. "They do it to get money." Stephen recalls that his father looked sad, apologetic, as if Mitchell's poorness were his father's own fault.

"How much money did Mitchell get?" Stephen wanted to know.

"I doubt he got any money at all. Some bigger *shmoe*, the one who told him to steal your bike, got it."

"I don't understand," Stephen said. He thought there was something his father was withholding.

When his father left the table, his mother drew a chair up beside him. In a sorrowful voice she said, "They're poor people, Stevie. That makes them very angry. They're so angry they do silly things like wreck a perfectly nice bike that they could enjoy. The older boy didn't get much money either. It's a child's bike; what could he get? They do these things because they're angry."

Stephen still remembers this scene in his childhood kitchen—where exactly his mother sat, just how the soiled dinner plates looked on the table—with the clarity with which we recall the most stunning epiphanies. He thought: There must be some way to fix this, an arrangement that would allow every boy to have a shiny red two-wheeler so that boys like Mitchell would not get angry and new birthday presents would not end up in pieces.

Stephen never saw Mitchell again after that day. The boy got swept away in the mysterious process of inter-school transfers that principals deploy to unload their problems on one another. But the story of that bike is one Stephen has played over many times. He used it in speeches he gave at Columbia during the protest rallies, he's alluded to it at City Hall. It has become a key chapter in the official authorized version of the story of my husband's life.

When he heard Hallie's bewildered voice in the snowy air, Stephen understood that, to answer her question, he would have to tell her about the anger that slashes its own hand, the senseless brutality of immense frustration. Even his own father had known it was impossible to explain this to a child.

-21-

Friday, November 26, 10:15 pm

THE SHRINK WAS TALKING about Mrs. Nightingale again, today. He said it would be a good thing for me to see her. Just for a short visit, maybe.

I started to get mad at him. I told him there was a problem I couldn't do anything about. Mrs. Nightingale told my mother to bug off. She's hurting too much from losing Cyrus and she can't stand to see my mother or even talk to her. I think she'd feel even worse looking at me, the kid who pushed Cyrus on the stairs. Maybe she even thinks I had the *mens rea* to kill him. She probably won't ever want to see me again.

My shrink said that would be unfortunate.

I yelled at him, "It's worse than unfortunate!" Then I started to cry.

I hated him for making me cry like that.

I hated that whole entire session.

Tonight, I tried to do a piercing myself. I got a needle and put it in the flame on the stove. Then I cleaned it with alcohol which we have in the bathroom. Then I pushed it hard into the skin between the big toe on my left foot and the one next to it. It bled like crazy and made a real mess. I stuck a band-aid on and gave up.

I'll try it again next week. I can get better at doing this. I have an amazing gold ring with a tiny black skull to put in once I get the hole to go through.

If it works, I can do my eyebrow, too.

-22-

CITY HALL, like any workplace, has its subterranean rivers and streams, and messages that sail, like notes in bottles, down through the corridors, spouting out at water coolers, drifting from one cluttered office cell to another, and creating what comes to be perceived as "the air."

"There's something in the air," people in the office say; "there's word going around."

What troubled Stephen was that there seemed to be nothing in the air, nothing bubbling through the corridors at City Hall about either Zack's case or the one Stephen thought it was linked to. Nothing from the mayor; nothing from the D.A. or from any of her assistants; nothing either—and that was Stephen's biggest worry—from the offices of Marcus Hake. The result was that the press carried no word at all about any of this. The stories, both Hake's and ours, had disappeared as if the spigot at the source had been magically, forcefully, turned off.

Hake had a large office uptown among his constituents, a prominent storefront about ten blocks from where we lived. But he also, under some arrangement that was never really clear, had an office in the municipal building, just across the street from Stephen's own office in City Hall. With the D.A. preparing her case against the three shooters, Stephen thought Hake's silence disturbingly odd. Dave, too, was uncomfortable. We should have heard something from Lindemann by now. About Hake's boys. About her investigation of the accusations against Zack. Some word or other should have been getting around, but neither Stephen nor Dave nor I wanted to inquire.

And then, there was Hake on the evening news! A press conference outside the municipal building. He had positioned himself at the curb so that the cameras, when they lined up to face him, showed City Hall in the background. He had such a marvelous flair for publicity, for every nuance, every detail. You had to admire that.

His announcement was not news at all, simply a reminder that three young boys were languishing in jail awaiting a trial. An update, he called it, for everyone tuned to their sets on the Monday following Thanksgiving—a night when no one would be out at the theatre or at the bars, but at home sobering up after the long holiday weekend. On the eight o'clock news, as folks were tuning in for Monday night football, there was Hake. It was the perfect night and the perfect time to remind the world that the shooters were children. Juvenile delinquents, certainly, he said, but juveniles all the same.

"You will hear people on the streets and in the District Attorney's office tell you they are criminals," Hake intoned, "and I'm not saying that these kids didn't commit a crime. I'm just saying they did not commit an *adult* crime. They acted out of ignorance, desperation and, yes, hunger. These were three young boys, boys just like your own and your neighbor's kids, who were simply out of ideas. Who was going to teach them right from wrong? Who was going to give them the love that builds self-esteem? Who was there around to model themselves after, to show them a good reason to behave like the boys you are raising in your own homes? These boys I'm telling you about didn't have any homes, not the kind of places you would want to live in and raise your kids in . . ."

It was a bravura performance and hit all the right notes, ending with a plea for the boys to be tried as juveniles.

"You see," I said to Stephen once the children were in bed, "he's not looking for a trade or any other underhanded deal involving Zack. He's out there beating the drum for his cause and, you have to admit, he's damn good at it."

"It's much too quiet down at the office," was all Stephen would say in reply.

-23-

THE NEWS CAME SUDDENLY. Like a tornado roaring up in a darkening sky. But the devastation felt personal. More like the work of a terrorist.

At suppertime, there was a phone call from Dave Rea.

Stephen looked pale when he returned to the table.

"We have a hearing," he said. "Tomorrow morning."

"But Viola isn't—"

"We have to be there. The three of us. Lindemann has presented a charge and Zack will have to answer."

"Zack? Stephen, you promised that—"

"Dave will prep him beforehand. There'll be some questions and Dave will make sure he's comfortable with his answers."

"Dad!" Zack's face was a mixture of fear and grief, a thirteen year-old boy trying not to cry.

Stephen wrapped both his arms around Zack's shoulders and jostled him lovingly. "It'll be okay," he told our son. "Dave will make sure you know what to say. Just do as he tells you."

"What questions will they ask? Is this going to be like the Port Authority guys?"

"Mom and I will be right there with you," Stephen said. "It'll be fine."

Juvenile Court Judge Marshall V. Thisbe had grown fat and lost a lot of hair but I soon enough recognized him as a guy Stephen and I had known at Columbia. President of the law school's Young Republicans, a guy who, even as a student, had worn a three-piece suit and spit-polished black shoes.

He was seated at a table in a small conference room and gestured to us to sit as well. Marian Lindemann had sent an Assistant D.A. to represent her office. While Stephen and I took seats on either side of Zack, Thisbe kept his head down, scanning the papers the A.D.A. had set before him. He was wearing a brown and green plaid flannel shirt, open at the throat, and a reddish brush of a mustache. All in all, he had a folksy look, I thought, and I almost felt relieved.

"Well, Zack," he said in a kindly, almost jovial, voice, "Why don't you tell me in your own words what happened that day at the Port Authority?"

While Zack told the short, simple truth that Dave had rehearsed with him, I kept my eyes riveted on Thisbe. His voice may have been jolly, but his eyes lacked any twinkle.

When the A.D.A. got his turn, he asked the Judge to charge Zack with the juvenile offenses of manslaughter and assault. My ears began to burn and then my entire body grew rigid, as though I were struggling to hold something tightly inside me, something that would otherwise fly out and burn up the room. While my heart sank, all the rest of me was about to explode.

It was Dave's turn next. He questioned Zack and Zack told the same story he'd told to Thisbe.

Thisbe didn't seem to be paying attention. He kept shifting the papers the A.D.A. had presented, dabbing his thick thumb with saliva and turning over one page and then another.

I could not keep silent any longer. "Your Honor, if I may? I don't understand why this hearing was put on the calendar at this time. We had no more than a few hours notice. As you must know, there is a witness who is vital to my son's defense and that's the victim's mother, Viola Nightingale. Mrs. Nightingale is still being treated for shock, but she's making excellent progress. She could certainly be expected to appear in person at a hearing after the New Year. If Your Honor would be willing to—"

Dave and Stephen kept signaling me to stop, Stephen, by tapping my foot under the table. I could not imagine why Dave had let this go forward without Viola, but I left my request unfinished.

Thisbe hadn't looked up at me for even a moment while I addressed him, just shuffled the papers and said, "Uh-huh." Finally, he shoved the papers into a pile and folded his hands on top of it.

"It appears that Zack here has on several occasions expressed contempt for the legal process," he began. "In his interview with Port Authority Officers Lunney and Thomas, and again with Lieutenant Vicarelli, he was uncooperative. I have to imagine this is an attitude he learned at home." There was no mistaking his expression of glee when he finally looked up and across the table at us.

Dave sprang to his feet. "Your Honor, I strongly object. Zack Grosjean has been perfectly cooperative with everyone and there is nothing in his home life that would—"

Thisbe cut in. "I was a law student at Columbia, Mr. Rea. I remember Stephen Grosjean, and Mrs. Grosjean, too. Troublemakers of the worst sort, and that's putting it mildly. Theirs is apparently not a home in which the law merits much respect. It is not an environment that produces law-abiding children."

Dave's face was flushed and his voice reached the level of a shout. "Your Honor, I want you to know that I share the Grosjeans' political views, and I shared their views when we were all at school together. If you want to start raising doubts about *my* character, Your Honor, you are creating a record you would not want to stand on. This history you're alluding to is absolutely irrelevant to the case of Zack Grosjean, and your comments are utterly outrageous. I must strongly object to Your Honor's remarks."

Thisbe struck a pose of boredom, and addressed Zack directly. "Young man, I'm afraid I'm going to have to recommend that you be bound over to the Parkside West Juvenile Detention Center to await trial."

My arm swung out automatically and pulled Zack close to me, shielding him, as I imagined it, from a horde of tomahawk-waving invaders. But the invaders had already descended upon us. The savage judge had already taken my child, already wounded him by demonstrating that his parents were powerless to save him.

Dave jumped up and objected again. I lost the sound of his voice as Stephen's long arm pulled me, along with Zack, into a three-way hug.

Finally, Zack's voice piped up from his dark surround. "How can the punishment fit the crime if they don't even know yet if I committed a crime? When are they going to listen to Viola, the only one except me who can tell them I didn't mean it? No one who knows anything about this got to say anything."

As he so often did, Zack was deploying his intellect to contain what must have been unmanageable fear.

Thisbe watched us absorb the shock, nodding his head and taking deep satisfaction in revenge that had been long in coming. "I'm sorry, Zack," he said, pulling some last few papers together and rising to leave, "but I don't think you will be better off in your home environment."

Zack elbowed Stephen and me aside, stood up, and called out to the judge. "I answered all the questions those two guys at the Port Authority asked me and I cooperated with Sergeant Al and I signed the report. I was polite to everyone and I told everyone the truth. My mother is right. If Viola Nightingale was here now she'd tell you it was an accident because she knows Cyrus was my best friend. This whole thing wasn't supposed to happen until Viola could get here!" His voice twisted grotesquely as he came to the end of his tirade because at last, he was crying.

Thisbe leaned heavily on the table. "Believe me, Zack, I get the picture. We'll arrange for you to be picked up in the morning. You'll have a call from your local precinct letting you know when to be ready. You don't need to bring anything. Just yourself. I do think this is best for everyone at this point."

Stephen wanted to stay behind to discuss the whole disaster with Dave, but I knew I had to whisk Zack away from the courthouse as quickly as possible.

In the taxi home, I let my body do the talking. My throat was parched and I had no words. Not even my mothering machine knew what to say. I held my son and stroked his arm and rocked us both as the cab bumped along through the wintry New York afternoon.

"Maybe it's the reckless behavior thing," Zack said somberly, "or the criminally negligent homicide thing. Maybe I was supposed to know that what I did on the stairs would kill Cyrus."

"No, sweetheart, you weren't supposed to know that. It was a freaky accident and no one could have known in advance how it would turn out."

"I didn't mean it, I swear!"

"No one thinks you meant it, Zackey. Not even that disgusting piece of . . . Something rotten is going on here that has nothing to do with you. Dad and Dave are going to get to the bottom of it. Just hang in, sweetheart. Something is terribly wrong here."

It wast not right for me to say things like that. I should not have appeared confused or shown disrespect for the workings of our government. I knew all that. But it was suddenly plain that Stephen had been right: Something far more malevolent was at work than the mischief of some neighborhood kids. The hearing popping up without warning, the judge not caring what was said, and the fact that the judge was Marshall V. Thisbe, a man Stephen had heaped contempt upon all those years ago—I could not keep from spilling some of this to Zack.

The truth will set you free, Mr. Di Perna liked to tell his class. Zack had even learned the saying in Latin. I had to tell my son the truth now, bitter as it was: Something was nightmarishly off key. Had it run off the track at the outset, as Stephen had insisted? Or was it simply Thisbe's turn at the Juvenile Court, an unfortunate twist of fate?

No, it was definitely evil, the sort of thing my mother would have read in the air when she woke that morning, something that would have sent her into her china closet, a scarf bound tightly around her head.

"When is Dad coming home?" Zack asked as I tucked him in for the night, trying to keep things normal as Stephen would have advised. Stephen had phoned before supper to say he and Dave were heading to Queens to see some other judge, some friend of Dave's who might be able to reverse Thisbe's order.

We'd decided not to tell Zack, not to fill his head with hope, just prepare him for the next day which we'd decided to describe as "like going to camp." It would be a temporary thing, a few days at most until Dave could rush an appeal through and get a second hearing.

"Dad and Dave are trying to fix this so you don't have to go," I said, and stroked his back.

"I just hope they can work something out because if they don't, I'll be locked up in a zoo full of uber bad animals."

"Let's stay strong," I said.

"Illegitimi non carborundum."

"That's it!" I said. I kissed his hair and pressed my face against his.

Oh, God! I said in the darkness of my heart.

-24-

WHEN STEPHEN ARRIVED HOME later that night, he first visited Zack's room, and then settled into our sagging bedroom chair, and spun out his story.

"I guess His Honor, Judge Thisbe, was keeping his hatred on ice so it could hold its flavor for three long decades," Stephen said. "If Marcus Hake had hand-picked that guy himself, he couldn't have done better than that horse's ass."

I didn't want to get back on the Hake track again, although I was willing, by then, to concede that what was happening was entirely personal: People settling scores.

"What happened with Dave?" I said. I was exhausted in a way that wanted to stop listening and simply sink into a deep featherbed and vanish from the conscious world.

"Dave said this hearing should never have happened on such short notice, that someone rushed this whole thing through, and he was sure he could get Zack released on the basis of those shenanigans alone. He wanted to put together an appeal, but that could take weeks. I wasn't about to let Zack go to that place, even for a day or two."

Stephen's voice dropped away. I supposed he was even more fatigued than I; he would have had to be.

"I wanted something we could do *now,*" he said.

Finally, Dave drafted an *ex parte* order setting forth Thisbe's "judicial misconduct," and requesting that a judge restrain the cops from executing on Thisbe's order. It would stop them from coming for Zack the next morning.

Dave and Stephen took the new papers up to the office of a judge Dave was tight with, Morris Weintraub. Dave said if Morris wouldn't sign that order, no one would.

But it turned out that Weintraub taught a course in Ethics at his synagogue out in Queens on Wednesday afternoons. His secretary refused to give them the name of the synagogue, but offered to have the judge sign Dave's papers in the morning. By morning, of course, the police van would be outside our door. There'd be days of procedures to go through just to get Zack released.

Dave, that old Irishman, remembered the judge once telling him it was an Orthodox synagogue, and Stephen could only think of one in Queens, the one a few blocks down from where he'd grown up. They had no idea what time the judge's class was scheduled to end; they could have been charging out to the Queens for nothing. But they were ready to try anything, even crashing a judge's Jewish Ethics class in an Orthodox synagogue in one of the outer boroughs!

At the synagogue, Stephen slapped a yarmulke on his head and one on Dave's, and they found the conference room where the judge's class was in session.

On the blackboard, in Hebrew, Stephen spotted some familiar Hebrew words. He tried to sound out the letters. There were very few he felt sure of, but the pattern, taken as a whole, came back to him. It was the subject of Stephen's Bar Mitzvah speech, the one with which he'd addressed the congregation as a newly-minted, thirteen year-old man: "Whoever saves a life, it is as if he has saved the entire world." Maimonides, The Master.

Stephen's mind, he told me, had wandered back to his own thirteenth year. How can it be, his rabbi had asked, that a single human life could be worth all the lives in the world? How can one equal millions? The question had sent Stephen to his father and on to *his* father. In time, the entire family was drawn in. It was Stephen's uncle who had finally given the answer Stephen offered at his Bar Mitzvah: A family that has lost a loved one, has lost their entire world.

When the discussion ended, Dave ushered Stephen over to the judge and introduced him.

"So, Stephen, what did you think of our little discussion?"

Stephen told him about his Bar Mitzvah speech and the answer his uncle had provided.

Weintraub said he thought there was a difference between the loss people might *feel* and the actual soul that is lost. "A single soul, The Master said, is as millions. The loss of a single soul is upon the entire world."

But Stephen insisted the emphasis should be on the act of *saving*. The grace of saving one human life is immeasurable.

Weintraub was impressed. He slapped Stephen on the back and thanked Dave for bringing him "a real scholar." Stephen took the compliment as a wonderful omen; it was a great piece of luck to be talking about saving a single life with the man who could keep Zack out of detention.

But when Dave showed the judge the papers he needed signed, Stephen's hope evaporated.

"The word is out," Weintraub said. "Stay away from this one. It comes from a very high place."

"How could you know about this already?" Dave asked. "It only just happened this morning!"

"David." The judge's voice was grim. "David, David, David. That moron Thisbe was the only one they could get to take this. No one else would touch it. It's been in the pipeline for a few weeks now and everyone knew to keep their hands off. The judicial grapevine, you know, is a noxious plant that starts in the dusty corners of courtrooms and wends its way through the sewers to all the courthouses of the city. This one is from very high up; you won't get a single judge to stop it."

He turned to Stephen with an apologetic look. "I am very sorry for your problems," he said, "but you should go home now and take care of your wife and child. There's nothing I can do for you. If there were anything, anything at all, I'd be the one who would do it."

In the cab ride back to Manhattan, Dave managed to say that he thought we'd exhausted our legal options. "The courts," he said, "are pretty much in the other court, if you know what I mean. I'm sorry, Stephen."

Stephen moaned as he rose from the worn old chair. It had cost him his last bit of strength to tell me this.

Exhausted by sadness and incomprehension, we huddled on the edge of our bed. Yet, even as he held me close and rocked me, as I had rocked our son in our taxi home, I could hear my husband's wheels whirr. Someone very high up was behind all this. From his office in City Hall, Stephen would find out who that was. While Dave was drawing up the appeal papers, Stephen would be dismantling the entire municipal government, leaving no stone unturned.

And I? I finally had to admit that we were up against the kind of evil I was helpless to undo. Stephen was the person for the job, now. Zack would be taken away in a van in the morning. I worried that even Stephen would not know how to bring him back home.

-25-

Thursday, December 2, 11:05 am

THINGS GET WORSE AND WORSE.

My father was hugging my mother, and my mother was hugging me when "you-can-call-me-Al" and his partner, Don, came to get me. At the hearing they said not to bring anything. They give you everything, even underwear and a toothbrush. But I had my book bag with my journal and my Latin book. I was hoping I wouldn't cry and I didn't. We all said, "See you later." It was a hugely bizarro scene at the Grosjean family's apartment.

Last night, when my father told me I'd have to go with the cops in the morning, he said, "Dave is going to get you out of there in a day or two. In the meantime, you should look at this as a great adventure. Make notes in your journal. You're probably the smartest kid to ever see that place from the inside. People will want to know all about it."

"One Boy's Time Doing Time" is the title my dad thought up. Maybe they'll make it into a movie someday.

Parkside West Juvenile Detention Center is not in the kind of park you might think. It's in the middle of an *industrial* park with old run-down factories and offices that have all their windows broken. Al took me to the director's office and said, "Well, good-bye, fella."

The director is Ms. Caldwell. She's tall and skinny and has no breasts. She's what Cyrus would call "ironed flat." She made me empty my book bag on her desk. She wanted to take my journal and give me a little black notebook they give all the kids here for writing down their thoughts. I said I'd rather keep going in the journal, and she said okay, but I'd have to give her my pen and write with a rubbery one she gave me instead.

My room is real tiny, with a bed, some cubbies, and a table and chair. My Parkside clothes were in the cubbies already and

Ms. Caldwell told me to put them on and give her my regular clothes and shoes. She said I'll get my stuff back when I'm discharged. When she left, she locked my door from the outside. I wasn't ready for that. My shirt got wet with sweat.

Locked in. I'm now stuck in juvenile detention. The truth did not set me free even though I didn't have the *mens rea*. This is the nastiest place I've ever been in. It's cleaner than that basement where I got my tattoo, but even so, it's way scarier than that. My throat keeps getting dry and my stomach is knotted up like a tight fist. I better do a lot of writing so I can calm myself down.

Thursday, December 2,   9:10 pm

There are sixteen guys in my hall and they're all thirteen or fourteen. I didn't expect to be the only white guy here, but I am. Our rooms are around the counselor's desk and the counselor's on duty all day. There's another one on all night and there's also a supervisor for each hall.

All the doors here have thick glass windows, even in the bathroom and the shower. No matter where you are, someone is always watching you. If you want to go to the bathroom, you press a buzzer and the counselor lets you out and walks you there. When you're done, he's waiting to walk you back.

When they let us out of our rooms for meals or classes or these meetings they call rap sessions, we have to line up and count off and march in a straight line so they know no one's cutting out. All our clothes come from Parkside, so we all look the same, a line of guys in too-big orange suits.

This whole place is like a prison I saw once on a TV show my father made me stop watching, but still, I heard some kids at lunch say they like it here. They said it's nicer than at home. Maybe that's because here you get your own room.

I didn't go to any classes this morning because I had to get a physical. The doc asked me about the tattoo. I said, "My

mother let me have it 'cause it's for my best friend that died."
He gave me a weird look but didn't say anything. Then he saw
my foot where I messed up with the piercing. I said I cut my
toe on a piece of glass that was left on the kitchen floor at
home after my sister dropped her orange juice. Finally, my
sister came in handy for something.

Lunch was better than the hot lunches at my school. The
cook, Layla, told me even the bread they have here is baked
right in this building.

Layla's the only halfway decent person I met this morning.
Ms. Caldwell is a dork and the kids in the cafeteria? Forget it.
They're the most hardcore animals ever. Stupid kids who are also
mean, the scariest kids you could imagine. My entire job at lunch
was to keep my head down so no one could see how freaked I
was. I kept chewing my food but didn't want to swallow it.

After lunch we had a rap session with Mr. Digby, the case
worker. I like Mr. Digby even better than Layla which is cool
because he's the one I'll be seeing the most. They were talking
about the point system. You start with thirty points which is
Level Two. You can lose points for bad behavior like cursing,
spitting, shoving, refusing to call out your number at line-up,
refusing to shower, or having contraband which is anything they
don't have in the commissary. If you lose thirty points you drop
a whole level. Fighting puts you on Level One automatically. If
you earn thirty points doing chores and stuff, you go up a level.
Level Three kids get special privileges on the basketball court
and in the commissary, and they get to use the pinball machines
at recreation. Level One kids don't get any recreation and
sometimes they lose visiting, too. I was wondering if there's a
Level Zero, but I wasn't about to ask anyone.

The kids were telling Digby there should be more chances
to get points because it's so easy to lose them. Digby said he'd
give that some thought. Like I said, Digby is a cool guy.

After the session, a short guy named Nestor Santiago came up to me like he wanted to be my friend. So far, he's the only kid here who even speaks to me. He's Spanish and, next to me, he's the whitest kid here. At lunch, I found out I'm the only white boy in the whole of Parkside West. Maybe that's why Nestor decided to talk to me. There are some white girls here, but Nestor says they are uber bad, the worst criminals, and they're going to be here for a long, long time.

I said, "What'd they do?"

Nestor said, "Never mind. You'll see."

Nestor says he got sent here because he was with some other kids who robbed a *bodega*. The other guys were seventeen, so they got sent to the regular jail. Nestor says he just happened to walk in with them and didn't do anything wrong. I don't believe him. He's got that sweet kind of face you see on kids who lie so much they don't even know when they're lying.

At rec time this afternoon. I found a chess board and tried to teach Nestor something about chess, but I could see right away that it was useless. Devone, a fifteen year-old kid from another hall, came up to us and said he could play. I won the first game which made him hugely mad. I let him win the second game and then I pretended I wanted a play-off. I let him win that, too. He still walked away in an ugly mood, like winning twice didn't do it for him either. I was missing Cyrus so much, I didn't feel like winning anyway. I'm sorry I ever started up with chess. From now on, I'll stay with checkers and knock-hockey and try to keep everyone happy by losing.

I didn't feel like talking at supper. I was missing my parents. Even my sister. I missed them asking about school, and telling about my dad's day and my mom's classes. I even wanted to hear about Hallie's dopey friends. The cafeteria here is noisier than the one at school, but there's not a single conversation you would care to get into. Just a bunch of jerks mouthing off.

We had another rap before bedtime. Digby said to introduce myself and tell why I'm here. I said there was an accident at school. All the guys, even Nestor, hooted. I guess everyone here claims that what he did was an accident.

Digby said, "Tell us about it."

I said, "Me and my friend collided on the stairs and he fell down and got sent to the hospital. His name was Cyrus. He died in the hospital."

Then the kids all started yelling, "Assault! Assault!" and "Murder Two!" Some of these guys know the Penal Law same as any cop. I said I filled out an *accident* report.

Jason, who Nestor says is in a gang, yelled, "If it was just an accident they wouldn't of sent you here." Then he said, "Is this kid Cyrus white or black?"

Digby said, "That's a pointless question. You shouldn't answer it, Zack."

I think Digby must have the complete picture of what happened. I said, "Cyrus was my best friend."

Jason said, "Yeah, so that means he was white."

I didn't answer him. I wished Cyrus was here so Jason could see for himself. But maybe if they saw Cyrus was black, they'd beat me up. Probably they'd try to kill me.

I thought maybe I should show Jason the tattoo with Cyrus's initial over my heart. You don't have that unless a guy is your kemosabe. But what would Jason know about it anyway? Jason is a jerk who I don't want to think about.

Before we quit the rap, Digby said, "Let me remind you that you can discuss race in these sessions but racial remarks made anywhere else in Parkside will cost you a lot of points."

I just got here, but I can see that race is a huge thing with these kids. It's like the most important thing about a kid is his race. When Digby said that, everyone looked at me. Even Nestor.

Right after the count-off, in the lineup for showers, Jason pushed in front of me. He looks older than fourteen—very tall and buff—but I thought he must regularly lose points for not showering because he had such a nasty smell. He leaned back against me a little. He said, "You *know* that was no accident on those stairs. You know it, and now I know it." Then he bounced away. Jason gets me freaked. Terrified, I would say.

It's after lights out now, and I'm trying to write in the light from the counselor's desk. I keep thinking about that teeny second at the top of the stairs where I could have done some other thing. In my head, I've made maybe twenty different DVDs of things I could have done different when Cyrus got up behind me. I don't know why I did that little bounce-back thing. I never thought about him falling down the stairs. Reckless. Criminally negligent.

Mr. Rea says they prove intent from the circumstances. The circumstances were that Cyrus wanted to have some fun with Ronnie and Louis and LeVar and I was helping him with that. Now those are the guys saying I wanted to hurt Cyrus so he couldn't play in the championship. That's just *absurdum*.

This was the fourth year in a row me and Cyrus would be going to the championship. Anyone who was ever there would know we weren't out to beat each other. We were friends. How can a lawyer prove how proud I'd have been if Cyrus even got to the semis?

I don't want any new friends.

I wish my parents were here now. Or, really, I wish I was home with them. I know I won't fall asleep here. Even with the counselor sitting out there, this place is way too scary. This skinny mattress is way too hard. I feel sick to my stomach. I just need to get home.

-26-

THE EMPTINESS, once Zack was out the door, sank into my belly and my bones where it lodged, an unceasing ache.

Stephen held me close and tried to comfort me, but I could feel his body stiffen; he was ready to spring into action.

"It's time," he told me. And, in spite of my tears, I had to agree: There could only be one explanation for that hurry-up hearing and that was Marcus Hake. He would never admit to fixing a judge, but Stephen was going to pay him a visit, get him to say something that would prove to the D.A. that she was being manipulated. Stephen was more furious than depressed. He tore out of the apartment right after Zack.

"Let's get it out on the table," Stephen said before Hake's office door had closed behind him. "I know what you want. I don't know how you got that judge to go along with you, but however you did it, it's not going to work.

"It's obvious you want a trade," Stephen continued. "Your three shooters for Zack. But just so we're very, very clear here, my son was involved in an *accident*. You can't trade apples for oranges, Marcus. A tragic accident occurring in the horseplay of two friends can never add up to the heinous disregard for human life those three hooligans showed. It's an equation that just won't balance."

Hake struck a thoughtful pose. He wanted to be perceived as taking Stephen's words seriously. "To respond to that, " Hake said, "I'd ask you to consider how those kids got to be so heinous and disregarding, as you say." That was a lesson he never tired of teaching.

"They're fourteen, fifteen years old," he continued. "Too young to see an R-rated movie. If you send them up on adult charges, a year from now they get moved . . ."

"I'm with you there," Stephen agreed. "They deserve to be tried as the kids they are. But I didn't make the law. It's not up to me. And it's not up to you, either. It's up to the D.A. In any case, it has nothing to do with my son!"

"Well, I just want you to understand where I'm coming from," Hake said. "I got a community where the youth is in despair. You can't grow up into a man if you're stuck in despair. I gotta raise these children up—"

Hake could give a ring to his words, and there he was, showing Stephen how he'd lay it out for the D.A., the papers, even the people in the streets when the time came.

"Save it for church," Stephen told him. "The D.A. has a constituency at least as vocal as yours, and a lot of the people she's answerable to are mighty upset that three jerks with guns got into a school building during school hours. There's a city full of parents out there who don't feel safe sending their kids off to school, and if you think that nailing Zack on some phony charge will square the D.A. with those parents when she tries to reduce the charges against your shooters—"

Hake's eyes grew wide. "Did you hear me say that? I never said anything like that."

Stephen said he wanted to punch that look right through the wall. "We both know what you're angling for," Stephen told Hake, "but the trouble with your scheme is that my son did nothing wrong, while those kids you're trying to help shot up a school cafeteria!"

Hake loosened his tie, unbuttoned his collar and leaned forward across his desk. "Look, Stephen," he said, "it's a game, okay? But I have to play it. *We* have to play it. I got three boys going up the river. You got a kid made a lot of black people pretty mad. My witnesses say he pushed little Cyrus Nightingale down those stairs and broke his head so he could be the chess champion instead of Cyrus."

"For chrissake!" Stephen bellowed. "No one in their right mind believes that! And you know those three so-called 'witnesses' of yours didn't believe it either until you sat down with them."

"Now, Stephen, settle down and don't get so excited. If you was me . . ." Hake interrupted himself and gestured to a chair. He wanted them to talk "man to man," Stephen thought.

"If you was me, what would you do? If you had three boys in need of help, and three who could help those other three out, are you gonna forget your three helpers and leave the three in need to take what the D.A. hands them? I doubt it. I've got three in need. The Lord provides in time of need, I always have believed."

"You seized on an unfortunate accident to manipulate some very confused kids and their families—"

"Whoa! Hold on! Those boys came to *me!*"

"At your invitation, no doubt."

"My office is always open to my community. I make myself available to anyone with a problem—"

"Right. And if they don't walk in through your always-open door, you walk yourself over to where they live and knock on *theirs.*"

"You're imagining things, Stephen. That's not how it happened."

"It happened," Stephen said. "How you got it to happen doesn't matter. You led those three witnesses into the D.A.'s office and you fed them their lines!"

"You'll never prove anything like that—"

"If it's true, I'll prove it. You're messing with the wrong man."

Hake switched on his angelic look and a voice to match. Stephen and I had both seen and heard it all too often on the evening news. "I'm not trying to hurt your boy," he told Stephen.

"Zack and Cyrus were like brothers—"

"All men are brothers," Hake cut in, "but brothers are oftentimes fierce competitors, isn't that so? Cain and Abel . . ."

Stephen had become a snorting bull and Hake was hurling spikes into his bleeding side. "That's *your* fantasy, Marcus. Zack and Cyrus were a *team*, for godsake. Why are you gunning for Zack, anyway? You've gone to an awful lot of stinking trouble to lock him away."

"Oh, now, Stephen, you know this is nothing personal."

That phrase, Stephen told me, rang in his ears like a gong. He leaned down into Hake's face and fixed him with his rage. "Of course, it's personal!" Stephen hollered. "You're targeting my son, a child who never felt one ounce of racial bias in his life. *WHY?*"

Hake pulled back to recover some breathing space. "C'mon," he finally said, "you know your boy is just a symbol. He's a white kid implicated in the death of a black boy. Zack and my boys *are* connected. By the power of the symbol."

"An accident can't be a symbol of a crime, Marcus. No one's going to fall for that!"

Hake shrugged, looking helpless and innocent. "Hey, that's how the community sees it. Lookit, Stephen, I'm a man of principle, just like you. We've both been on the lines fighting injustice for a long time now. And you know when you're in that kind of fight, it's nothing personal. People aren't fools. They know how to get beyond the personal and see the symbolism. We both know how it is, don't we?"

"There's no 'we' here, Marcus."

Hake stood up and walked across the room to his window. Without turning to look at Stephen, he said, "Well, so look, man, maybe what you wanna do is ease up and play the game."

"Your game, Marcus? No way!"

"It's not my game. It's the system's. My boys plead, your boy pleads. If Zack would settle for third degree manslaughter, for example—"

"No way, Marcus! I told you Zack is innocent. That means he won't plead to anything, is that perfectly clear?"

"Reckless endangerment, even. As a juvie offense that ain't so bad."

"Forget it! Zack will never take a plea. *Nada*. Got it? I think you'd better talk to whoever fixed that moronic judge for you and tell him the deal is off."

Hake circled around behind Stephen. "You know," he said, "for someone who's been in the city government as long as you have, you are surprisingly naive." He leaned his mouth up close to Stephen's ear, lowered his voice. "I have a lot of chits in my pocket, Mr. Grosjean, a lot of folks who owe me."

He strolled casually around the office to give Stephen time to let this weighty bit of information sink in. "There's a lot of trouble I've taken care of on the streets of this city, a lot of peacemaking I've done in my time. People in high-up places are mighty grateful for what I've spared them, you know what I mean?"

He placed a heavy hand on Stephen's shoulder. "Your son is up in Parkside today because I pressed some of the folks who know how much they owe me. And I can get your boy sent home, too, if you play along. It's like poker, just a game. You play poker, Stephen?"

Stephen had gone to Hake's office to lead him, somehow, into owning up to his scheme. Now, he was astonished—and revolted—to see how freely Hake was willing to acknowledge it all. There was nothing to gain by threatening to unmask Hake: Anyone who might stop him already knew!

"I'm not done with you, Marcus," Stephen said as he turned to leave. "In fact, I'm just getting started."

Hake, Stephen acknowledged when he arrived home, had an effective inside game. What we needed—what we quickly had to get moving on—was an inside game of our own. That would require some dirty pool, not what we could reasonably ask of Dave Rea or of any lawyer. It would mean action somewhere on the margins, in the domain where *Stephen* was accustomed to playing.

-27-

THURSDAY. FRIDAY. All I could think of was Zack. It was now a familiar feeling, almost the feeling I'd had in the lobby of the hospital, waiting to see Cyrus. Please, please, I kept saying to what I hoped, after all, was an almighty power. Please keep him safe; please let him come home.

At last, it was Saturday, visiting day at Parkside. We'd had no communication, and I was worn to a thread.

I knew I had to be cheerful for Zack. I tried to picture my mother, a brave enough woman when she needed to be. Or Aunt Charlotte who insisted that if she bit hard enough on her lip she could endure anything. Finally, I considered Mimi Yee, an iron will in an unwrinkled dress. Asian mothers seemed unflappable. They spoke quietly to their children, and their children turned out so well.

One thing I was certain of as Stephen parked our car: I could *not* be myself. I had no self for greeting my son in a juvenile detention facility. Everything would depend on my ability to make myself up.

Zack, I saw instantly, was doing just that. "Hi Ma, hi Dad," the breath behind each syllable too shallow. I hugged him tightly and kissed his forehead, grateful for the feel of him once again against my body, for the shiny head buried in my arms.

Stephen kissed Zack's head. "You don't look so bad," Stephen said. "How's it going with your journal?"

"I wrote in it last night. I can't really sleep on that bed, though."

I stepped back to take the full measure of my son. He was wearing prison clothes. Not stripes, but an orange uniform, something they could spot him in from a distance. The knot tightened in my throat and sank into my chest: My son suited up as a convict!

"Seems like you're trooping through well enough," Stephen said. It all came so easily to Stephen. "How's the food?"

"The food is actually pretty good," Zack said. "They bake the bread right here."

"This place sounds not too bad," Stephen continued. "Maybe you'll want to stay."

"Really, Stephen!"

"School here is a joke," Zack said, more soberly. "The kids must all have lead poisoning or something. Most of them can't even write a sentence. They sleep the whole time and the teachers don't care. And the ones who stay awake—they can't even read!"

"Maybe we could bring some of your books from home," I said.

"Better leave it alone, Bettina," Stephen said. "It's only for a short time."

Stephen in fact had no idea how long it would be. Zack should keep up with his class work. There had to be some way to arrange that; some exception should be possible for a child who could read literature in German as well as in English; a chess champion who had memorized whole sections of the Guinness Book of World Records. Surely there must have been some gifted child in this facility before!

No, I thought as my mental house of cards fluttered down. There was never any child like Zack in this place until now.

Zack was telling Stephen about a basketball game in which he'd scored a few baskets.

"High five!" Stephen said.

"High five!" said Zack, and then a shadow descended. "So, Dad, when can I come home?"

"Listen, son," Stephen said, "Dave and I are working on it, but there's a lot of political stuff that has nothing to do with you. In the meantime, keep yourself busy. Stick with your journal because you really will have a story to tell when you get out. Use this time as if it's something special because, in a way, it is."

"Zackey," I said, squatting down so we were eye to eye, "You know your Dad can get around anything in this city and he will, sweetheart. Just stay out of trouble, and we'll have you out very soon. Okay?"

It wasn't okay. But what could Zack say? It was time to say good-bye.

We kissed our son and hugged him again. All around us, mothers and grandmothers were doing the same. They spoke in slurry English and prattled in Spanish. They wept and cried out to their children to be good. I knew I felt more like those mothers than like Mimi Yee who I was trying to be. "Good-bye, darling," I said. "I love you so much."

Out on the street, Stephen said, "I think that went pretty well. Zack seems all right, and you were fine, too."

"I don't think there was anything fine about it," I said. "Zack looks terrible. He's not sleeping, and it's not because of his bed. He's too scared to close his eyes, Stephen. The other kids in there—did you see them? Zack can't possibly negotiate his way around kids like that. He was putting on a brave front for us, couldn't you tell?"

Stephen begged me to be patient. The place seemed well enough supervised. Zack was better than we'd expected.

"He can't stay there more than another day or two," I told Stephen. Then, like a small child myself, I said, "Promise me that's all it will be."

-28-

Sunday, December 5, 10:15 pm

I HAVEN'T EVEN BEEN HERE four whole days but it feels much longer. It's sure not going to be the sleepover party my father thought it would be. I'm counting the days, and that's sort of bizarro since I don't know what number I'm counting to. No one knows how long I'll be here. I just count to have something to do.

I count inside my head. I talk inside my head, too. If any of the animals caught me talking to myself, they'd beat me up. They beat on you for any reason at all. You never know when some loser will flip out and bust you in the face. Yesterday, a guy got cut over his eye and had to get stitches. He was just looking at another guy eat a piece of cake. Looking can get some of these guys mega steamed. I try not to look at anyone, especially Jason. Just writing his name down makes my mouth turn dry.

It's amazing how fast they'll whack you. There are guys here with some ugly injuries, even right smack on their faces, but no one gets points off for fighting because no one sees the fight. You're walking in the hall to your class and all of a sudden there's some noise behind you. You don't turn around. You just keep walking. Then you get to class and you see the guy coming in behind you is all messed up, but nobody saw it happen. The teachers don't ask questions. I guess they know they won't get any answers.

The week before I came here, two guys got knocked unconscious. One was Peejay Simms. Nestor said his jaw got broken and there was blood all over the floor. They had to call an ambulance. Nobody saw it happen, so nobody got punished. It happened in the hall while Peejay was walking to math.

Nestor said the guy who jumped Peejay is fifteen. He's a guy who lost all his points the first week he was here and he

never got any back. He's got no privileges and no visitation.
There's nothing else they can do to him because it's against the
law to punish him more than that. So the guy goes around
hitting on kids whenever he thinks of it. Nestor showed me the
guy and he looks like an ordinary kid. That's the thing. You
never know where it's coming from. It's a total zoo.

Even with all the fights in the boys' halls, the girls in this
place are worse. They bite and scratch and pull each other's
hair. Their language is filthier, even, than the boys'.

The girls don't have meals or recreation with us so we only
get together in class. What happens there is one of them says
something nasty to another one and suddenly there's this war.
They think up some uber sick things to scream while they fight.
Some of these girls are enormous and they swing with their whole
body. Yesterday, there was a fight between two Spanish girls
because one called the other a gorilla dyke. They were punching
each other mega hard and scratching each other's faces. The
teacher who tried to break it up got a tooth punched out.

The hugest girl I've ever seen is in my Social Studies class.
Her name is Egypt Emmons. She weighs maybe 300 pounds,
and I'd guess she's around six feet tall. She's got slanty eyes
and a huge wide nose that was broken a few times so it's
spread all over her face. I guess they gave her the biggest
uniform they have but it's still way too tight. No one ever picks
a fight with Egypt.

So, Friday morning, Egypt is in the back of the room as
usual and she's slumped way back in her chair. She's almost
lying down in it because that's the only way she can fit. One of
the other girls starts screaming like she saw a spider or
something. They all scream like that, kind of Ooooooh!
Ooooooh! Ooooooh!

Then, the girl who started it starts yelling, "Ooooooh!
Teacher! Lookit Egypt! She got her hand into her pants! I bet
she fingering herself there. I bet she doin' it to herself!

Ooooooh! Ooooooh! Egypt doin' herself right here in the Social Studies class!"

The teacher pretends he didn't hear anything but everyone turns around to look at Egypt. When she has the whole class staring at her, she pulls her hand out of her pants and holds it up and starts the Ooooooh! Ooooooh! stuff herself. She screams, "Ooooooh, teacher! Lookit my hand, all covered with blood! Lookit how I'm bleedin' to death! Ooooooh! Ooooooh! Ooooooh!"

The class goes crazy then, the girls all acting like they're dying of disgust and calling Egypt all the grossest names. Egypt stands up and starts waving her bloody hand around. Leshonda and her girlfriend, Rosaria, start yelling that Egypt is having a baby right there in the class. They say Egypt's so big, she's having four or five babies. So Egypt starts yelling, "You lying bitches. I can't have any baby 'cause I'm a virgin." Then the other two start calling her filthy liar names, and whore, and dyke, and anything they can think up.

The teacher just stands there. He for sure is not going to start messing with Egypt Emmons. The guys don't want to get into it either. They cover their faces and shake their heads because these girls are too much even for them. You don't want to go there. That was the only peaceful moment all day with all the guys sitting there laughing and throwing each other grossed out looks until the bell rang.

Last night, after supper, Digby asked who was going to religious services. That sounded sort of interesting so I raised my hand.

I started walking down the hall behind some other kids, but Digby pulled me over. He said, "I don't think you'll be comfortable at those services, Zack. We only have a Catholic priest and a Muslim. You'd be better off coming to the rap session instead."

I said, "I'd rather go to a service."

Digby said, "What service will you go to? There's only those two here tonight."

I said, "I think the Muslim service sounds interesting."

Digby said, "That's not the best idea, Zack. Why would you want to do that?"

I said, "My grandmother used to live in Beirut; she can speak Arabic, you know. Besides, I've never been to a Muslim service. I really want to go."

Digby shook his head. He said, "I can't stop you from exercising your freedom of religion."

The Muslim guy had a white robe and a white hat but there was none of the bowing and chanting I was hoping for. The whole thing was just a speech about good behavior and clean living. Clean living always means drugs. The Muslims are totally anti drugs and alcohol. Digby was right. I would have heard the same stuff at the rap.

And Digby was right when he said that I would not be comfortable. Jason was there and he kept throwing me a nasty eye. He walked behind me right up close when we were leaving.

He said, "Hey, snowflake, what you think you doing? You ain't no Muslim. That ain't nice, crashing on someone else's religion."

He kept it up the whole way back to our unit. "You better pump yo brakes, faggot. Start showin' a little recognition, you know what I mean?"

So I already have an enemy which is uber easy here. Every kid wants to have you for his enemy.

Jason is getting set to whack me, I just know it. I stay awake in my room all night because I'm trying to figure out how he's going to do it. My Dad better get me out of here fast, before Jason and his homeys mess me up. I think maybe he wants to kill me. I've got to get out of here and go home.

-29-

I WAS SPRAWLED on my bed with the Sunday newspapers. The Times had not bothered to cover Zack's hearing, but Hake would be pleased with the tabloids which had, predictably, given him pages two or three for the continuing saga of the cafeteria shootings, and printed Zack's story several pages back. It was only a matter of days before they would pick up Hake's spin and start covering the two stories as one. Already, one of the screamers on AM radio was suggesting a connection. Soon, I'd stop reading the papers just as I'd done when Stephen's job was on the line.

I grew drowsy and let the papers drop to the floor. The phone rang. Once, twice. Was it someone from the tabloids calling to speak with "The Mother of the Accused?" My answering machine clicked on and I heard the cheery greeting I'd recorded long ago. And then the incoming voice:

"I need to tell you something, Bettina . . ."

"Viola!"

We hadn't spoken since that awful phone call when she'd unequivocally pushed me away. But now June had just read her the news. Her voice was cool and matter-of-fact. "This isn't going to be a long conversation," she announced. "There's just something I want you to know."

"It's so wonderful to hear your voice, Vi. How are you feeling, now? I'm so glad you called."

Viola moved briskly on to what she'd called to say. "Zack is in all this trouble because of Marcus. It's Marcus Hake that's behind it. He and Pastor Oakes. They've been all over me since the day after the funeral."

"What do you mean, Vi, all over you?" I wasn't sure if it was Viola's medicine speaking or if she was telling me this with a clear head.

"Oh, they've been coming around, first one, then the other. Ever since that day. Both of them trying to have these little talks. Pastor Oakes mostly. He shows up here every couple of days. June lets him talk a little; then she sends him away. I'm way tired of that man. I know it's Marcus that's sending him here."

I'd hauled myself out of bed and was hunched over the night table, my feet searching beneath the bed for my slippers. "I'm sure the pastor is just looking in on you. He's supposed to do that, Vi. What makes you think Hake is involved?"

I pressed the receiver tightly to my ear, wanting to hear with absolute clarity what Viola had to say about Hake.

"The pastor wants me to talk to this lawyer he knows. He wants me to file a lawsuit. Can you imagine? For money! What is he thinking? It's really Marcus who's trying to get me to do that, though."

I drew a long breath. "You're entitled to compensation from the city," I told her, softly. "Stephen and I have talked about it with the lawyer who's handling Zack's case. You should get damages for wrongful death."

If that phrase had not come up a few times in our talks with Dave, I would not have been able to say it to Viola. Dave had said the city would settle for plenty to keep the matter out of court and out of the papers.

"I don't want to think about it," Viola said. "Getting money for Cyrus? I don't know; it just isn't right. Anyway, it's Marcus behind all of this, I know that. He's been meddling in ever since Cyrus went to the hospital. You saw him there for the prayers in that chapel? He's got some very ugly business in mind."

I could hardly breathe. "Yes," I said, "I saw him at the chapel, but he's an important member of your church."

"He wants me to go downtown and talk to the District Attorney. He says I need to file a *criminal* complaint on top of the one for money."

My heart slammed to a halt. The three accusers . . . and now, Viola, too! Hake was orchestrating an entire symphony. Words were about to leap from my mouth and I struggled to hold them back. "What do *you* want to do?" I asked, as evenly as I could.

"No way am I going to do *that!*" Viola said. "Marcus tries to make it seem like Zack did something mean, like he wanted to hurt Cyrus or something. But you know—and *I* know—that that's ridiculous. Where does he get his ideas?"

I began to feel dizzy and sat down heavily on the side of my bed. Viola Still Cares About Zack! I repeated these words to myself and let the warmth of them spread around my face, my throat, my chest. She said it would be *ridiculous* to blame Zack. If she was speaking from a lucid mind, I could believe she still cared for my son. Of course, she cares! She would not have phoned if she didn't.

But what was I to make of this strange theory about Hake? I'd struggled to maintain a balanced view of him, and now here was Viola, a member of *his* community—a member of his own congregation—saying she didn't trust him. Even Stephen could not have imagined that Hake would put pressure on Viola! Urging her to join the three boys in filing a criminal action? The man acted as if he owned the world. Assuming, of course, that Viola wasn't simply imagining this.

"Vi," I said, "whatever the consequences for Stephen and me, you have to act in your own best interests. We'll understand, I promise. The teacher on that trip to Washington was an employee of the Board of Education and if he was negligent, then the city is responsible. You'd be entitled to damages, Vi. There's a lot of money involved and we want to be sure you'll have it."

"Well, I'll never do what Marcus Hake wants!" Viola said. "Maybe that negligence suit you're talking about, maybe someday. But even that just doesn't feel right—"

"It definitely *is* right, Vi. You're entitled to that money."

"Well, whatever it is, that's for later," Viola said. "Right now, I just wanted you to know that your boy is in that place because of Marcus. I just can't believe they would take Zack away. In juvenile detention! A boy like Zack!"

"I appreciate the call, Vi, " I said. "It's really wonderful to hear your voice.

Viola had been on the verge of saying goodbye when one more thought crossed her mind. "But just tell me this," she said, "are the folks down at the school being supportive?"

I wished she hadn't asked me that. I told her about the petition.

"So how many signed it?" she asked.

"Oh, Vi, it doesn't matter anymore. It was a stupid idea I had."

"Just tell me though, did Dorothy and Wintell sign on? I want to know: Did those Morrisons come through?"

"They weren't there," I murmured. Did she understand that the Morrisons' son was one of Zack's accusers? "The Morrisons have been a big disappointment. They and Sheila Holmes—"

"I never did trust that bitch, Dorothy! All that smiling, and always baking those damn cakes! That woman never was for real!"

"I used to think Dorothy was okay . . ."

"That boy of hers is a smart kid. He could come out okay if she'd stay away from him, her and that dandied-up puppet she's got for a husband. Damn! I hate that woman!"

I had no idea what had passed between Viola and Dorothy, but I'd never heard her badmouth anyone the way she was talking about the Morrisons.

"So who did sign your petition?" she demanded to know.

"It doesn't matter," I said. "Not enough to make a difference. I was an idiot to start."

"It's not you," Viola said. "It's a whole lot of other stuff. But even considering everything, I'd have to say I just don't believe this. After all the work we put in...."

"I know," I said. I wondered how I'd break the news, someday, about Deandra.

"Damn them! What a pack of traitors! Marcus got to them all. I know he did!"

"Viola, we don't know that . . ."

"Dorothy and Wintell are always sucking up to him at church, like they want to get something from him. Don't ask me what that could be. It's like he's a celebrity and they just want to get close in with him. I'll bet you anything it's Dorothy who cooked this whole thing up with her son and those other two boys and handed it to Marcus so he'd pay her some attention. Then Marcus got to talking to the Pastor and it all just ran down from there. That's what happened to your boy, Bettina. I just know it went something like that. That Morrison woman doesn't care what she has to do to move herself up."

"Viola,"—my voice was barely a whisper—"do you know any of this for a fact, I mean really *know* it?"

"I know it 'cause I know Dorothy Morrison. And I know that dumb Pastor, and I know that congregation. These are my people, Bettina. Don't ask me if I know them."

I pulled my pillow up against my stomach and curled myself around it. There was no way to prove any of this, of course, but it made sense to Viola and, as she'd just told me, that should be enough for me.

"Stephen had an idea Hake might be involved," I said. "He can't stand that man."

"Stephen is a very smart person," Vi said.

Her suggestions about Hake and the Morrisons were making my head throb.

"You'd better get back to bed, Vi," I said. "You need to get well so you can come off those meds. And Vi? I love you. I've missed you terribly and I'm so happy to hear your voice now even if it's about this mess."

"It's this story in the paper that got me to call you," she said, and I heard her voice begin to drift away. "It's Marcus and Dorothy taking away your boy. I just thought you should know, that's all."

I sat on the bed, still folded over my pillow. Clearly, Viola still cared for Zack. I wasn't sure of *our* friendship, but some of her feeling for Zack had survived.

I imagined Viola had had to wrestle with June about making this call. June did not understand my friendship with Viola; nor did she believe what she'd heard about the friendship between our boys. Where June came from, friendships like these were likely impossible. Somehow, Viola had picked up the phone in spite of her sister. I had to hope she could do that again someday.

I found Stephen on the sofa, fidgeting with the TV remote, and sat down beside him. "That was Vi on the phone," I said. "The first time we've spoken and she's the one who made the call."

"Does this mean she's feeling better?" Stephen asked hopefully.

"She read about Zack in the papers. She told me a very strange story."

"But is she better yet?"

"It's hard to say."

I told him about Hake pressuring Viola to file a criminal complaint.

Stephen was only mildly surprised.

"Isn't that against the law? Shouldn't we let Lindemann know he's been harassing her?"

"I'll pass it on to Dave," Stephen said mildly.

"Stephen! Can't this be *our* inside game? Wouldn't this put Hake out of business? It's illegal to stir up law suits and criminal complaints, isn't it?"

"Hake walks right past the law and nobody stops him," Stephen said with disgust. "He's pretty much admitted to fixing the judge, so I'm sure he'll admit he pressured Viola. He fears nothing. Everyone owes him too much."

"Well, the good news is that Viola was trying to help Zack. She called me because she still cares. It'll be a good thing to tell Zack when we see him next week. It'll make a big difference, I know it will. It makes a big difference to *me*."

"Take is easy, Betts," Stephen said. "Getting upset about an article in the paper is one thing; signing an affidavit is something else entirely. It's a legal document. She'll have to swear to it under oath. It's a much bigger deal than calling you up with some dirt about Hake. Viola's still unstable. You don't even know if any of that gossip is true."

"Still," I said, "I wish I could let Zack know she called."

-30-

I CHARGED INTO HAKE'S OFFICE and demanded to see him. I had no specific plan, only my raw maternal rage.

"He's not taking any more appointments today," his assistant said. "It's almost four. We're getting ready to close."

"He'll see me," I said.

"May I have your name, please?"

"It's not important."

The assistant knocked at a door at the rear of the office, then nodded in my direction.

When he appeared in the doorway, Hake was wearing a red carnation in his lapel, undoubtedly snipped from the bouquet on his assistant's desk.

"Can I help you?" I thought he bowed slightly.

"I'm Bettina Grosjean."

He smiled his photo-op smile and ushered me into his office.

"So, Ms. Grosjean, we meet at last . . ."

"I've admired you for years, Mr. Hake. You might say you've been one of my heroes . . ."

"Very nice of you to say that, Ms. Grosjean." He shut the door behind us.

". . . but now you're a miserable disappointment. You've let yourself fall prey to a conniving woman who only wants to use you for her own social advancement. With Dorothy Morrison's help, you've kidnapped my son and induced his classmates to tell filthy, vicious lies. You've been harassing Viola Nightingale who has got—God knows—enough pain to deal with. What is Dorothy to you, anyway?"

"Ms. Grosjean, can I call you Bettina? Bettina, please sit down." The famous smile appeared again.

"I didn't come here for a polite conversation, Mr. Hake. I came here because you are the one who is going to get my son released from that holding bin. So, no, I'm not going to sit down."

Hake gestured vigorously toward the chair opposite his desk. "Please, Bettina, have a seat. Let me tell you what I think you're missing here."

I sat down at the very edge of the chair and leaned forward. "I will listen, but only for a minute. Then you will tell me how you plan to get Zack out of that place."

"The point is, Bettina, you come here looking for justice. You and your husband, you got a big idea about justice. But this is not the time to be talking about justice. What you two are missing is that there can't be any justice until there's equality. It's been my life commitment to—"

"Your idea of equality is to equate an innocent kid with three murderous criminals. There's no comparison!"

"That's because you can't compare black children and white children, and that's because there's no equality. That's what I've been trying to fix, you see."

"Aren't we past all that by now?"

"No, dammit! We're not even near it! What you don't seem to get, Bettina, is that everything that goes down every day is about inequality between the races. We're nowhere near done with race."

"Your three boys were locked up because they're felons, Mr. Hake, not because they're black."

"It's not that simple," Hake said. He got up and strolled around his office. He was going to start talking down to me, the paternal pose. I stood up and started circling around with him.

"You do understand," I said, "that when there's no race issue, trying to fabricate one makes a farce of your whole enterprise. If you want to be taken seriously, you have to make accurate distinctions."

Hake whirled around to show me a face distorted with anger. "I don't need you to tell me how to manage my career! Who the hell do you think you are to come barging in here telling me how I have to think? You two hippies with your heads in the clouds? You lecture me, but it's *your* son who's in detention, not mine."

"You do have enormous power," I said, my nostrils flaring, my voice a menacing hiss, "but you've completely lost your moral compass. When you start to act like the people you despise, you've lost your soul. How long do you think it'll be before the people who look up to you get disgusted and walk away? Dorothy Morrison is just one woman. The community is full of people who will judge you differently."

"Don't worry yourself about my people, Bettina. They understand power a lot better than you do. Nothing like being disempowered to give you a big education in the workings of power. Nothing like being on the downside of inequality to learn all about the meaning of equality."

He strode back to his desk and lowered himself ceremoniously into his chair. Then he leaned back and studied me with a disdainful sneer. "Maybe you better leave this office, now. I have serious work to do here."

But I bent over him, my face close in on his. "You *know* my son is innocent," I said.

"I know a little black child is dead. I know your son was the proximate cause of that. And that's all I need to know."

"This is not about race, godammit! Zack and Cyrus Nightingale represented everything you've been working for! Zack is not your enemy. Dorothy Morrison, who brought you her son as a witness, is your enemy. Why can't you grasp that reality?"

"I could ask you the same question," Hake said. "You're missing reality totally. The reality is what I just told you. Race is in there every day. It's hard-wired into everything. Let me ask you something: You walk down the street and see maybe ten people. What did you see? Well, five were black and five were white. That's the first thing you notice, and most times it's the *only* thing.

"The lady holding those scales of justice is blind. But nobody in this whole country is *race*-blind. It's maybe gonna take ten or twelve generations before anyone is race-blind because it's going to take at least that much time before the races blend down to a continuous spectrum of colors. Until then, everyone's gonna see race before they see anything else. So, until then, there's no equality.

"Now, you wanna talk about justice? First, you gotta make things equal. Until things get blended down into that continuous spectrum, I gotta put my hand on those scales to force them to balance out. Right now it's about *power*."

By the time he finished, I was reeling.

"I'm sorry I had to be the one to open your eyes," he said. "I mean, seeing as you are the professor and all."

"You *are* sorry, Mr. Hake," I said more quietly. I was speaking to a madman, I decided, a lunatic who had taken my son hostage. "A man who has lost all principle is a sorry, pitiful wretch and I do feel very sorry for you. You obviously care nothing for children like Zack who have to grow up here and now. As for your ten or twelve generations of racial blending, that is undoubtedly the nuttiest idea I've ever heard!"

I stood up, hurried to the door, and slammed it hard behind me. In the brilliant white light of my rage I saw with perfect clarity what my next step would be.

Stephen had cautioned me to stay away from the papers. But the twelve generations we'd have to wait for racial peace? That was something the people of our city should know about. This news could embarrass Hake enough so that the mayor might walk away from whatever debts he thought he owed him.

In the Broadway Luncheonette, I ordered a muffin and a decaf and dug my phone out of my bag. Somewhere in my files was the number of our old friend from the Movement, Lester Kanovitz.

Lester was the editor of a widely-read leftie weekly. He lived in his office, never spared a moment away from the cause. So I wasn't surprised to find him there, even though it was past six. Of course, he knew all about Zack; he read every paper in town.

"It's terrible," I said, "the worst time of our lives."

I recounted my conversation with Hake. "It's a shameless power play, even by his own description. He calls it 'putting his hand on the scales of justice.'"

Lester seemed to chuckle when I said that, an ambiguous sound I couldn't quite decipher.

I laid out Hake's theory of the "continuous spectrum." "In a couple more centuries, he says, there will be no races, and only then will there be equality. Until then, justice is a pointless ideal."

"He's probably right about that," Lester said, and the chuckle was more pronounced.

"What? Lester, you're making a joke that's not funny. Not to me. Not with Zack locked up—"

"It's no joke, Bettina. He's right when he says that people will have feelings of distrust and hatred for generations to come. Unconscious, irrational emotions pull hardest on our strings in times of crisis. If there were ever a time when everyone was satisfied with their portion, those differences wouldn't make any difference. But, you know, that's never going to happen."

"Lester," I said, practically spitting, "this is not what you and I are about! We're trying to get everyone past the irrational stuff! It's our job to make the unconscious conscious so people will act fairly!"

"Well, look Bettina," he said, "it doesn't matter what we do about consciousness just now. The bottom line is that what you're asking me to do is impossible. I'm not going to run an article ridiculing Marcus Hake. This magazine has always been a great fan of his."

"I was a fan, too," I said, "but now that I see what he really believes—"

"Bettina, baby, the liberal media is never going to take down Hake."

"Lester! He's doing just what he always says whites do to him!"

"Whites can never be the victims of injustice the way blacks are, Bettina. The history of slavery in this country is the real source of racial injustice, and that goes in only one direction."

"Lester," I screamed, "the man has no scruples at all! It's all a power game to him. That's why he's kidnapped Zack. And now I've told you, and you're giving me all this highbrow political theory—"

"Highbrow political theory is this magazine's stock in trade. And isn't it what you're teaching up there at the university?"

"Oooooh, Lester! Lester! To hell with you, Lester!"

My hand, as I switched off my phone, reverberated like a gong. Lester Kanovitz, our old friend from the Movement, was only in it for the game; he had as much moral fiber as Marcus Hake. The great leader of his people and the defender of moral values—all they really wanted now was power!

Had I not been inhibited by the other customers in the booths all about me, I would have let out an enormous bellow. I was a lioness again, rattling the bars of her narrow cage. My son, the lion cub, was also a prisoner, but in my son's cage, there were bigger, stronger, animals who might be setting up to devour him. If Lester Kanovitz couldn't hear what I was saying, who could?

-31-

Friday, December 10, around 11 pm

THERE ISN'T MUCH LIGHT in my room, and I'm mega tired, but I have to write this down. If I write it down here, I won't spill it when my parents come tomorrow.

It happened right after inspections. That's where you line up with your towel wrapped around you and get your whole body checked. After you shower off, the nurse dusts you with some de-lousing stuff. Nestor told me sometimes it hurts. I said, "So what?"

I could feel that something was wrong. Everyone was looking at me like they knew something I didn't. It's on the way back from inspection. Jason is there. He gives me the nasty eye and then a whole nasty face. He says, "You not coming to no Muslim service no more, you got that, faggot? So don't be comin' on a bubble-poppin, cause I'm a bust yo bubble."

I nod my head yes, but I don't look at him. He's not down with getting looked at.

So I'm looking at the floor instead of Jason's ugly face and he says, "Yeah, I think you burned me some comin' to that service. Someone gotta teach you 'bout showin' a little recognition. You needs to check yourself, white boy, cause I think you 'bout to bite it."

Then, real fast, he jabs me with something and I get this mega pain on the side of my body. Then he rips the jabbing thing right down to my leg. When he jerks it away, I see it's the curly part of a rusty corkscrew. This whole thing takes maybe two seconds. I make my teeth totally tight so no sound comes out and I walk back to my room like nothing happened.

When I unwrap my towel, there's this big, crooked cut going down my right side, bleeding hugely. I think that's probably good because blood cleans out a cut, but I grabbed a couple of pages out of my journal and pressed them onto the cut. Jeez, I couldn't believe this was happening. I almost passed out, but I rocked back and forth to stop from screaming and it kept me going.

I had a tetanus shot last summer so I figure I won't get tetanus. But I could get a bad infection. Jason for sure isn't keeping that corkscrew uber clean.

My chess coach, Mr. Avery, says worrying is the worst use of a good imagination, but the pain keeps me imagining an infection and that gets me worrying.

Spero mori, Jason. I really do hope you die.

My side burns. It's the bad pain that makes me nauseous. I know I should get it washed out with iodine or something, but if I tell the night counselor and they take me to the infirmary, they'll want to know what happened. Even if I don't say it was Jason, there'll be mega flack. Not something you would want to get into with Jason or any of them.

Saturday, December 11, around 2 a.m

I took a fresh page out of my journal and stuck it on the cut. Then I got my pajamas on and rang the bell for the night counselor to take me to the bathroom. They watch you all the way there, so I had to press my arm against my side to hold up the paper.

When you're in the bathroom, they watch you through the glass window. I went into the stall and pretended to pee. When I came out and washed my hands, I took some extra liquid soap. Then I went back into the stall like I'd left something there. I pulled off the journal paper and rubbed the soap down the whole cut. The burning went right into my stomach again and up to the top of my head. It made tears pop into my eyes.

I didn't want the counselor coming in to get me, so I flushed the bloody paper down, stuck some toilet paper back on the cut and walked mega fast out of there. When I was locked in my room again, I dropped down on my cot and clamped my teeth uber mega tight. I tried to breathe real slow.

My Dad says it's okay for boys to cry. He says men have feelings same as women, and boys get their feelings or their bodies hurt the same as girls. But if I cry now someone's going to hear it.

I'm thinking maybe Cyrus was feeling some terrible pain like this when he put his head back and closed his eyes on the bench in the Port Authority station. And maybe when he didn't open his eyes in the hospital, he was feeling like he wanted to cry. I am so sorry I hurt you, Cyrus. So, so, sorry.

The *illegitimi* are totally wearing me down. I think maybe this is my punishment for what I did on the stairs, bouncing back against Cyrus so he fell to the bottom and got his head banged up. It was reckless. *Mea culpa, mea culpa.*

I have to stand up and walk around a little. It hurts like crazy when do that but I have to practice walking so no one figures out what happened.

I just hope my dad finally got something figured out with Mr. Rea, some good plan to get me out of here. I have to get out before I get killed.

-32-

WHEN I CAME to that entry in Zack's little green-covered diary, I shuddered. How could we not have known?

Almost a week had passed since we'd seen him. Stephen had promised to get him out quickly, yet neither Dave nor he had found a way to accomplish that. I had not slept all week, and had spent my nights shuttling between the refrigerator and the couch, trying to distract myself with my students' papers on the aftermath of the Great War. As the week wore on, I'd found it more and more difficult to speak to Stephen because all I wanted to say was "When will you bring Zack home?"

The night before our second visit to Parkside, Stephen and I had had a terrible argument. As in so many of my tangles with Stephen in those years, I was fighting for a *principle* and Stephen was being pragmatic. Such a silly business, really, when our son's life was in peril. But on that evening, we had no idea what had happened to Zack.

Stephen switched off the ten o'clock news and sat staring at his lap.

"We have to make a decision," he said at last.

"About what? What could there possibly be that's still up to us?"

"We have to let Dave know if Zack is willing to take a plea."

I remember that I barely registered his words. The idea was an inconceivable one. "Oh, c'mon," I said, or something like that.

"Well, you know," Stephen said, "Dave has to file the papers very soon. Zack must either take a plea or opt to go to trial. If he pleads to some mild offense, it'll give Hake something to work with. He and the D.A. will figure out some deal for his three shooters and, well, it's a way to limit the damage, I suppose." Stephen looked miserable when he lifted his face to look at me.

"Are you serious? The damage is being done as we speak! Zack is locked up with criminals; he's not sleeping and not attending school He can only see his parents once a week! That's the damage so far. You're not actually considering playing this game, are you?"

Stephen stood up. His face was haggard, his hair peaked up at various angles. "I'm sure Hake's got the mayor by the balls, and the mayor has the judges sewed up. He even got Lindemann to rush through that hearing. All of them must be sure we'll have Zack cop a plea once we understand where the chips are. They'll work out their deal with Hake and then everyone will quiet down."

"So, Zack is everybody's pawn!"

"I'm afraid that's it."

I got up and made for our bedroom.

Once again, I stood at my favorite window, staring out at the city's lights. I was hugging myself when Stephen came up behind me and wrapped his arms around mine. I could feel that incredible softness that happens in his body when he's in a sweet mood. He buried his face in my shoulder, brushed his lips along my neck, begging for something he did not dare to mention.

I threw my elbows out wide to push him away, and turned to face him. "No!" I told him. "This will never happen!"

"Bettina—"

"NO!"

"Bettina, sweetheart, do you really think this is what I want for Zack? Don't you think I'm as horrified as you at the thought of this? But be realistic. Hake's holding all the cards here. Of course, I want to get it all dismissed outright. But our chances in the courts are terrible, as you know. One sure way to get Zack out of Parkside is—"

"Out of Parkside and into a reformatory to serve time for whatever he pleads to? How does that help?" I could feel the steam rise up around me. "No! We'll go to the papers, blow this bullshit agenda of his wide open!"

"It's not just Hake we're up against here. Dave has to have our decision. The clock is ticking and, frankly, there isn't that much 'inside' stuff left for me to play with."

I took a deliberate stride up to Stephen and burned him with my eyes. "Never," I told him, "is our son going to plead guilty to harming Cyrus Nightingale. It's the wrong thing in every way. So let's just put this idea back in the box, okay?

"How could we explain this to Zack? What would we tell him about the world he's growing up in? You want to tell your son to lie? He'll think we're buying into the story those boys are telling. Can't you see what an abandonment that is?

"Talk about damage, Stephen, this will damage Zack so deeply the scars will never heal. And what'll we tell him when he asks why we're advising him to do this? No," I said, "no plea! If the only other option is a trial, we'll take our chances there. And if the trial goes badly, we'll appeal. At least Zack will know we're on his side. Let the D.A. try her case. That would be a civics lesson I can make sense of to our son."

My brain was whirling, a volcano setting up to blow.

"Look, I hope we'll get out of this without going into court at all," Stephen said, "but we have to be prepared to go through with whatever choice we make now. Have you any idea what a trial will be like? How long Zack will be kept waiting in Parkside while the system ticks through its calendar?" He was drawing near to me again and I felt I should warn him about the impending volcano.

"I think so…" I stepped forward as well, narrowing the gap between us.

"It will be horrible for everyone," Stephen said. "Most of all for Zack. Ugly, awful things will be said. Neighbors, people at the school, will testify. Teachers. The three accusers will blast their lies everywhere. It'll be all over the papers. Zack won't be able to go back to school. You won't want to go out in the street—"

"And if he states for the record that he thoughtlessly caused Cyrus's death, what do you think will happen then? Do you imagine him just slipping back into the Program after reform school? What about the record, Stephen? How is a reformatory going to play for the rest of his life?" My face was so tight in on Stephen's I could feel his breath on it.

"You must be kidding!" I roared. "I won't let him plead, and that's the end of it! If you need a plan right now, then plan on a trial. I'm amazed at you. How can you even *think* of doing this to Zack?"

Stephen took a small step back. "Bettina . . ."

And that's when I slapped him. A cold, hard smack on his cheek that startled me as much as it did him.

While my family slept, I roamed our apartment. In search of a blanket . . . a hug . . . my mother. But the blanket on our sofa was one of Aunt Charlotte's crocheted afghans, full of lumps and stains; and my mother was still in rehab with a fault line in her hip to match the one in her mind. Nature, I thought, was calling her home.

I pulled the afghan around me. The most evil elements of humanity were stealing my son. I might wreck everything by insisting on justice, but I would have to bet on decency to triumph. I could see no other option.

My husband was simply being himself, a man who would rather settle than fight. Everything he'd ever accomplished he'd won through negotiation. We were, as Dr. Franks often reminded me, two very different people. Yet, even for Stephen, there had to be a limit: There are some things over which you simply don't bargain!

I'd acted unforgivably toward him and, in the darkness, a lush paranoia blossomed forth, born of fear and shock at what I had done. I dared to wonder: Could I spend the rest of my life with a man who would play with our son as a pawn?

The loneliness that followed that thought was unbearable. My husband was a stranger. My mother was fading. Zack was locked away. Even Viola, my haunted mind dared to imagine, might decide in the light of day to follow her pastor's urgings and file that criminal complaint after all.

It was not yet light when Hallie appeared in the hall. I first glimpsed her as a wraith, her flannel nightgown chalky-white, the wan glow from the nightlight in her room glinting off her hair.

"What's the matter, Ma?"

"Nothing, sweetie. Just can't fall asleep tonight."

"It's Zack, isn't it? Is he going to get convicted?"

"No, of course not. He's going to be . . ."

I ran to where my daughter stood, scooped her into my arms, and whirled us both around and around, stumbling into furniture, tripping over the worn Indian rug, spinning crazily through the room.

"You smell delicious, you know that? It's that apple shampoo. You smell good enough to eat!" I was delirious. "Come," I said as I set her down, "let's get you back to bed. I'll lie down next to you. You can help me fall asleep, too."

We tried. First, we lay on our sides, spooning. We switched to lying flat on our backs. We turned the pillows to the cool side, and back again.

"We're not going back to sleep," Hallie said. "We're too worried."

"Well, we're worried," I said, "but we need to stay strong, as I've told you."

"Yeah, and now you're fighting with Daddy. I heard you, you know."

"Oh, Hallie, it wasn't a fight. Daddy and I have different ways of seeing some things. All married people do. It happens when there's a lot of pressure around."

"Daddy isn't getting Zack out of that place, is he? Zack was supposed to come home before this and he's not here."

"Daddy's doing his best, but it's enormously complicated."

"You're angry at Daddy because—"

"No, Hallie, I'm not angry. I'm upset just as you are because I want Zack to come home. And he *will* come home. Please, try to go back to sleep."

I got up and bent over to kiss her blossomy hair. She pulled the quilt up to her chin and turned her back toward me.

"Is Zack going to stay there?" I heard her muffled voice from behind the pillow.

"No," I said. "But you need to be patient, okay?"

She turned back to face me. "I miss him!"

I kissed her hair again. "I know you do, Nell. You can come along with us when we go to see him tomorrow, okay?"

I closed Hallie's door behind me and stood in the hallway, opposite the door to Zack's room. It had remained shut since the morning he left in the police van. Cautiously, I opened it. On the ceiling, his model planetarium with its brightly-colored planets stood at rest. There was a remote starter for it, I knew, a button that would set the planets moving again around the big yellow sun at their center. On his bookshelves, the collection of books that my thirteen year-old had already plowed through, and the Gilbert chemistry set with which he'd nearly blown them all away. His laptop sat silent on his desk. How I longed to see those planets circling their sun again, and hear that laptop hum!

I returned to the sofa and Aunt Charlotte's afghan. For the worst of what my parents had endured, I reminded myself, they'd had each other. And then, my mother had had Charlotte—and then all of us—to help her through. I would never get through if I had to do it without Stephen.

-33-

Saturday, December 11, 3:12 pm

I WAS FEELING not too good when my parents showed up but I was uber happy to see them. My Dad ran up and tried to pull me into a hug, but I knew it would hurt my side where the cut is so I pushed him away a little and gave him a kiss instead. I had to work mega hard not to cry because I couldn't let the animals see me do that. I'm already a wuss back at school for passing out in the hall. I can't let something like that happen here or I'm dead meat.

Then my mom wanted a hug too. I gave her a kiss and we all sat down on one of those wood benches they have in the meeting hall.

My mom said, "So, how's it going?"

I said, "Not terrible." Then I thought about what a lie that was, so I said, "I don't know what to tell you, Ma. The kids are the dumbest and the meanest. The teachers don't do anything. The bed is still way too hard. I hate this place."

My dad looked like he was glad I decided not to keep kidding around. He said, "I know, son, but it will be over very soon. Is there anyone here you like? One of the counselors, maybe?"

My mom said, "Really, Stephen, we have to talk. We don't have much time."

I didn't know what was up with them. It was like they both wanted to tell me something and each one was waiting for the other one to do it. This got me pretty freaked. I couldn't think what was going to be so bad.

Then my mom said, "I'm afraid the politics have become messy, sweetheart. It looks as though we may have to have a trial."

I thought, I'm supposed to get out of here and the lies those kids are saying about me are supposed to get thrown out. When did this trial thing happen? Just like at the hearing with that judge, I could feel some hot blood pumping into my earlobes.

My dad took my hand and said, "Look Zack, Dave and I are trying to get this whole thing to go away. But just in case we can't do that, we have to tell the D.A. whether you want to have a trial or do something called taking a plea. Mom and I have been considering both options and we'd like to know how you feel about each one."

I couldn't understand what he was getting at because the burning in my ears was shutting down my mind. I said, "I just want to come home." My voice was kind of shaky.

My dad said, "We want you to come home, too, and Dave and I will make that happen. But right now, we have to let the D.A. know about this. So please listen carefully. We'll do whatever you want. Okay?"

Then my mom got hugely agitated. She said, "Stephen, we didn't agree to this. How can he possibly be the one who—"

But my dad said, "Please, Bettina, let's hear what Zack has to say."

My mom was not down with that. She said, "He's too young to decide about this."

I said, "I want to decide. I want Dad to explain it, Ma. Let him tell me."

My dad explained the two choices and said he hoped we'd never have to do either one. He said if I plead to something, I have to say I did a crime. And if I don't get into any more trouble for six years, the whole file will be sealed and there'll be no record of anything, including what I say in the plea. So if I'm good, it'll be like I never said I did it, but the law is that first I have to tell a lie. I got a sort of buzz in my head just trying to understand how this was going to work.

He said if we have a trial, Ronnie and Louis and LeVar would swear they saw me push Cyrus. So either those kids get to tell lies about me, or I have to lie about doing something bad to Cyrus. Absurdo!

My dad said if I went for the trial, I could wait for it at home but if I went for the plea, I could get out even faster. He was rooting for the plea, I could tell. He doesn't like fights and he didn't want me to fight against those three liars.

My mom didn't like him making the trial seem like a bad idea. She doesn't mind fighting for stuff she believes in, so of course she wanted me to tell the truth and pick the trial.

I was starting to stress out totally. How could I pick between these two choices? They were both so bad. The worst part was choosing between my parents with them both sitting there while I made up my mind.

I said, "If I choose the trial, are you sure I can wait for it at home? House arrest or something? Because I really want the trial, you know."

So then, my dad got upset. He said, "I know you think a trial will be exciting, Zack. You're imagining what you've seen on TV, but—"

I cut him off. "NO! It's not about TV! It's about Cyrus!"

It felt like my face was burning up. I said, "I won't tell them I hurt Cyrus on purpose. Isn't that what I would have to say in a plea? That I had *intent*? That I meant to hurt him? Because I didn't! I keep thinking about that time on the stairs. I keep wondering why I backed up like that. And I wasn't trying to hurt him. I WASN'T! And I'm never going to say that!"

Then my mom jumped up and did her big-blanket hug on me. She said, "We know that, darling. You would never hurt anyone, least of all Cyrus. I agree the trial is the best way to go." She was rocking me and it felt good even though my cut was a mega pain.

My dad said, "Zackey, you won't have to say you meant to hurt Cyrus. You could plead to a lesser offense. Carelessness. Not having regard for the consequences."

So just when I thought I had made the choice, the thing got hugely complicated again. I got out from the blanket hug and started walking around, trying to think about all this. I said, "I don't know. After I do the plea thing, they'll put me in some work camp or something, won't they? How long will *that* be? And when I get out, I'll have a record. They'll tell the colleges, right? The file will still be open when I apply to college."

My mom said, "A trial will clear all the charges and establish that you are perfectly innocent. As you are."

All of a sudden, I felt like I didn't have any air to breathe. I started running down to the end of the visiting hall, this long room that hasn't got much light. My cut was hurting like crazy but I kept running to the end of the hall. I was concentrating on not crying because it wasn't like I could count on getting out of here anytime soon.

My dad came over and squatted down in front of me. He kissed me on the cheek. I knew he could taste the salt because, in a real quiet way, I *was* crying.

He said, "I'm so sorry, Zackey, that I'm not doing better for you. And I'm sorry to be rushing you through this. But Dave Rea needs to know so he can prepare."

I know none of this is my dad's fault. I said, "I know you're trying. I'm not mad at you or anything."

He said, "This mess we're in has absolutely nothing to do with you, son. I wish I could stuff you under my raincoat right now and run past the guards with you, but—"

I said, "Hey, wanna try it?" I was giving him some Groucho eyebrows when I said that and it made him laugh.

He said, "You tell me what you want. From the choices we have, you pick."

I sat there pretending to think. I already knew what I was going to say but I didn't want to tell him. Then I came out with it. "I can't stay in this place anymore, Dad. There's kids here I know want to get me. If I can wait for the trial at home, I want the trial. Otherwise—"

"Otherwise?"

"Otherwise we better talk some more, okay?"

"Okay."

I have to get out of here. After the rap, I'll ask Digby to find me some books about trials. I'll figure out something Dave Rea might not think of.

A jailhouse lawyer. I saw a movie about one.

I truly need to get out of here. Out, out, out!

-34-

ZACK HAD BEEN SO BRAVE at that visit, he'd completely hidden his injury from us. But our daughter, who had not even seen him, knew something was amiss. All these years later, I cannot say how she knew.

Hallie and our neighbor, Roberta, were waiting in our car when we left Parkside.

"How is he?" Hallie asked before I could shut the door. She had waved to Zack from the street and he had waved back, but the windows had bars and were dirty, and she hadn't been able to see him.

"He looks tired," I told her. "It's miserable in there. We have to get him out ASAP."

"Mr. Rea could get a writ," my daughter said. "*Habeas corpus.* They use that to get prisoners out."

Roberta, who had just retired from teaching, loved that.

Stephen chuckled. "Umn, that's very good research, Hallie," he said, "but I don't think that's what we'll use in this case. We have to work out a *deal* for Zack."

"Oh, yeah. Politics," said Hallie. "Or you could get a writ *corum nobis.* I found that online."

"It's great you're doing all this legal work, sweetie," Stephen said. "You'll be great at defense work some day. But for now, would you buckle up that seatbelt please?"

"I'm just trying to help," Hallie said. She slumped back in her seat, refused to let Roberta help her with the belt.

"You have to be careful of the internet," I said. "It's not a law school."

"Well, you better get him out really fast," Hallie said. "He must be getting beat up in there. I know he—"

"Oh, Hallie, please!" Stephen said. "We appreciate you trying to be helpful, but please don't get carried away."

"I'm not getting carried away," Hallie said. She leaned forward between Stephen and me, and spoke directly into my ear. "He's little, he's smart, and he's white. How could they not beat up on him?"

"Please, Hallie!" I struggled to keep my voice level. I reminded her of the positive attitude we'd promised each other.

"But MA," she said, "they have to be hurting him." She hurled herself back into her seat and added, devilishly, "Besides, do you think he'd tell *you*?"

"Zack looked tired," Stephen said quickly, "but I didn't see any cuts or bruises. I don't think you should get worked up about this, Hallie. You're only upsetting your mother."

Hallie grew silent, but only for a while. "Do you think he'd show you his marks?" came the voice through a megaphone. "You didn't see the marks on him because they do it where it won't show. I saw it on *Prison Gangs in America*. The prisoners hurt each other WHERE IT WON'T SHOW!"

We were stopped at a traffic light and I looked over to see Stephen swallow hard. "Hallie, that's enough," he said.

"Okay, but don't say I didn't warn you. Zack better get out of there 'cause he's getting hurt whether you know it or not."

"I said that's enough," Stephen told her. "I don't want you watching those shows anymore. They're giving you some terrible ideas. Zack's facility is carefully monitored and he's fine."

His words drifted by me like old, dry leaves. I could not dismiss what my daughter had said. Perhaps I was thinking something like it myself.

"Now, tell me, Hallie," Stephen was saying, "don't you have some homework? A book report or something?"

"Yeah, Clarence Darrow. A lawyer. Maybe you don't want to know about that either."

"Hallie!

Stephen was caught in some tricky traffic and I knew that I was the one who should be mollifying our daughter. But I only wanted Stephen to turn the car around and race back to Parkside.

The voice of my daughter was the voice of my mother, the seer: You would never be able to see the marks.

"What do you think?" I asked Stephen once we were alone at home.

"I think Zack is frightened and lonely, but I don't think he's hurt. He would have said something. He might not have told me, but he would have said something to you."

The boy who had left with his back pack for Columbus Day weekend was a child who shared everything with me. But this Zack with the sallow face and weary eyes was another child entirely. Who could say what he would do now?

I had taken more time, on our second visit to Parkside, to look around at where my son was spending his days. How, I had asked myself, could we have laid such a heavy burden on him, asking him to choose between bad and worse? I remembered the feel of his body as he'd slumped down between us in the visiting hall, his long, skinny arms dangling between his knees. He was intellectually precocious but, at thirteen, his shoulders were still the shoulders of a child, delicate bones still trying to form the frame of a man, nerve endings barely sheathed and heartbreakingly tender. I hated myself for troubling him with that awful decision. I was proud and happy that he'd chosen the trial, but I could not imagine how he—or any of us—would get through such a thing.

After lunch, I took Hallie to her dancing class and then headed for home. Stephen would pick her up and take them both for pizza when the class was done. I'd be alone for the afternoon, perhaps not the best thing on that particular day.

One of those ugly wet snows had been falling half-heartedly all day, just enough to remind us that it was almost officially winter. The traffic along Broadway was slow, buses wheezing and groaning, drivers leaning on their horns. Along the curbs, an inch worth was already sooty, and the roadbed was drenched in that nitrate soup that city traffic always makes of the snow.

I wanted to go straight home and have a nap. The few hours sleep that had been my portion since Zack left were dreamless and empty; they always left me unrested, as though the deepest part of me, where all the fear and hurt was lodged, had remained awake. Yes, I thought, a long, brisk walk home, and then a nap.

Columbus Avenue, I knew it like my own hand. Public School 165, my old grade school, stood down the street. A block away, in a second-floor tenement, my old dressmaker still took up my hems and pinched in my shoulder seams as she'd been doing since I was fourteen. Why did the street look so strange?

I walked to Broadway and turned toward home. The colors in the shop windows and the signs above them were peculiarly dim and distant. The people moving past with their overstuffed shopping bags were larger than usual and they moved more slowly. At Broadway and 112th, I passed Susu's Yum Yum. Susu had served up at least one of our dinners each week for the past twelve years. Had she changed the exterior of her restaurant? It looked terribly odd.

A few doors down I found Haft Brothers' Meat Market. How much tough meat had we chewed through before I learned to stop in on Mondays or Thursdays when Ralph, the good butcher, was on duty? Haft's had the usual sausages and thick steaks laid out in the window. I pushed the door open. It was heavier than I remembered, much heavier. The sawdust on the raw wood floor sent up a sugary smell that was sickening in the presence of all that meat. I stood, watching mounds of ground beef swim in the glass case, my hand cemented to the door handle for support. George, the brother who never trimmed the fat sufficiently, was saying something, asking me to please close the door.

"And what can I do for you today, Mrs. Grosjean?"

I wanted Ralph. But it was Saturday, not Ralph's day. In the rear of the store, stood a pair of wrought iron delicatessen chairs.

"I just need to rest for a moment, if that's okay."

George stared at me over the stainless steel countertop. "Yeah, sure, Mrs. Grosjean. You feelin' poorly?"

"Just need to catch my breath," I said. "It's awfully cold out there, isn't it?"

"Sit right down," George said. "Holiday season wears everyone out, don't it?"

I remained there for several minutes, closing my eyes and then opening them to see if the meat had stopped moving. Finally, I hauled myself up, thanked George, and dashed out onto the pavement.

At the corner, Nelson stood by his lamppost, wrapped in a khaki blanket, his nose dripping into his bristly mustache. I wished I could stop and chat, but my heart was lurching madly; I could feel it clap against my ribs.

I began to count. Three, four . . . eight . . . fifteen. The number of steps to our building's front door. Then again, the steps to the elevator: eleven, twelve . . . The steps to our apartment . . . the kitchen . . . Oh, God! Zack is being hurt! Somewhere it doesn't show! They do it where it doesn't show!

I suppose that was my signal to stop, like the red light that flashes when your brakes are about to fail and send you careening into the busy intersection, or the beep from your oil gauge when you're running on empty and about to grind out your engine. You are supposed to pull off the road then, or proceed with caution to a place where you can ask for help.

I sat down in the kitchen with my coat still on, and stared at the front page of the New York Times. I read the same headline over and over. I closed my eyes and forced my mind to stop the senseless ticker. I was glad Stephen was out; it would have been awful for him to see me this way. Over what? An *imagined* threat to Zack?

There had been no marks . . . Stephen was sure Zack was okay . . . Hallie was a highly imaginative little girl.

I called my mother at the rehab. It was the usual air: Aunt Charlotte was being bad; the nurses were worse; the food was the worst she'd ever had. I lacked the strength to dispute any of this and so I told her I hoped she'd be happier tomorrow. I wished she were able to ask about me. And how are you, today, Bettina?

As soon as I hung up, I chided myself for being unable to tend to my mother, for having a mind more in tatters than hers.

-35-

I HAD FALLEN ASLEEP. Right there on the sofa with my winter coat on, my scarf in a soft loop around my neck. I even had my boots on. But the incessant ringing finally broke through and I picked up the phone.

"Who? Who is this?" It was not a voice I'd heard before. Someone for Stephen. A person from his office who was working on the weekend. "Yes," I said. "I can take a message."

I jotted down a woman's name. One of the women who'd been shot in the school cafeteria, the one in a coma. She'd died.

"Oh, how awful!" I said. "After all this time! What happened?"

"Septicemia. A hospital infection. Last night at Methodist Hospital. I thought Stephen would want to know."

"Yes. Of course. This is dreadful news. I'll tell him. Yes."

I had never seen, or even known, that woman. But there are times when a death, any death, can send you spiraling down.

I tapped a familiar number into my phone.

"Hi, June," I said, "how's Viola today?"

"I thought we agreed you wouldn't be calling here."

"I'm sorry. I just . . . June, I just need to know. Is she okay?"

I didn't know why, exactly, I'd overstepped and made that call. I was frightened for Zack. And frightened for me. An absolutely impersonal bug had just dropped from the air to kill a woman nearby. I wanted *someone* to be okay.

"She's sleeping," June told me, her voice flat as a lake.

The she heaved a deep sigh. "Those lawyers were all over her this morning. Got her all tired out. Word must be out that she might sue for money. I guess they all know she'll eventually do that. And if there's a lot of money, there's a lot of lawyers coming out of the woodwork. They figure it'll be easy. 'Slam dunk,' one of them said. 'The city's going to settle for sure.'"

"That guy is right," I told June, "but she will have to file a notice of her intent to sue or she'll lose her right to do it. The time to file that notice is going to run out, June. She'll definitely have to file very soon."

"Yeah, the guy she was talking to did say something like that."

"You have to make sure she does it. The city *will* settle, but you'll have to file a Notice of Claim."

"Well, you know, the last thing Viola needs to do right now is talk to these lawyers with their tongues hanging out. I told this one—he's the only one we thought was civil enough to talk to, Elias something—I told him we'd be back in Georgia before Christmas and we'd talk to him when we come back to pack up the apartment. Let him do that suing while we're someplace else. Let him do it after we leave for good. Lawsuits are mean enough and this one being about Cyrus, well, Viola's just not up to that now. She needs to get home for a good long time."

"Yes, I understand," I said, but my breath caught. Pack up the apartment? Leave for good? I hadn't come around to that yet. The table where Viola and I had put the Program together, drinking wine and iced tea? Viola and that table, going away forever?

"These lawyers," June rattled on, "think this is some kind of auction. Each one has a different number in mind. Each one wants to top the one before so he'll be the one we choose. Can you believe it, them telling Viola the price of her child, the price in dollars? I just had to get them all out of here."

"I was hoping to talk to Viola," I said, "just to say hello."

"Well, she was feeling pretty good before those lawyers got to her. Like I said, she needs her sleep now. I'll tell her you called."

And then the phone went silent. This, I realized, had been the longest and most agreeable talk I'd ever had with June. To my frantic, whirling mind, it seemed an excellent sign.

But, of course, June, herself, was overwrought and in need of a sounding board. I just happened to be the one who called.

So, Viola and June would head south for the holidays. They would leave before Christmas and be gone for weeks, June had said. We would have to bring Zack home before that.

We would have to go on without Viola's affidavit. And Zack would have to make do with my assurance that Viola did care about him, even if we never could see her again.

I looked down and saw the name I'd written a few minutes before. A woman I now knew to be dead.

I rested my head on the kitchen table and wept for us all.

-36-

As soon as Stephen returned home, I showed him the name on the paper. Methodist Hospital. Last night. Septicemia.

Stephen sat down heavily.

"Did you know her?"

"Not at all."

"It's awful, though, isn't it?"

"A death is always bad," Stephen said. He was pondering something, I couldn't tell what."

"Well," I said, "I'm sorry."

"I didn't know her," Stephen said again.

I went to the bathroom and washed my face. I looked miserable. Unslept, red-eyed, puffy.

Stephen was still staring into space when I returned to the living room.

"About the trial, Stephen," I said, "I hope it will—"

"There won't be a trial," Stephen said with surprising finality. "I've been thinking about it. It's fine that Zack decided to go for it. It's something we can tell Dave and Dave can tell the D.A. and it'll be a good thing Zack decided to do it. But it won't ever really come to that."

Stephen believed the D.A. had locked Zack away as a means of forcing us to have him take a plea. It was Hake who had pulled her strings so he could set up a sort of package deal that would include both his three shooters and Zack. Once the news came down that Zack was *not* going to plead, the D.A. would have to face the prospect of actually proving Zack had intended to hurt Cyrus. "I just don't think she wants to risk that," Stephen said. "This whole charade has been an attempt to get Zack to plead. Now it's over."

"God, I hope so," I said.

But there'd be so much more to getting our son home. Once someone's locked away, getting him unlocked would take forever. Even if Zack had foiled Hake's plan, Hake would still be out there, pressuring everyone he could get his hands on. If he could fix a judge, he could probably fix a D.A., even someone as sterling as Marian Lindemann. We weren't much closer to having Zack at home than we'd been before Zack made his brave decision.

"That's it!" I heard Stephen cry. He smacked his hand smartly on the coffee table, rattling his empty wineglass and knocking a stack of blue exam books to the floor.

"My God, what is it?"

But Stephen was already on the phone to Dave, telling him that one of the shooting victims had died. Dave confirmed what Stephen had been thinking: At least one of the shooters would now have to be charged with murder, not reckless disregard, or assault with a deadly weapon. The one whose bullet hit that poor woman would be up for Murder Two; the other two would get Felony Murder. They would both have to be charged as adults.

"There's a silver lining in it for us," I heard Stephen say to Dave."

Now, the D.A. couldn't possibly try any of those kids as juveniles. That, Stephen explained, would squeeze the D.A. to get rid of Zack's trial.

Dave must have reminded Stephen that Lindemann never did see the two cases as connected. Dave had tried to get her to view it that way, but she'd kept resisting.

But Stephen was thinking as a politician. "She can't have these two trials running back to back," he told Dave. "Both involving kids? Both with racial implications? The *optics* connect the two cases no matter what Lindemann believes. The mayor won't ever let these two trials come on in the same year. The city would go up in flames.

"When the mayor and Lindemann learn that Zack wants a trial, they'll start looking for some way out. The case against Zack is all hearsay. They'll want to get rid of it and concentrate on the one she can win. Get started on our papers," Stephen told our lawyer. "Let them know Zack is going for that trial."

So, that's what had made the death of the cafeteria worker so interesting! It played wonderfully into a strategy to get the charges against Zack dropped. And now Stephen was suddenly happy to have Zack take a plea. It would force the D.A. to confront two high-profile trials at once! What I'd seen as a victory for sturdy principles—our son choosing to stand on the truth—was nothing more to Stephen than another political tool.

For years, this conflict had lain lodged between us, surfacing from time to time to roil the marital waters, but never had our own child stood at its center. It had always been more an argument about ideas, a difference of values. Values were important to both of us, but they had never cut so close to the bone. Stephen's merciless strategizing counted both that poor woman in the hospital and Zack's brave choice as just a pair of aces in his hand. I wanted to stand by my husband, but he was making that terribly difficult.

-37-

FOR ALL THOSE WEEKS, I had managed to meet my classes and give my lectures, pulling out old notes and speaking as if on automatic pilot, but now the semester was drawing to a close. There would be term papers to plow through and bluebooks to grade. This, I always thought, was teaching's most awful chore: discovering how little my students had learned in the course of thirteen weeks. Grades, I was shocked to discover, were due at the end of the week.

My office was located in a warren of cubicles whose walls did not extend fully to the ceiling. It was close to four in the evening and the department secretary had left early to do some Christmas shopping. Almost all my colleagues were gone as well. At the far end, somewhere near the corner of the space, I could see that just one other cubicle was lit, someone else dutifully grading papers. I opened my bag and pulled out the Feminist History papers and a stack of Modern History exams.

I had read the first five Feminist History papers and was at that dreaded point of deciding where the lines should be drawn: Where did A-minus end and become B-plus; where did the B's degenerate into C's?

But then, a buzz from my cell phone. Stephen. It was probably the rundown of his Monday afternoon with the mayor. Ever since Zack's hearing, Stephen had come to dread those meetings. But that particular Monday, he'd been looking forward to it. He planned to let it drop that Zack was going to trial; then he'd inquire about the plans to try the shooters.

At first, I listened with only half an ear, ready to laugh at all the right points.

The mayor, Stephen said, looked ridiculous, sitting at his desk in a Santa suit, ready for his annual visit to a children's hospital. He had pushed his Santa beard up to his forehead and tossed the fake white hair back over his pate like some zany version of a woman's hairpiece. As Stephen entered, Hizzoner yanked off the beard and folded his hands sedately in front of him. That's when Stephen knew this was not going to the usual Monday meeting.

But even my husband could never have guessed that he would be relieved of his job!

"You need some time with your family," the mayor said. "It's got to be terrible at home, what with your son . . ."

The words the mayor wanted to pronounce carefully were "temporary leave of absence." He said he understood all the strain Stephen and I were under. He made it sound as though he was being kind. Stephen couldn't imagine anything less kind and sat staring at the absurd Santa suit, trying to understand where this sudden kindness had come from.

"It's getting complicated," the mayor said. "With the D.A. sure to prosecute at least one of those shooters for murder, this thing is going to heat up very fast. Your son is the other side of that equation, I'm afraid. It's going to look terrible, no matter what Lindemann does, if you're still here at City Hall. You're too close in. Anyway, you could certainly use some time off."

Of course, the mayor's math was terribly wrong. Zack was not the other side of *any* equation.

"Don't worry about the money," the disheveled Santa told Stephen. "It's a paid leave , completely arranged. You can go home today, right now if you like."

"Oh," said Stephen, "is this about what *I* would like? That's very good of you. But you see I've got three projects ongoing at this point and what *I* would like, as if that mattered, is to keep moving those projects forward. I'm a guy who cares about his work and that's what *I* would like."

The mayor was unmoved. "Look Stephen, this could be over in a few weeks and you could be back here a week after that. But I have to do this. Be nice, Stephen. Go home to your family for a while and don't make my ulcer bubble over."

"I think this stinks," Stephen told him. "There's nothing nice about it."

"The pay is good, Stephen. And there's a nice Christmas bonus for you, too. Take a nice vacation. You and—"

"Right," Stephen said, "a Christmas vacation with my family. You're going to owe me, Mayor. You're going to owe me big. Ho, ho, ho!"

But the mayor had no idea, yet, that Zack was choosing to go to trial. Soon, Hake would be causing a heap of pain. Santa would start wishing for a team of reindeer to carry him far, far away.

"Thank you, Mr. Mayor," is what the mayor probably expected to hear, but Stephen decided to leave it at "Ho, ho, ho."

It was a very short phone conversation because I could only listen in silence as Stephen relayed the news.

"My God," I said, "my God!"

What could I say? "I'll see you at home."

My poor husband! It wasn't the money, there'd be enough of that. And Stephen seemed more infuriated than hurt. But in all the years I'd known him he'd been fired up with some project or other. A man like Stephen could not be without his work.

Perhaps he could pick up a consulting job, maybe agree to that course New York Law School had always wanted him to teach. My husband was in the earliest stages of absorbing a terrible blow. When it finally hit home, the temporary leave arrangement would be a nightmare for him.

I began to pull my things together and pack up my bag. I *had* to get home. The lioness shuffling home to the den. Stephen, my lion, had just been declawed, set out to pasture to hoof the hay. It seemed I could feel very little. A pure, crystalline rage is like that; it cancels everything.

In my doorway, lit from behind, the figure of a man. An unmistakable figure. An unmistakable man.

Elliot Raskin was a star. The son of a well-known labor leader, one of the old lefties who'd brought the garment industry bosses to their knees back in the union days. Elliot served on every important university committee, on national panels, and on the board of the American History Association. He was a frequent guest on radio and television, the guy they called for an intelligent comment on just about anything because not only was Elliot brilliant and congenial, he was gorgeous as well. At fifty, his thick, curly hair was gray and his eyes had become bluer as crinkles formed in their corners. Other men his age had grown chesty, and the less fortunate had bellies that spilled over their belts. But Elliot had remained a tall, skinny kid. You could still see his hip bones protruding through his jeans, and I could have sworn those jeans were the same ones he'd worn in the days when we shouted slogans together from the steps of Low Library.

Elliot and I were the only ones in the History Department from those days and, although we never mentioned it, we had had a history of our own. It was an insignificant history because back then those things were always insignificant— little ripples on the deeper seas of our cosmic struggle. Still, it was there, carved in time like initials in a forest tree, and it made things slightly awkward for us to, well, to confront each other at department meetings, for example. I always felt a slight disturbance whenever I ran into him.

And there he was, leaning in the doorway of my office.

"Oh, hi," I said. I was in no mood at all for one of his witty chats.

"Hi," Elliot said. His voice resonated richly from the prominent Adam's apple that bobbed above the open collar of his plaid flannel shirt.

"Exams?" I said. I was still choking back my grief, and just wished he'd trot off to the men's room or wherever he was headed when he noticed my office was lit.

"No. I'm trying to finish the book. I really have to get it off my desk."

Elliot kept a huge, cluttered desk which would not be noticeably cleared when this book of his was done. There was, of course, another book in the works, and there'd be another after that. Elliot had the book-a-year rhythm that made him the envy of us all. I had gotten quite depressed about it, but when his tenth book came out, I'd given up comparing my life with his.

"This is the one about, uh, 'The American Character?'"

He laughed. "Yeah, whatever *that* is."

It must have been terrible, always having to denigrate your work to your colleagues.

"You here to work on your grades?" he asked

"Yeah," I said, "but I'm ready to go home now." My eyes burned, my forehead throbbed. Move on, Elliot, I wanted to say.

He remained in the doorway, looking sexy as hell.

I stood up and continued to pack my bag. "I have to get going," I said.

"Oh, sure, sure. You okay, though?"

"Yeah, I'm okay." I crammed the papers into my bag and started to buckle it.

"It's rough, huh."

"It's really awful, since you ask."

"How's Zack doing?"

"He's surviving, that's about it. Elliot, please, I have to get home." The news about Stephen's job had made me into a blubbering mess. Now Elliot was crowding me. Couldn't he see I was a wounded lioness?

I needed to lock my top desk drawer, and fumbled in the pocket of my bag for my office keys. That's when Elliot stepped into my cubicle and drifted around, pretending to take note of the titles on my shelves. Finally he settled into the chair beside my desk, the one reserved for students who wanted to discuss a paper or dispute a grade.

I looked up and found a pair of baby blue eyes, all sympathy and concern. The dam that had been blocking my throat gave way. "Oh, God, Elliot," I cried, "it's absolutely the bottom! My son—you know how I feel about Zack—they're killing him in there. This whole thing . . . Elliot, what should I do about Zack?"

That was an absurd question. Elliot's own kids were not yet school age, and I had no reason to believe he was a particularly good or resourceful father. It was that disturbing little step down I always took in his presence; I looked up to him no matter what the subject.

"It's going to iron out, you know," Elliot said. "There isn't *that* much evil and insanity in this city. You do know that, don't you?"

I fell back into my chair and buried my head in my hands. "I don't know anything anymore. Marcus Hake, the D.A., the mayor… even that jerk, Lester Kanovitz!"

Elliot, of course, knew Lester from the old days, and I quickly related the conversation we'd had about Hake and the "continuous spectrum."

"You need the Neo-Cons," Elliot said. "You want to put Hake down, you need *Commentary*."

"I hate those people," I said.

"They're not my favorites either, but they'd love this story. You're in a mess that makes strange bedfellows."

"They'd never give me the time of day," I said. "and the feeling is mutual."

"You'd be surprised at what they'd do to get some dirt on a guy like Hake," Elliot said. "Or maybe you should just go to the tabloids. They love smut, and have no loyalties at all." Elliot started to laugh.

"What?" I said. "What's funny?"

"I was just imagining Hake's nutty phrase smeared across the front page of the Post, that's all. They'd love to portray him as a loonytoon. And, you know, it *would* make the City Hall people back away from him. For a while anyway, and that's all you'd need."

Elliot stood up and walked behind my chair. He rested a brotherly hand on my shoulder, and I leaned back against him. "You need a break," he said, his voice a perfect softness. "Can't you get away for the holidays?"

"With Zack up in Parkside? Are you kidding?"

"They have to let him out soon. When they do, you should get away for a while, if Stephen can take some time off. . ."

That mention of Stephen smashed through whatever armor I had left. "Oh, Elliot!" I turned, threw my arms around his waist, pressed my forehead into his skinny body and began to weep.

Elliot lifted me out of my chair and held me close while I cried. After a moment or two, as I grew quieter, he began to stroke my back. It was a natural enough gesture. I myself had performed this very service for friends who'd lost loved ones, or were going through divorces, people overwhelmed with grief. So I can't entirely blame Elliot for starting the weird and terrible sequence of events that followed.

The pressure of his strong fingers along my spine was instantly familiar despite the all the years that had elapsed. And so was the smell of the skin at his throat when I stood up to plant a dry kiss there. And the feeling of his hand, those long, thin fingers spread wide across the back of my scalp, so sweetly pressing my head against him, sheltering me. That was pure Elliot. No one else had ever held me that way.

It felt wonderful to be crying, the first release I'd had in months. I burrowed deeper into the plaid flannel, letting my breathing slow and my tears run out. At last, I pulled back a little and looked at him. No wonder everyone adored him! He was a feelingful friend, a man who knew what to do, and when and how to do it.

"Thank you," I said. "I'm sorry to be coming apart like this. I . . ."

Elliot looked down at me with that dreamy, drowning look we all recognize. He leaned toward me again and brushed his cheek against mine. He kissed my neck. That was fair enough, I supposed; I'd already kissed his. But then he really kissed me, deep and hard, all tongue and expertise, and didn't stop.

For just a moment, I was swept up in it. When was the last time I'd been kissed that way, my head held like a bowl of precious liquid and I, imbibed? But then, I felt his hand traveling under my sweater.

Elliot, goddamn it! What do you think you're doing, you narcissistic peacock? Who do you suppose you are, you chauvinist pig? You're supposed to be my friend, damn you!

I pushed him away with all the force I could muster and Elliot, stunned at this affront, reeled backward, whacking his head on the corner of a book shelf. He flung out his arms to brace himself but could not maintain his balance and slid, helpless and foolish, down into a gangly heap on the floor.

I didn't wait for him to pull himself up. I gathered everything—papers, bag, blue exam books—into an awkward bundle, grabbed my jacket and scarf, and dashed out of my office. Tears streamed down my cheeks and my nose dripped as I tugged on my lumpy down coat and fled down the hall.

Oh, the shame of it, the idiotic, clumsy shame! I was only half together, but I raced down the stairs and out into the heartless holiday air.

From the bus, I watched the façade of St. John's Cathedral slide across the window pane. Fleetingly, I considered once again how helpful some sort of faith would be. I was a ragged, defeated pulp of a thing, ashamed, even, to nod hello to Nelson, and here I was, slouching home to comfort a husband who had just an hour ago lost his job.

-38-

EARLY THE NEXT MORNING, I begged Dr. Franks to make time for "an emergency mini-session," and dashed from home while the streetlights were still lit. After rattling off in a single brief paragraph the story of my confrontation with Hake, my dismal failure with Lester and Stephen's terrible news, I arrived at the reason for my emergency.

"This is the bottom of the pit," I said, "the worst humiliation, the worst degradation, and I inflicted it on myself! I encouraged him. I know I did. I hate myself!"

"You were stupid," she said. "Nothing worse than that."

I was astonished. "Thank you," I said, "I needed to hear that."

"Do you understand why it happened?"

"I was vulnerable, I guess. Everything was falling apart." I looked up at Dr. Franks whose expression had not changed.

"Are you angry at Stephen?"

"No, no, it wasn't about Stephen. I just feel so . . . so . . . By the time Elliot walked into my office, I . . . I was . . . *drowning*. I can't really explain it, because I've never felt like that. And this morning, I *still* feel that way. If I knew what it felt like to die, I might say I feel like I'm dying. Everything's slipping away. And Elliot—"

"Yes?"

"Do you think I have a thing for Elliot Raskin? Something left over from the old days? Because I can tell you, all I saw when he came into the office was a trusted old friend. And now I have to face him at faculty meetings, on committees at the A.H.A. . . . Oh, Christ!

"And he'll be thinking of me with my books and papers tumbling out of my arms and he'll be stifling a laugh. Any warm feeling I may have had for him before this," I told Dr.

Franks," it's altogether gone. G-O-N-E. I don't know how I'll
face him now. I was a moron!"

"It *was* stupid."

"What am I going to do?"

"I think the most important thing for you to do now is
figure out why you were falling apart, as you put it, at the time
Elliot happened by."

"Well, I think that should be obvious. Zack is in terrible
danger, probably getting hurt where it doesn't show. Stephen
and I have been having some serious arguments, and now he's
lost his job. To say nothing about losing Cyrus . . . and Viola . . ."

"But all that was happening before yesterday. Cyrus died
almost two months ago, Zack has been in detention for two
weeks. Viola seems to be getting better, and Stephen's layoff is
only temporary. Even he doesn't sound too upset about it. You
won't be facing any money problems. What made you feel like
you were *falling apart*?"

"Oh, God!"

"Oh God, what?"

"I feel so sorry for Stephen! He's out of a job and was
already feeling humiliated, and now I—"

"It's not about Stephen, Bettina, you already said so. Now
pay attention because this is about *you*. What made you feel like
you were dying?"

"What?"

"Before Elliot came by, you were coming apart.
Everything, you said, was falling apart. What happened that
made you feel that way?"

"I had that terrible talk with Marcus Hake, a man I once
admired, who turned out to be a racist and also utterly insane.
Then I told Lester about it—Lester who was one of the best
people I knew back in school and who puts out a really good
magazine now—and Lester, of all people, ended up telling me

that Hake was probably right! Can you believe it? I couldn't believe it, I really could not!"

"But it sounds as though he meant it."

"Well, he did. That's what was so...so horrible. Horrible!"

We sat staring at each other.

Dr. Franks had the habit of letting things cook for a while to make sure I was working. She'd soften me, and then move in for the kill.

"So," I finally said, "are you saying it was Hake and Lester who got me into that mess with Elliot?"

Dr. Franks would never answer a question like that; she would ignore it.

"What made you feel you were coming apart, Bettina? What made you feel like you were dying?"

"What are you getting at anyway?"

"It strikes me that something very important to you, something close to your heart was, well, let us say, under attack. Hake, and then Lester, had gotten at your core. Elliot's bad behavior was more of the same, wasn't it?"

"Yes! I was furious! I *am* furious! After all our years on the same side of things, Lester—"

"That was a long time ago."

"Yes."

"People get older. They mature."

"Yes," I said. "I know that. But . . ."

"Yes?"

I was going to say that Elliot was not at all mature; he was the same old narcissist he had always been.

"They're all so disappointing! All those passionate fighters for everything good? They're all just a pack of power-hungry, self-seeking...*players*!"

I said nothing else, only sat with my eyes closed, feeling everything turn dark.

Finally, an immense sob tore out of me. It ebbed and flowed until it had spent itself.

Dr. Franks sat quietly, watching me with what seemed like enormous sympathy.

"And so now what?" I finally said.

"Well, now that you've fallen apart, we can begin to put you back together." She nodded and smiled a very sweet smile. "But I'm sorry to say that—"

"Yes. Of course. Our time is up."

As soon as I got home, I ran a steaming hot bath. I'd had two showers since fleeing from my office—one when I got home to Stephen, another before heading out to Dr. Franks—but still did not feel clean. I sank down in the tub and scrubbed my neck and shoulders and arms with the pumice stone usually reserved for my feet.

"Good riddance, Elliot, you preening jerk," I said. "Good-bye, Lester-from-the-Movement; good-bye Marcus Hake, Bold-Crusader-For-His-People! You are over, the whole thing is over. Totally over!"

I held my nose and dunked my head under the water. Good riddance, too, to that wanton hippie; send her down to the sewer with those others!

Then, I added some of Hallie's bubble bath, that bright pink goo with the girlish apple scent I love in her hair. I ran some more hot water until a white bubbly foam rose to my chin.

My husband is also a player, a person who succeeds because he figured out things I never did. He can get people to give him what he needs because he's a grown-up who knows how to play the game.

I scooped up a huge blob of bubbles in both my hands and buried my face in it. Damn! Stephen's as good a man as there is. A far better man than I could have hoped to find.

I stepped out of the tub and pulled on my terry robe, yanked the plug from the drain, and let the foamy water drain away. I rinsed the tub with a fresh, cold jet, pressing my finger to the faucet to squirt water all around until every last puff of foam was gone.

I thought I saw Stephen, then, standing before me, an excellent man with small, ordinary flaws. And I saw myself in the mirror on the back of the bathroom door, a woman in a terrycloth robe who had recently fallen apart.

I settled myself on the sofa. On a stained Rolodex card, the number of the slimeball who'd slipped me his card at a conference years ago. I'd never called him till then.

The folks at that Neo-Con magazine promoted wars. They hung with the corporations and loved their guns, and I was handing them a gift. Why should I give them this? Why me?

Because it was *my* son, the lion cub, that Hake was holding captive, that's why!

I picked up the phone and dialed. I said I was going to write a story, a firsthand interview with Marcus Hake. I was put right through to the slimeball-in-chief.

"Nice," he said, "and nice to be hearing from you."

(Oh, go to hell.)

"Why don't you write me up a little proposal, some highlights, you know how to do that, right?"

"I think so," I said. (Of course I do, you moron. I'm published in all your opponents' journals, as you well know.)

"Fine," he said. "I'll look forward to seeing it."

"Let me have your email address," I said, "and I'll get you something tomorrow."

"What's the rush? Is this a personal beef?"

"No," I said in an over-the-top casual voice, "I just want to jot it down while it's fresh in my mind. Maybe I'll just dictate a little something tonight. And this will be under my pen name, of course."

"I'd much rather have it from Bettina Grosjean . . ."

(Yeah, of course you would.) "We'll talk, okay? I'll send you the material and then we'll talk." (That's how Stephen would have put it.)

It was the sort of thing I'd never done before, and it was thrillingly empowering.

-39-

Thursday, December 16, 8:05 pm

TOTAL SUCKO. This morning, things got totally horrible around here. I was feeling really proud that I figured out a way to keep the cut on my leg a private thing, but this morning it started pounding something fierce. When I got to the bathroom, I saw it was a pukey greenish color. The skin was puffed up, and stuff was oozing out. Infection time. Not all worrying is a waste of a good imagination.

I figured I had to show it to Digby. I told him I got it on the railing of my bed. He marched me down to the infirmary right away.

On the way down, he of course tried to get me to spill. But I could see he didn't really expect to get anything out of me.

I said, "There's a pointy metal thing sticking out on the end of my bed. Some part of the springs, I think."

Digby said, "There's a canvas sack that encloses the whole frame. Nothing sticks out. You could be very helpful here if you'd tell me the truth, Zack."

I said, "I'm telling you the truth the best I can."

He said, "Okay, I get it."

The Parkside nurse got a special car to take me to the hospital. It had two guys in uniforms sitting in back with me in case I decided to bail. The hospital doctor gave me a shot and some ointment and pills to take four times a day.

As soon as we got back to Parkside, they took me to Ms. Caldwell's office and, to make a bad thing worse, my parents were there.

My Mom swooped down on me like a huge bird. She said, "Zackey, darling, why didn't you tell us?"

I said, "When you were here on Saturday, I was okay. It just got nasty this morning." I pulled down my sweatpants and showed her the white bandage I got at the hospital. I said, "See, it's fine now. I have some pills to take to cure the infection. You didn't have to come here, you know."

My Mom squatted down next to me and put both her hands on my cheeks. "Zackey, you have to tell them who did this to you. They need to know who's to blame. You're not doing anyone any favors by letting this go unpunished."

I didn't want to look at her. I didn't want her giving me that eye she has when she talks about truth and justice and stuff. I just looked away and said nothing.

Then my father came over and walked me into the corner. He said, "I understand why you won't talk, Zack. Really, it's the smartest thing right now. We'll be getting you out in a day or two, so just keep your head down and stay as safe as you can. Mr. Digby is looking out for you. Ms. Caldwell is, too. I feel terrible that we couldn't get you out sooner."

I said, "I need to come home, Dad."

My father looked like he was almost going to cry. He said, "I'm making that happen, Zack. I promise. Two, three days maximum. Just watch yourself, okay?"

It was really cool that my dad understood about not ratting on you know who.

Even before I got back upstairs, the word passed around that I'd been whacked.

There was mega yapping and hooting when I came to the rap.

Jason yelled out, "What hater done that to you, Zack? Tell us who done that and we gonna bust his grill, whoever done that."

I said, "I got it on my bed."

The whole bunch kept trying to get me to tell so they could have an excuse to pile on me. I waited to see what Digby would do. The place was turning into a riot.

Digby yelled out that he thought we needed a little reminder of how we were supposed to behave. He said our unit would have mop-up duty for the next two weeks, me included. I figured he was punishing me for not telling, and the other kids for breaking up the rap. In regular schools, next week would be Christmas vacation, but now we'd all be mopping floors. The guys were uber steamed and they blamed me.

Digby said if we didn't all shape up fast, we'd lose visiting on Christmas, too. I got the feeling I'd be getting whacked again real soon.

Just before lunch Digby came into my room. He said, "Well now, Zack, I think we have to find something to do with you before that bedspring cuts you up again."

I didn't say anything back.

So he said, "Okay, Zack, you think about it and so will I. We've never had a kid like you in here before. It's a problem for me and I hope you'll help me solve it."

I said I did have one idea. I asked him if he had any books about trials. I said, "I need to read up a little for the trial that's coming up."

He said, "You're kidding, right? You're going for a trial?"

I said, "Yeah, and I need to get ready. Can you get me some books?"

He said, "Well, I've never had a request like that but I'll see what I can do. In the meantime, try to think of some other way to keep yourself out of trouble."

This afternoon, I went up to talk to Digby. I said, "I *did* think of something but I don't know if you would want to do it."

He said, "Try me."

I told him I wasn't learning anything in the classes they have here. It's all stuff I already know. I said I was thinking maybe I could get transferred to someplace where I could learn something.

Digby said, "I can't transfer you out of here, if that's what you mean. I'm afraid you and I are stuck with each other for the time being."

I said, "Yeah, but maybe I could work in the kitchen. Maybe Layla could teach me to bake bread. I don't know if that's allowed, but it's the idea I came up with."

Digby said, "I like that idea a lot, Zack. There are all kinds of security problems with a kid working in the kitchen, of course, but I'm going to look into it. That's a nifty piece of thinking, Zack."

Digby came around during rec time and said I should come to his office because we needed to talk again. He said I could start working for Layla in the morning. It was all set up. I'll get up an hour earlier and go to sleep earlier, too. He said, "That's the beauty of it. You won't be showering with those guys, or lining up with them, or walking to classes either. You'll be on a different track. That's the best part of this plan of yours."

Then he bent down like he wanted to whisper something. He said, "And we're going to tell the other kids that this is your punishment for not being honest about who whacked you. You have to back me up on that, understand?"

I said, "Yeah, I get it." Let the punishment fit the crime.

So right away I reported to the kitchen. They let me measure stuff in a cup and level it off with a spatula. I dumped it into the bowls and they mixed everything up. Then Layla set the bowl up on a shelf where the hot air from the stove could stimulate the yeast. Yeast is a very cool thing, a living organism that multiplies real fast and makes some amazing gas which is what puffs up the dough so it's bread. Layla punched the dough around a few times and put little bits of it in the oven. What came out was some very good rolls.

At dinner, one of Jason's homeys said, "Hey, Zack, you make this here?"

I said, "Yeah. You like it?"

The guy pretended like he was gagging. He said, "It's the worst stuff I ever ate. It's prison food. You making prison food, snowflake, 'cause you a liar."

Nestor was there and he thinks what the other guys think, that me working in the kitchen is a punishment. When the other guys left, Nestor said, "How you doin' back there in that kitchen?"

I said, "It's not too bad for a punishment."

Nestor said, "Maybe you oughtta tell them it was Jason that cut you. Everyone knows that anyway. Then maybe you can get outta there."

I said, "No, I'm not squealing. I'll take the punishment."

This afternoon, there was some bad news about Nestor. His case got reviewed and the judge sent him to reform school. He still says he didn't even know the guys who robbed that store, but they all said they knew *him* so the judge said Nestor needed to figure out how to tell the truth. So now, the only kid at Parkside I ever talk to is getting set to leave, and Jason and his homeys are still out there shooting me their nasty looks.

Thursday, December 16, 10:20 pm

Tonight I'm in bed an hour early. I'm thinking about what plan my Dad has to get me out because this thing of working in the kitchen isn't going to keep Jason away forever. All of a sudden, I hear this creepy sound like something scratching across the outside of my door. I wait a little and then I buzz for the night counselor to walk me to the bathroom. When I get back to my room, I check out the door. There's this crooked line across it where the paint is cut away and the metal shows through. I know it was Jason. He still has that rusty corkscrew and he wants to make sure I know.

-40-

WHEN WE RETURNED from that emergency visit to Parkside, I only wanted to tell Stephen I'd known all along, and he only wanted me to know he was doing all he could. We both knew all this; it surely didn't need saying. We sat staring at the TV, the sound on mute.

I noticed Stephen's hands were busy at his scalp, scratching, mussing his hair, pulling his fingers through to form those funny clumps he'd become famous for in our household. This was how he cranked the engine when a difficult problem urgently needed a solution.

"We have to have Viola," he finally said. His voice was very soft; he was still somewhere far away.

He sat forward and turned to look at me. "I need something more here, something that will get Zack out right away. I need that affidavit to tell the D.A. about Hake harassing Viola Nightingale. What we have so far is just not enough."

Stephen had pretty much ignored Viola's news about Hake putting pressure on her when I told him about it, but Stephen stores things away and waits for a time when they can be useful. Now, with the image of Zack's big white bandage burning in both our minds, Stephen was ready to pull out any tiny shred of an idea, even Viola's "gossip" about Marcus Hake.

I thought he should go back and scratch his head again. "Stephen," I said, "you were the one who doubted Viola really knew what was going on. You and Dave both said she'd probably never sign anything under oath, especially about Hake. Anyway, we can't wait for her to get off those meds. Zack has to come home a lot sooner than that.

But, with this new bee buzzing in his ear, Stephen was unstoppable. He picked up the phone and called Dave again. It was easy enough, as I listened to Stephen's side of the conversation, to piece together what Dave was saying in reply.

Stephen had interrupted Dave's evening of college football. Saint John's, Dave's alma mater. Dave, probably working his way through a beer, couldn't have been happy to talk to a client after hours.

Stephen told Dave right off about Zack's injury. "It's not enough that he has chosen to have a trial," he said. "A trial won't happen for a long time. Zack can't stay in there any longer."

Then Stephen unveiled his new plan: They would serve the D.A. with an affidavit from Viola that would include the news about Hake's interference and at the same time they would serve a notice of Zack's decision to opt for a trial. If Hake had harassed Viola, any prosecutor would guess that he'd probably also pressured the three kids accusing Zack. If that were true, those boys would fold at cross-examination and the case against Zack would turn into a farce.

The idea, Stephen said, was to turn up what was already a lot of pressure on Lindemann, given that the shooters would now have to be tried as adults.

Stephen could probably hear Dave's TV in the background and the sounds of the St. John's game. "We need a squeeze play," he told Dave, "really pile it on. Come at Lindemann from both sides and make her scream. A *pincer operation*: Let her know Zack is opting for a trial, and call in Viola Nightingale for the squeeze.

"You hear me, Dave?" Stephen hammered on. "Lindemann needs to see how Hake operates. I'll leave it to you to get the words right, but make sure it's in that affidavit."

Dave had to object. He was not Viola's attorney. She would have to hire a lawyer of her own and then, maybe, Dave would try to talk with him. But in the end, it would be Viola's own lawyer, not Dave, who would advise her what to say.

Stephen was relentless. "Call the D.A. tomorrow morning," he told Dave. "Tell her we have new evidence: This story about what Hake's been up to."

And then, still pacing with the phone to his ear, he recalled the news about the woman from the cafeteria. "Actually, Dave," I heard him say, "it's a three-way squeeze. A *triple pincer!* Lindemann is going to be happy to drop the charges when you tell her Zack is going for a trial, and also that her witnesses made their accusations under pressure."

When he set the phone down, I stood staring at him in disbelief. "How are you going to do this, Stephen? Viola's not ready to testify and we have no way of knowing if that will ever happen. Only her doctor can say she's ready to make a statement, and only her own lawyer can tell her what to say. So far, there's nothing from the doctor and she's not at all interested in hiring a lawyer. She's really not even talking to us! How can you tell Dave to call the D.A.?"

"I'm going to talk to Viola," Stephen said. "We've been tiptoeing around, but now we have to do it. If she won't talk to you, I'll get her to talk with me."

"But Stephen . . ."

"She cares about Zack. You said so yourself. She wouldn't have called with all that dope about Hake if she wanted to stay out of this. And what is it she told Zack at the funeral? That he's like a son to her? Her other boy, she told him."

"Yes, but that was before . . .

"No, it was *after*. It was after Cyrus died. She still felt that Zack was like her own child. With Cyrus gone, I'm betting Zack is even more important to her."

"You're the one who said she probably hates us all. Forever, maybe. And now you've got this new plan and you're changing your whole idea about Viola."

"I've been thinking this over for awhile," Stephen said, "and I believe Viola is terribly mixed up, torn by all sorts of conflicted feelings. She hates us for her loss. She may even blame Zack for it. But at the same time, I think, she might still want a child in her life, something good to hold on to. She just needs someone to help her straighten it all out."

"And you're going to be that person? You're going to tell Viola she needs to snap out of her funk and write the affidavit that Dave will dictate? No, Stephen, you can't do that!"

Viola was so fragile and so resistant to dealing with us. This new plan of Stephen's could make things far, far worse.

The next day, it seemed Stephen's new plan would surely fold.

Dave rang from the lobby and Stephen buzzed him in.

"To what do we owe the honor?" Stephen said.

Dave said his wife was shopping up on Columbus Avenue and he had some news to share. "So I grabbed the chance to tell you this in person."

"I've been phoning around," Dave said. "It seems Lindemann is leaving town for a two-week holiday starting next Tuesday. Her office will be closed to any new matter starting then. We'll have to wait until after New Year's. I'm sorry, folks, I thought I'd better tell you right away."

"You have to find another way," Stephen said. "Can't we do this with an *Assistant* D.A.? Lindemann has a whole staff there, right? It's almost a week until Christmas."

Dave had the sad, worried look of Bassett hound. He said he sympathized with our anxiety but that only the D.A. herself could make the decision to release Zack. "Nothing," Dave reminded us, "gets done this time of year. And I have to warn you," he went on, "you shouldn't count so heavily on Viola's testimony. She'd have to cross a lot of old lines to rat out Hake in a public document. People clam up when they have to sign official court papers. I just want you both to be aware—"

Stephen said we'd considered all that, we'd discussed it more than once. "I know you're being a friend," Stephen said, " but I also know you need to cover your ass. You lawyers are all alike. Whenever I send up a balloon at City Hall, it's always the lawyers who shoot it down. I appreciate your trying to keep our expectations low, but I feel I can do this. I'm going to talk to Viola and make her understand how much we need her."

Still, Dave wanted to be certain we understood: Even if Viola agreed to sign an affidavit, the papers would not reach the D.A. until after New Year's. That was more than two weeks away.

"What time does that office close Tuesday? Five o'clock, right? Today's Friday. We have four whole days."

Stephen didn't need Dave or me to remind him: Two of those days were the weekend. I wanted Stephen to bring Zack home. But, surely, this was not the right plan.

-41-

"LET'S GO, BETTS," Stephen called from the kitchen. It was Saturday again, another visiting day at Parkside. I couldn't imagine what we would tell Zack. At the emergency visit, Stephen had promised to have him out in a day or two. Again, we'd disappointed him.

Stephen had been up since dawn. He'd already picked up our car at the garage and double-parked it right outside our building. "I'll wait for you downstairs," he said, and raced out the door.

"Why such a hurry?" I asked. I had a thermos of coffee in one hand and a hairbrush in the other. The visiting session wouldn't start for at least an hour.

Stephen's face, his gestures as he opened the car door for me, were all business. Efficiently, he steered us into the uptown traffic.

"We're picking up June and Viola," he said. "I'm taking them with us."

"But, Stephen . . ."

I knew what he was about. I thought he was probably mad.

Viola and June looked wary as Stephen escorted them to our car. He opened the back door and helped each of them in. June said, "Good morning." Viola said nothing.

I turned around in my seat. I hadn't seen Viola since the funeral. Her body seemed to have shrunk; her face, after weeks of powerful drugs was swollen. Her eyes, always so sharp and alert, looked dazed.

"Hello, Vi," I said. "Hello, June."

They both nodded.

Zack was waiting in Ms. Caldwell's office when we arrived. He walked toward us and stood squarely in front of

Viola. His head tilted slightly to the side, he said, ever so softly, "Hello, Mrs. Nightingale."

"Zack," Viola said. Her voice was hoarse.

I walked around to stand behind Zack, kissed his hair, and rested my hands on his shoulders. I wanted him to know: Whatever happens here, I'm ready with a hug.

"How are you feeling?" Zack asked.

"Oh, not so bad. It comes and goes. How're you feeling yourself?"

"I'm okay."

Stephen and I stood with our eyes on Zack, hanging on every word that passed between them. June had settled into a small folding chair near Ms. Caldwell's desk. She perched at the edge of her seat as if her sister might fly apart.

The most ordinary of greetings, the simplest words, spoken by a child and a woman who had become very small. Yet June and Stephen and I feared an explosion. We glanced nervously at one another, as if we were watching two walkers on a tightrope.

Viola listened intently as Zack told her a bit about Parkside, the bread he was learning to bake while he helped in the kitchen. Then she turned to June.

"That's the little boy," she said, gesturing toward Zack.

Automatically my arm wrapped itself more tightly around Zack's shoulders and clutched him close to me. The little boy who . . . What little boy was Viola about to name? What child did she see before her?

June nodded her understanding. "Yes," she said, "that's Zack."

"That's the one I've been telling you about," Viola said.

I held my breath. What had she been telling her sister? What had they been discussing in that dim apartment, day after day, night after sleepless night?

"I tell my sister," Viola said, turning back to face Zack and me, "I tell her every day. Cyrus loved this boy like a brother. It would do anyone's heart good to see the two of them together. So much love, you just would not believe it."

She leaned forward and held out her arms to Zack. "Come here, boy."

I let go my son and he stepped toward her.

"He loved you like a brother," she told him. "You are my other boy, I guess. Doesn't that make you my other boy, Zack?"

Zack did not flinch. He seemed to know exactly what Viola needed. It was what he needed as well. "Yes," he told her, "I'm your other boy."

What followed swept all of us in—Viola and Zack holding tightly to each other, and me, fumbling for my tissues, trying to stifle my sobs and stay strong.

But then I, too, rushed forward and joined them, and then Stephen piled on as well. For many minutes we remained folded around one another like that, hugging, swaying, pulling back a bit, then falling again into a lumpy, warm heap.

I stepped obediently out of the car when Stephen stopped in front of our building. June and Viola were still in the back seat, and I opened the back door to give Viola a kiss. Stephen, I knew, wanted to escort them up to their apartment. It would be his chance to make some sort of pitch. Perhaps he'd get lucky. Viola was in a happy enough mood. She had talked about Zack during the entire ride back from Parkside.

But would that be enough to make her call her doctor? Would it get her past her dread of hiring a lawyer? If Stephen could bring her around to signing an affidavit, would she, in this still-fragile state, be willing to put on paper the accusations she had leveled against Marcus Hake? With the D.A. heading off on holiday on Tuesday afternoon, what good would that affidavit be, even if Viola agreed to testify?

Trust your husband, I told myself. He's as good a man as there is.

-42-

ON SUNDAY MORNING, I simply could not settle down. I darted around the dining room table, noting the stacks of bluebooks that needed grading, knowing grades would soon come due. It was impossible to work, impossible to think.

Stephen could not help noticing. "I told you everything went well," he reminded me. "She's calling the doctor and getting in touch with some lawyer she knows. She even gave me the guy's name. First thing tomorrow, Dave will get in touch with him and they'll draft the affidavit. I think Dave can convince them to give us what we need. It's happening, Betts. Why are you so edgy?"

"It's too late," I said. "The D.A. is the one we need and she's leaving town. Zack can't stay in there—"

"You know," Stephen said, "there's something you could be doing now instead of frying your brains."

"The bluebooks," I said. I sounded disgusted, and I was.

"No," Stephen said. "You could be making things up with Viola. Take one of those nice walks you two used to like. Keep her interested and talking. Keep the wheels greased."

"Oh, Stephen!" This political lingo sounded awful applied to Viola and me. But Stephen was, after all, a politician. And a canny psychologist. He was playing the game to win. It was probably a good idea.

I phoned Viola and asked if she and June might like to join me for a walk in Riverside Park. I promised myself, as I stepped out to meet them, that I would just make small talk and try to keep everything normal. Again, I had to wonder just what that word could possibly mean. Viola was no longer the woman who had once been my best friend. And June? There were a lot of wheels to grease.

At three-thirty, we met at our old spot. It was blustery, and Viola pulled her muffler up over her nose. After a very short walk, we were all too cold and wanted to head back. But Viola asked if we could duck into the little shop that sells her favorite tea.

The tea shop occupied a narrow space on Broadway. Shelves running to the ceiling were stocked with jars of fragrant dried leaves. Another set of shelves formed a divider along the length of the shop, creating two long aisles to the back. We ambled slowly up one aisle, lifting jars off the shelves and opening them to inhale the pungent black teas, the spicy red ones. Vi and I used to sit at a tiny table in the rear on cold days like this, sipping something hot and delicious. Where was the tea Viola loved so?

Suddenly, from behind, a customer charged past, shoving us out of her way.

"Hey!" June called after her. "What do you think you're doing?"

The woman turned to us, a horrible scowl on her face. "What do you think *you're* doing?" she said. It was Dorothy Morrison, I realized a bit too late.

Viola recognized her instantly and started up the aisle after her. "Why're you being so rude?" she called to Dorothy.

Dorothy turned again and snarled. "Why are you with that woman, anyway? Are you crazy or something?"

"That's Bettina Grosjean and my sister," Viola said. She had reached Dorothy and the two women were standing almost toe to toe, Dorothy, in her high-heeled boots, glowering down at Viola in her muffler.

"That's the woman whose kid murdered your son!" Dorothy spat out the words.

In a flash, June and I were on them both, pulling Viola back as she lunged for Dorothy. Dorothy muttered something about Viola being out of her right mind, and managed to land a blow to Viola's face before scurrying down the second aisle and out of the shop. Viola strained to get free, but June and I held firm. Eventually, she relented and stood, panting and wheezing, leaning on us both. A trickle of blood ran from her upper lip.

I helped June get Viola home. We washed her face and made an ice pack for her to hold to her mouth. Through all of this, June spoke only to Viola. I could only imagine that she agreed with Dorothy, that she thought it was somehow wrong for Viola to be out walking with the mother of the boy responsible for Cyrus's death. I could understand June feeling that way, but Dorothy surely knew, and understood, my relationship with Viola.

Dorothy Morrison, the cake-baking, highly educated, banker's wife and respected figure in our Parents Association and in her own church, had just drawn blood from the woman I regarded as a sister, a woman still grieving the loss of her only child. There could be absolutely no doubt about it: At Dorothy's instigation, Hake had marched her son, along with Ronnie and Louis, down to the D.A. to lie about Zack.

When I left Viola's apartment, I wanted to head straight to Dorothy's place and confront her. But, then I remembered my first visit to the Morrison's apartment, the smarmy sweetness of Dorothy offering me a slice of cake. If someone was going to get Dorothy to come clean, it would have to be Stephen. I raced home to give him the news.

Breathlessly, I recounted the events in the tea shop, my lower lip quivering as I spoke. "She drew blood, Stephen. She actually made Viola bleed! First Zack, now Viola, this is just too much."

And then the phone. Viola. She wanted to see Stephen right away. Something important she wanted to talk about.

Oh, no! She's feeling overwhelmed. One day back out in the world, and she's sorry she did it. She's going to take back her offer, I just know it. And who could blame her? She's already had enough!

-43-

Wednesday, December 22, 6:15 pm

YAY! YAY! YAY! YAY! YAY!

Since Jason scratched up my door, I was thinking any day I'd get whacked all over again, maybe even killed. The cut still hurt and Nestor was gone and there was no one to talk to but Layla who is really old. I was getting ready to go down to the kitchen when I looked through the window in my door and saw Digby coming toward my room. He was carrying a cardboard carton and smiling. He balanced the carton in one arm and unlocked my door.

He said, "Well, that's it, Grosjean. I guess you're outta here."

I said, "Huh?" Really, I thought he was joking.

He said, "Here are your clothes. Get dressed and take your Parkside clothes down to the checkout. Your folks are waiting, so hurry it up, okay?"

Unreal! I was totally and extremely ready to roll.

I stopped at Digby's desk on my way out. I said, "Bye. It was nice knowing you. I mean it."

He said, "Yeah. I liked knowing you, too. But I'm really happy to see you go."

I said, "Yeah, me too."

Digby gave my shoulder the little scrunch thing he does. He said, "I'm sorry I couldn't find any law books for you. I guess you'll have time for that when you get home. So just take care of yourself, okay?"

I said, "Yeah, I will." I wasn't thinking about the trial or about how I would read up on it. I was just so happy to be getting out of that place and going downstairs to my mom and dad.

On the way down the corridor with Ms. Caldwell, I was thinking maybe I should let Digby know it was Jason who got me. But then I figured it wouldn't do any good. Jason has no more points to lose and besides, he's the kind of kid who could maybe come after me when he gets out.

When I was almost at the swinging doors, Digby yelled out, "And don't let those bedsprings bite, okay?" Funny guy, Digby.

My mom sort of jumped off the ground when she saw me. She gave me a mega blanket-hug and I hugged her back. She kept ruffling my hair while my dad and Dave took care of the paperwork at the front desk.

She said she wanted to see the bandage on my cut again, but when I showed it to her she said, "Now you have to let them know who did it."

I told her that Digby already knew, and I'm sure that was the truth. Digby always knew everything that was going down in our unit.

So my mom calmed down. But soon there were tears rolling down her face. Even when we walked outside and got into Mr. Rea's car, the tears kept coming.

While Mr. Rea drove us home, I said, "So what happens now? When do I have the trial or whatever?"

My mom was sitting in the back seat with me. She said, "No trial, Zackey. It's all over, sweetheart." Then she pulled me so close I could hardly breathe.

I pulled back a little and said, "Huh? I thought you were getting me out so I could wait for the trial at home."

My dad said the District Attorney never got a chance to decide about a trial. He said the whole thing was taken out of her hands by the mayor. They just shut down the whole investigation and sealed the file. Case closed.

My mom said, "It was all politics, Zack. It was never about you." She wrapped me up in another hug and we both hung on for a long time. I cried a little, too, and she gave me a Kleenex. Later, we laughed these weird little laughs.

I said, "So, do I go back to school now, or what?"

My mom said, "We can talk about that tomorrow. We have a couple of options. There's a school in Greenwich Village that Daddy and I like. What do *you* think, Zack?"

I said, "I don't know."

And I don't. I'm done with the punishment and I'm still getting used to that.

Non mea culpa. Non mea culpa. I have served my time.

It's great to be home again and not have to worry all the time about what Jason is up to, but I don't know about going back to school. I've sort of had it with Ronnie and Louis and LeVar, and I think my mom is about done with their parents, too. But a new school won't be any picnic either. Cyrus is never coming back and there's no one else to play chess with. There's no one else I even want to hang out with.

Everyone in this city knows me from the newspapers. I don't know what I'd say if someone asked me what really happened. I bumped my best friend on the stairs in a bus terminal and he accidentally fell down and died? That's the truth, so it's the story I'll be telling for the rest of my life, I guess.

Now I'm back in my regular room on my regular bed, and I'm a free man. I know I didn't have the *mens rea* to harm Cyrus. but the story of how we got to the top of those stairs, and the reason I was feeling not completely friendly toward my best kemosabe at that particular moment, that's a story I don't think I will ever tell anyone. It's the story I have to keep inside my heart, right under the Gothic letter "C."

-44-

On Zack's first night at home, we had a little celebration. Viola came to dinner with June, and I brought my mother over to join us.

Stephen had said Viola would tell us the story of just how Zack had gotten out of Parkside. "Just wait," he kept saying, "she wants to tell you this herself."

Until that moment, I really hadn't cared about the political games Stephen had set in motion, all those inside moves. All that mattered was that Zack was finally home and the charges against him had been dropped.

Viola helped herself to a second slice of pie and a second scoop of butter pecan ice cream. You could tell she enjoyed keeping us all in suspense.

But Hallie, the attorney daughter, could barely stay in her seat. She wanted to hear every detail. "Sprung," was her word. "How'd you get him sprung, anyway?"

Viola told us that after her visit to Zack, she'd called the lawyer, Elias Townshend, the one she and June had liked best. Early Monday morning, because of the emergency, Townshend arrived at Viola's apartment to advise her on the affidavit Stephen had asked for. After she signed that, Townshend presented her with another set of papers he'd prepared as well, papers he wanted to discuss.

The city's counsel, Roy Shaffer, would be expecting her to bring a lawsuit charging negligence in Cyrus's death, Townsend told her, but she'd have to file a Notice of her intent to sue, and it would be best to do that before she left for Georgia. Time to file was running out.

Attached to the Notice Townsend had prepared was a copy of the Complaint to show the city what Viola would be filing when she finally brought her suit to court. It was standard practice.

Viola hadn't wanted to look at any of it. "I told Townshend I'd just sign whatever he wanted me to sign, but then I wanted to leave town. I just had to be out of here before Christmas."

But Townshend said she ought to have a look. A lot of money was involved. "Shaffer knows to expect a big number in this case," Townsend explained, "because it's about a child."

"I told him I don't need any money when I haven't got my child," Viola told us. "June was getting ready to show him to the door, but when I saw that big number he was suing for, I said I wanted some time to think about it. Thing is, I had another idea that I wanted to check out with Stephen."

Viola looked at me apologetically. "I'm sorry, Bettina. I didn't want to get you involved. No need to get your hopes up if it wasn't going to work.

Viola left Townshend in her livingroom and went to her bedroom to phone Stephen. "It was a twist on Marcus's idea, really," Viola told us. "The whole thing, I have to say, came to you courtesy of Marcus Hake himself!"

"We're not mentioning his name in this house," I said.

"Well, then, you can also say it came from Stephen and Mr. Rea because they had the idea of exactly how to do it. Stephen and Mr. Rea put it to work for us."

Hallie was jumping out of her seat by then, and Zack hunched forward in his.

Townshend helped Viola draft a cover letter to be delivered to Corporation Counsel Shaffer along with the Notice and the Complaint. In the letter she let Shaffer know that she would be away for a very long time and absolutely unavailable to discuss a settlement. "You can make this lawsuit go away tomorrow morning," Viola's letter said, "if we can discuss this immediately."

"It was that letter that did the trick," Viola told us.

On Tuesday afternoon, Stephen and Dave and Viola met at Townshend's office. Roy Shaffer, as they had all expected, had read the letter as soon as it was delivered and had phoned Townshend immediately. Now they were assembled for the conference call Townshend had arranged. Townsend put Shaffer on the speaker phone so the others could hear.

All Shaffer could hope to do was keep Viola's negligence from going to trial, a sensational trial in which the city would be found guilty on every TV channel and in every local paper. A racial issue, a dead child, a prodigy dead because of the city's neglectful employee. Containment was the best Shaffer could hope to achieve.

What would it take to settle? he wanted to know. He needed a number. He needed to know Viola's bottom line before the close of business.

At that point, Viola seized the conversation. "I think I can speak for myself, now," she told him. "I don't see any reason to trouble Mr. Townshend with this. Unless you people refuse to agree to my settlement conditions, Mr. Townshend here won't be making very much money on this."

"What do you want, then?" the chief lawyer for the city asked.

"I want you to give me back the only child I have left," Viola said. "I want you to get them to drop those stupid charges against Zack Grosjean and release him immediately. That's the only way I'll settle this."

"Now, Mrs. Nightingale," Shaffer began. He told her he had no authority in criminal matters; only the District Attorney could strike bargains of that sort.

"Don't Mrs. Nightingale me," Viola said. "Just get that child out, you hear? I lost my son. My son! There's no amount of money you can give me that will buy him back. The only thing that has any value now is Zack Grosjean.

"You talk to anyone you have to talk to. Just get Zack out before the sun goes down tomorrow, and pay Mr. Townshend his fee. If you do that, this whole ugly lawsuit will go away for a very reasonable amount. But this offer of mine expires tomorrow at sundown, 'cause on Friday, I'm leaving town. I want to see Zack out of that place before I go, and I want all those phony charges dropped. That's the deal, take it or leave it!"

Shaffer tried again, and once more after that, to explain that the D.A.'s office and his had nothing in common. "We're both lawyers and we both work for the city, Mrs. Nightingale, but the similarity ends there. This is an office for civil matters; I'm not involved with criminal investigations. The District Attorney and I rarely even see each other."

"You're a smart fellow," Viola told him. "You'll figure something out."

"That's nice of you to say, Mrs. Nightingale," he said, "but whatever I figure out, as you put it, would have to wait until after the holidays in any case. The District Attorney's office will close later today for a holiday break."

"Well, there you go, then," Viola said. "I knew you were closer in to her than you were letting on. I hope I hear back from you tomorrow because after that we'll be going for a trial and a much heftier sum."

When Shaffer was gone from the line, Townsend and Stephen shared a raucous high five.

"I wasn't so sure we should celebrate. I told them we better wait and see what the city will do with it," Viola told us as she polished off her pie. "You never can tell about this city of ours."

"I guess we saw alright," Zack said soberly, when our laughter had finally died down. Zack had been sitting quietly beside his grandmother, looking down at his plate and pondering this most incredible story. He hadn't laughed as much as the rest of us. "I guess I'm an expensive second son," he said, looking across at Viola with sweet sad eyes.

"No, baby," Viola said, "you are not expensive at all. What was I going to do with a great big lawsuit anyway? I'm going home with June for good next month, and we're going to be fine."

"Vi," I said, "I really must know that this will be a good thing for you, too."

"Don't worry, honey, I'm getting enough for everything June and I are ever going to need or want."

"It was a dicey game we were playing," Stephen admitted, "but when I saw what was happening to Zack, I decided we had to risk it."

"It was seeing Zack up there in that detention place," Viola said, "and Stephen telling me some kid had taken a stab at him. And I've got to say, I also wanted to get back at that bitch, Dorothy. When I looked in the mirror and saw where she punched me, I was ready to do anything to make sure that plan of hers wasn't going to succeed."

"This is extremely interesting," Hallie said. She'd been pondering the story, trying to be certain she understood where all the pieces fit. "Are you saying the lawyer for the city, that guy, Shaffer, just told the D.A. to drop the case against Zack and she did it, just like that? On Law and Order, the District Attorney . . ."

"Not just like that," Stephen said. He explained that when Zack decided to have a trial, the D.A. had to be sure her witnesses were believable, but that what Viola said in her affidavit about Marcus Hake made the D.A. realize that those boys she had as witnesses were not a good bet. By the time Shaffer asked the mayor, and the mayor asked the D.A., to drop the charges against Zack, she was probably very happy to do just that because she knew it wouldn't be a winner.

"That's totally amazing," Hallie said. I knew she'd want this explained a few more times in the days ahead.

"Like everything in politics," Stephen said, "like everything in life, really, it was a lot of things all coming together. Even the cafeteria lady helped a little."

"How?" Hallie wanted to know.

"Daddy will explain that another time," I put in. "It's complicated enough as it is, right?"

Hallie's brow furrowed. She felt she was being underestimated. "How much do they have to pay Mr. Townshend?" she demanded to know.

"Oh, I wouldn't worry much about Mr. Townshend," Viola said. "They're going to pay Mr. Townshend whatever figure turns up at the bottom of Mr. Townshend's bill!"

"Neat," Hallie said admiringly.

It was time for my mother to claim her share of credit. "And we won't worry anymore about Zack, either," she said. "I feel like the air around here is finally clearing up. I could tell there were very bad things traveling around, you know, but now I think they're almost gone."

"Thank heaven for that!" Stephen said.

"Really, Dad, you have no proof that Grandma's wrong," Hallie said.

"I was right," my mother asserted firmly, "I was right all along."

No one was about to contradict her.

"We got 'em!" Viola said as she and June were getting up from the table. She looked frayed and weary; it had been a long couple of days. "Those bastards! And Marcus is a bad apple, you know. I've been saying *that* all along. He wanted to use this same fancy idea to get those delinquents out early! He wanted me to file a huge lawsuit and then offer to drop it if they'd agree to try them as kids. You know, that woman from the cafeteria who died was the aunt of a friend of mine!"

Then she broke into the first real smile I'd seen in a long time. "I think we improved on that idea, of course, but I first heard it from Marcus, you could say."

"Let's just say you got a much better result this way," Stephen said.

Even June allowed herself a small, uncertain smile.

The following day, Stephen had a call from the mayor demanding to see him right away. We'd both felt certain he'd be summoned back to City Hall, the mayor slapping him on the back and claiming it had all been a big mistake. Merry Christmas and welcome back. As if nothing had happened, just nothing at all.

"You've got a lot of nerve, Grosjean," the mayor began as soon as Stephen was seated opposite him, "a lot of nerve pulling a stunt like this. I give you time to take care of your family and you turn around and hand me *this*? Just who in creation do you think you are?"

"What the hell are you talking about?"

"I'm talking about blackmail, Grosjean. About you cooking up the Nightingale lawsuit to get your kid out! You could have trusted me, you know. I had already talked to Lindemann. She was going to allow a plea. What made you think you could do a thing like this?"

"I don't know what you're talking about. Mrs. Nightingale is represented by counsel. Her decision was made in consultation with him. In any case, you should know, for whatever it's worth now, that my son was not disposed to take your stinking plea."

"It's blackmail, pure and simple. I never did trust you, Grosjean. Forty years in politics and I never met a guy who wasn't out for himself. You're just like everyone else, but you're too uppity-up to admit it!"

"You truly are berserk!" Stephen told him. "It's a great settlement for you. Viola had a valuable lawsuit against the city. She'd have made out like a bandit, and you know it. The only one who might have lost here is Viola. She was crazy not to ask for a hundred million, and you know that, too. What is she walking away with, now? A lousy twenty mil? For her only child? The city came out way ahead on this, you disgusting piece of filth!"

"Well, you're out of here, Grosjean. Fired! No more leave of absence! And I'm going to see what I can do to make it 'fired for cause.' Damned if you're getting a pension after you pull a stunt like this. Get outta here!"

Stephen remained where he was. He put his feet up on Hizzoner's desk and folded his hands in his lap.

"You aren't going to fire me," Stephen said, "because you'll look like a big enough moron just losing me from your administration. Instead, you're going to go to the media and say how hard you tried to persuade me to stay on, and how really sorry you are to see me go. You know perfectly well that those charges against Zack were fraudulent. They were a measure of how much you owe to Marcus Hake. With the death of that cafeteria worker, all that was going to fall apart.

"The only damage you've suffered is to your ego," Stephen said. "Someone got Zack out before you could make a big display of doing it yourself. And you lost the chance to make me think I owed you something. But I never would have thought I owed you. I stopped owing you anything the day you failed to intervene to keep Zack out of this mess.

"In any case," Stephen said, feet still up on the furniture, "I've pretty much paid my debt to this city. And I couldn't stand another minute in this odoriferous little clubhouse you're running. So I'll ask you to accept my resignation, and after you finish trying to persuade me to withdraw it, we can both call a press conference and give them the sad news."

Then, my extremely cool husband lifted his feet slowly off the desk, one at a time, stood up, and walked out.

That night, I reached across the bed for Stephen. It was a tentative gesture, fraught with complicated layers of hurt, misunderstanding, distrust—there was no way to peel them all back. The best I could do was to work my way forward through them all, and pray that Stephen would be there, the man I had months before fallen away from because—what was it then?—we'd had a sharp disagreement over the city's priorities? Sanitary waste projects versus school cafeterias? Had we actually stopped making love because of that?

Would he reach for me when he sensed my fingers creeping gingerly toward him? Would I have the courage to continue? Or were we both too deadened by hurt and recrimination? My hand traveled slowly, but determinedly, forward.

Stephen's thick, warm hand settled over mine, covering it softly. For a time, it was enough to be held like that, welcomed and protected. And then, it was not at all enough.

I inched myself closer until his arm, furry and strong, was around me, and then his face was on mine, and soon it all came flooding back to us. Like riding a bicycle. But a new bicycle. A Fire Engine Red one like the one Stephen always talked about. Deliciously familiar and comfortable and old, but also exquisitely, excruciatingly new. Which is, I have learned, the way marriages move.

EPILOGUE

HOW SHOULD I make sense of that awful time? In all, it went on for less than three months, but it made, I have to say, all the difference.

The narratives we historians construct to explain life's events always fail, somehow, to tell the whole truth. We include in our story what we believe is needed to complete it, but completeness is a matter of personal choice, a question of judgment or taste.

What is the story I should tell myself when I think back on the year Cyrus Nightingale died? I could say that I was betrayed by the parents at my children's school, by the city, by the society I had worked so hard to improve. But if I enlarge the frame to include the expectations I brought with me, that story changes. With a different view of human nature, I would not have felt betrayed at all. Perhaps I trusted in people to be better than people ordinarily are.

Is faith in human nature written on our DNA? Does it persist in spite of experience? My son began as a twig on his mother's tree, but life taught him too much, if such a thing is possible. When that year finally ended, I was left to wonder: Would Zack lose the habit of optimism? Would that be his price to pay?

I rose from the chair where I'd been reading, set my son's journal aside, and resumed sorting through the musty cartons. I wanted to decide what to keep and what to discard—what was part of our family's history and what was not.

At the soft sound of a step, I turned to find my mother making her way, haltingly, down the cellar stairs.

"You still at it?" she said. "I think maybe you should have it all carted away. Who wants that stuff anyway?"

I told her about the green-covered journal that had engrossed me for the past several hours.

"I'm trying to figure out a story," I told her. "The story of us. What do you include and what do you leave out? Zack's little chronicle here is all that remains in writing, I suppose. Our only primary source."

"Not true," my mother said. "Hallie wrote a composition once, remember? 'My Year In The Sixth Grade.' Something like that. She got an A."

I wracked my brain but, surely, I was growing old.

"Yes, yes," my mother insisted, looking around the cellar for something she knew must be there. "The teacher gave her an A, but it should have been an A plus. I know I saved it in that hat box. The big round one with the flowers on it."

Without uttering another word, my mother and I began rummaging through the remaining cartons.

"There!" my mother cried. "Up on the top shelf!"

I pulled down the box, lifted the cover and stood back while my mother took out strands of irridescent poppit beads, a loosely-bound stack of childish drawings, photographs, bits of dollhouse furniture and, finally, a homemade booklet held together with three brass paper fasteners. Purple letters had been carefully stenciled on the pink construction paper cover. My mother folded back the cover and handed the booklet to me to read:

My Sixth-Grade Year: Where I've Been And Where I'm Going

It's been a year and a half since our friend, Cyrus Nightingale, died. Everyone will tell you the world has changed a lot since then, and I know it has. For the Grosjean family, the changes have been huge because we now live in Vermont, which is next to New York on the map but is a completely different kind of place. My brother Zack had a very bad year and after the trouble was over, my father and mother decided we all needed a fresh start. So they rented out our New York apartment and we all came up here.

We found a house right down the street from our old friends the Haseltons. Their daughter, Maddy, was my best friend in New York and now I see her almost every day. This is about the neatest thing that could have happened to me, being reunited with my blood sister. My mother asked Selma Haselton for the names of all their doctors and stuff to help us get settled. Now, Maddy and I even have the same orthodontist, which is totally terrific.

My father used to work for the City of New York, but now he is a consultant for some of the towns around here. Most days, he's at home on his computer. Other days, he travels around meeting people and having lunch. Vermonters eat tons of veggies. My brother likes veggies too, but he's the only one in our family who does.

My Grandma Clara came from New York to live with us. Next to having Maddy almost next door, the second best thing about Vermont is having my grandmother right here in our house. She tells me stories about my grandfather, stuff even my mother doesn't know. She tells me how she learned to see in the dark, and how she can see the future which are two amazing things she really can do.

She also lets me wear her fabulous costume jewelry. She has a ring that's covered with opals which are these little stones that have actual fires burning inside them. It's bad luck for anyone who wasn't born in October to wear opals, but Grandma was born on October twenty-fifth, and I was born on the fourth, so the Ring Of Fire will be mine someday.

My grandmother brought my mother's old dollhouse here with her. I used to see it in her apartment, but it always had to stay in my mother's old room. Now, I can play with it in my own room and I absolutely love it. My mother says I'm too old for a dollhouse, and she's right; my grandmother should have given me this a long time ago. But Maddy and I still love arranging all the mini mahogany furniture and setting the table with the teensy blue glass dishes.

Grandma and I think alike because I'm gifted the same as her. She says I can sense things that no one else can. I hope she's right because that would be a totally excellent advantage when I become a trial lawyer. Grandma says not to be so sure of that. People don't listen to the gifted as they should. They act like we are the ones who are crazy when we try to tell them what's really going on. I've noticed that this tends to be true.

A good thing about Grandma coming to Vermont is that now she kisses everyone. Not just air kisses. She really puts her lips on your cheek and you can feel a real kiss. So I guess I taught her something good in exchange for all the stuff she's been teaching me.

My parents' friends, the Haseltons, teach cheese-making at a community college near here, and Selma helped my mother get a part-time job teaching American history. My mother would rather teach Women's Studies and Feminist History, the stuff she's actually an expert in. She had a talk with the dean and next year they are going to let her teach one of those classes as an experiment, which she says is at least a start.

Last month, Cyrus's mother and her sister, June, came to visit us from Georgia. My mother took them hiking up the mountain and they came back complaining about all the flies, but they were laughing a lot. This year, we're all going to visit them at Christmas, all of us except my grandmother who will stay with the Haseltons. My advice to them would be to lock any big closets they might have, but don't ask me to explain why.

My brother Zack was sad for a long time after we got here. I felt sorry for him because he wasn't making any friends at this school. After school, he would walk around in the meadows where the cows are. I think he was actually talking to those cows, but I wouldn't swear to it.

Sometimes, he'd go up the mountain road to that old graveyard that has a bunch of creepy headstones from three hundred years ago. The stones have drawings of skulls on them and these funny little poems about death. Zack told me the most interesting stones are on the graves of children. In colonial times, it wasn't so unusual for very young children to die. Zack wanted me to walk around that graveyard with him but I told him, "No way!"

For a couple of months he went up there with his laptop. He said he was writing his memoirs. He was always a weird kid, and it looked like living here in the mountains was going to make him even weirder.

But then, last month, his class took a trip to Portsmouth, New Hampshire to visit the Maritime Information Center. They spent the whole day getting lectured about endangered species of fish. When Zack got home, he looked up all those fish on the Internet and made lists with each fish's Latin name, and the numbers of them in the world ten years ago, and the numbers that are left today. He and this kid Noah in his class found all the species that are getting overfished or killed off by toxic waste and they put them on a spread sheet in their laptops.

Now Zack's whole room is covered with pictures of fish and he goes around saying their names in Latin. He's showing off with the fish names the way he used to with the names of baseball players. So he's definitely getting back to his old obnoxious self. He says he's going to be an ichthyologist which is a Greek word he taught me to spell that means an expert on fish. Even with my special gift, I can't tell how Zack will turn out. My grandmother also says we'll just have to wait and see about Zack.

But I do know all about me. Maddy and I saw a film a few nights ago about high school kids who go to Africa to show people how to plant the right crops so they'll have enough to eat. I'm learning a lot about the environment here in Vermont and I'm going to spend my high school summers in Africa helping the people there.

I'm going to major in Environmental Studies at the University of Vermont, and then I'll go to law school. I'm going to marry an awesomely cute and smart lawyer and open a practice with him. We'll have two kids—one of each—and we'll raise them in New York because I still think the city is a great place to grow up, even if I can't be there at this particular time.

My husband and I will drive a compact, environment-sensitive station wagon and I will wear a piece of my grandmother's jewelry every day. I will use my gifts to help bring justice to the poor and a healthy environment to the Earth. I have special knowledge, same as my grandmother does, and I'm going to use it to put more goodness into the world.

I won't let my special knowledge scare me, though, the way it does my grandmother. I'm not going to be scared by anything ever, that much I know.

Acknowledgements

It's hard to imagine how any work of fiction finds its way to publication without Anita Warren or someone very much like her. If not for her tender insights, steadying hand, and abundant heart, always at the ready, this book would not be here today. Through the years and across the miles, she is the friend whose wisdom, energy and devotion guided this book and preserved its author. *Eishet Chayil!*

The Virginia Center for the Creative Arts twice hosted me for lengthy stays. Their hospitality and nurture allowed me the peace-filled freedom to truly imagine.

Bobbie Cohen brought her keen sense of humanity to her careful reading of an early draft and offered many thoughtful suggestions; so, too, did the late, great Ellye Bloom.

Hannah Bendiksen generously contributed her astute sensibility and an invaluable point of view.

Bronx County Assistant District Attorney, David Greenfield, miraculously arranged for me to spend a day inside the Spofford Juvenile Detention Center (now, Horizon Juvenile Center) where the staff graciously provided an exhaustive tour and helpfully answered all my many questions.

Lynn Blumenfeld and Ghilia Lipman-Wulf lent valuable assistance in the last lap.

As always, my husband, Jack Weinstein, supplied the patient love that sustains me.

More books from Harvard Square Editions

People and Peppers, Kelvin Christopher James
Gates of Eden, Charles Degelman
Love's Affliction, Fidelis Mkparu
Close, Erika Raskin
Anomie, Jeff Lockwood
Transoceanic Lights, S. Li
Living Treasures, Yang Huang
Nature's Confession, J.L. Morin
A Little Something, Richard Haddaway
Dark Lady of Hollywood, Diane Haithman
Fugue for the Right Hand, Michele Tolela Myers
Growing Up White, James P. Stobaugh
Calling the Dead, R.K. Marfurt
Parallel, Sharon Erby

Printed in the United States
By Bookmasters